# CAFE AU SLAY

## ORCHARD HOLLOW 

A.N. SAGE

CAULDRON
PRESS

Cafe au Slay

Orchard Hollow, book 2



ISBN 978-1-989868-31-7 (Paperback Edition)

ISBN 978-1-989868-30-0 (Electronic Edition)

Cover and interior art by Cauldron Press

www.cauldronpress.ca

Editing by Inessa Sage

www.inessasage.com

# CONTENTS

# CHAPTER 1

No matter what they tell you, nothing beats a quiet afternoon where things simply fall into place. It was a shame that, despite having my act more or less together, my afternoons were still as far from quiet as one could get. Being a witch in a town full of hidden paranormals was not all it was cracked out to be—especially when said witch had a new employee unable to pour a simple cup of coffee.

"Not again!" Rory's shrill voice carried over the lunch rush lineup and made its way to my eardrums.

I rubbed my temples, surveying the cafe to see what damage the young barista caused this time. Things have never been more chaotic here at Bean Me

Up. Since I hired her a week ago, Rory spilled more lattes than she made, set a scone on fire, and kicked a patron's suitcase into a bucket of filthy mop water. As far as employees went, Rory was not winning awards any time soon. But she had one thing going for her, the main thing that made me not kick her butt to the curb and call it a day: Rory was a witch, which meant I could count on her not to tell the humans about my extracurricular activities.

She was also Cilia Craven's niece, and I was certain if I fired her after a mere week of employment, the witch's entire coven would come after me. Hard.

"Piper! A little help!"

My head spun, and I rallied myself back to reality, facing Rory head on. The front of her apron was covered in a dark, oozing liquid, and I could smell the rich scent of caramel all the way from where I stood. In Rory's hands, a steamer overflowed with more of the sticky substance. *Wonderful. She made something else go boom-boom.* Sliding the tray of drinks I held onto a nearby table, I maneuvered my way through the crowd and rushed to Rory's side. "Are you alright?"

Rory rolled her shoulders, put the steamer down, and pointed at her apron. "How does it look?"

It looked like a hot-mess-express train ran through here.

"Why don't you fill the pastry display and take the

table that sat down?" I suggested. "I can man the front for a bit."

In my gut, I knew now that I said it, I'd be stuck here for the rest of the afternoon. Rory's face lit up the second I told her she could abandon the disaster she created, and she bounced away to grab a fresh box of muffins. I closed my eyes, begging the powers that be to watch over my clumsy assistant before we lost the muffins like we did the coffee. Apologizing for the wait, I scrambled to get everyone's orders ready. By the time I made the last of the oat matcha lattes—a new staple in the cafe—I had blisters on my thumbs from holding the metal steamer. I intertwined my fingers and stretched my hand out, cleaning up the counter quickly before searching for Rory.

The teenager was exactly where I thought she would be, chatting up a young couple sitting at the front bar by the window. Rory's dark-lined eyes twinkled as she listened to whatever gossip the girl spilled, and she nodded enthusiastically, eager to hear more. I shook my head and untied my apron, tossing it on the counter. Sweat beaded on my brow and I wiped it with the back of my hand, leaning against the back wall for balance. It wasn't even noon, and I was already exhausted.

I thought hiring someone was supposed to make my life easier.

One more glance at Rory told me it might be awhile before she tore herself away from the conversation. I hoped we didn't get hit with another wave of people in the next hour so I could grab a quick snack for lunch. I hadn't been able to do that in weeks. Between training Rory, or cleaning up after her, and practicing my yet to function magic; I was swamped.

It didn't help that my ghost familiar insisted I try to get out and socialize on the regular. Because apparently, when you're dead, it's highly important to butt your nose into other people's lives or they take away your ghost license.

"I see our new helper is staying busy."

*Speak of the devil....* I whipped around to face the office where Stella, the aforementioned familiar, stood with her arms crossed. She was almost fully solid today, and I breathed out, relieved she was in good spirits. The simplest way to tell Stella's moods was to look at her. If you could see right through her, walk the other way unless you wanted your head bitten off, which happened more often than I could keep track of.

I crammed a piece of the butterscotch cookie in my mouth and fixed my falling ponytail. "She's learning. Give her time to figure it out."

"It's a shame you don't pay her to gossip," Stella

sniped. "Because she has that down. Maybe you can use your zippity zap magic to give the kid some skills?"

"Stella, how many times do I have to tell you? Don't call it that." I rolled my eyes. "And I can't zippity anything—"

"Incoming!" Stella announced, vanishing into thin air.

Groaning, I turned my attention away from the empty doorway and back to the cafe. Bean Me Up had a few stray customers lingering, but it was empty enough that the front door whooshing open startled Rory. Her eyes met mine, and she excused herself from the lengthy conversation, hurrying to the counter and pretending to busy herself with the pastry display. I wasn't sure what she was doing there since I already filled it up when she'd forgotten about my earlier instructions.

My teeth slammed together, and I snuffed out the anxiety swelling my chest, fixing a warm smile for the newest customer.

When I saw who it was, I stopped breathing.

Sheriff Romero strolled slowly toward me and my heart beat fast against my ribcage; so fast I thought it was trying to escape. My eyes darted to the office door, fear weighing me down like an anchor. *Please don't let someone else be dead.*

The last time the sheriff showed up at Bean Me

Up, there was a dead body in the back alley, and I was the prime suspect. Despite the case being closed, thanks to yours truly, I still got goosebumps every time I saw Romero. It was as though his presence and death went hand in hand.

The sheriff closed the distance between us and took off his hat, nodding. "How are you, Miss Addison?"

Romero was the only person in town who called me by my last name, no matter how many times I asked him not to.

"Oh, no," Stella said, reappearing behind me. "Who died this time?"

I shoo'd her away and concentrated on Romero. "Good day, sheriff. What brings you by?"

"I'm on my way down to the station and wanted to pick up some coffees for the team," he explained. "Why else would I come to a cafe?"

*Because someone else kicked the bucket.* I reined in my wayward thoughts and smiled deeper. "No reason," I said. Then, raising my voice loud enough to carry through the cafe, added, "Rory will get your order."

I couldn't be certain, but I was pretty sure the young witch growled under her breath. She pocketed her cellphone—the same one I asked her not to be on while working—and flashed her teeth. "Welcome to Bean Me Up! What can I get you?"

"Let's see..." Romero eyed the blackboard menu behind the counter. "How are the oat matcha lattes?"

"They're okay."

I fought the urge to zippity zap my assistant.

While the sheriff placed his order, I snuck into the office and closed the door. Usually, around this time, when it was safe to leave Rory alone in the front, I would take my break and try to do some research on my newfound magic. The electricity I was able to summon was an anomaly and unlike any witch magic I'd heard of. Every day I wished gran was here because if anyone knew what was going in my body, it was her. Gran knew everything there was to know about magic and the paranormal community. But she was gone, and it was on me to decipher what kind of freak I was. Because at the end of the day, no matter how great Stella thought this development was, I never felt more of an outsider.

Sucking at witching was one thing; being able to pull power from my very core without the use of a conduit, that was some weird stuff. Even for Orchard Hollow.

Which said a lot, considering our town was a hub of paranormal activity.

The back door squeaked and slid open right as I

settled into the office chair. I side-eyed the slim open-ing, big enough to fit a certain clumsy raccoon body, and smirked. "Hello, Harry."

My welcome was answered by a series of chitters followed by the sound of sharp nails scratching against the tile floor. I rose off the chair and looked beyond the desk to where Harry Houdini ran at record speed to make his way across the office. His eyes locked on the shelving unit against the wall, narrowing with a singular purpose.

A box of cookies.

The raccoon had a sweet tooth like no other, and it was impossible to keep food around without him somehow getting his grabby paws on it. It was even more difficult to keep the thief at bay when Rory insisted on leaving a bowl of snacks for him nightly. Though I had to admit, the teen's love for the furry beast was one of her more redeeming qualities. Espe-cially since Harry coming around ruffled Stella's feathers and, as far as I was concerned, the ghost could use with a little ruffling.

I slid into the chair, the sound of the wheels rolling making Harry notice my presence for the first time. His eyes slid from me to the cookies and back again as he calculated his chances. Fist in the air, I shook my hand and said, "Don't even think about it."

The next two things happened simultaneously.

Harry Houdini launched himself for the box like he was leaping off a cliff. His large body cut the air with surprising speed, and he got himself airborne enough to clear a carton of paper napkins I stored at the base of the shelf. Tiny, thieving fingers wrapped around the cookie box and Harry's chitter intensified to a pitch I could only describe as alien S.O.S.

While Harry performed his circus act, I grabbed my trusty old broom now stored under the desk for occasions such as this. With the raccoon busy admiring his loot, I tiptoed across the office, ready to sweep him out of my life.

Suddenly, Harry's body froze.

I stopped breathing.

The furball dropped the cookies, shocking, and made a beeline for another shelf. His eyes widened and my heart sank when I realized what he had his sights set on.

"Harry, no!" I yelled.

I was a second too late. Before I could reach him, Harry grabbed a potion bottle off a shelf and crammed it into his mouth. I watched, half horrified, and half amused, as the monster twisted the bottle every which way to attempt fitting it into his gaping jaw. Lucky for Harry and me, the potion bottle was much too robust, though that didn't stop him from gnawing the neck with his sharpened teeth. I put the broom down and closed some of the distance between us. "I'm not taking you to a vet if you eat that," I said. "We don't know how you'll react to witch potions."

"And if *Piper* made it, we don't know if anyone can survive the hit."

*Think of rainbows and puppies. Think of rainbows and puppies. Think of rainbows and puppies.* I turned around slowly. "We get it, Stella," I said, annoyed. "I suck at witching."

The ghost grinned and flipped her long ponytail over her shoulder. "Zippity zap."

"Uh! Fine!" I yelped. Flipping around to face Harry, I pointed a finger a few inches from his bushy tail and concentrated on visualizing a spark. Electricity built in my body, and I directed it to my fingertip as Stella and I practiced many times before. "Sorry, buddy," I said, and let the magic go.

A flash of lightning lit up the office as an electric wave burst from my finger and scorched the wooden shelf Harry perched on. His eyes flew open, waking him from the thief coma he was in, and he dropped the potion bottle on the floor, scurrying out of the office and into the back alley. The bottle Harry dropped hit the side of the shelf, cracked, and continued to roll until I stopped it with my boot.

"Happy now?" I asked Stella.

"Never," she answered, disappearing again.

Checking the bottle for spillage, I placed it on a higher shelf and closed the back door. There was truly no point in locking up since Harry somehow managed to ninja his way inside regardless, but this had become a routine of sorts and as gran always said: if you want to get your life sorted, start with a routine. After giving the office one final glance, I returned to the cafe, a smile on my face.

That smile quickly vanished. Scratch that; the smile slapped me in the face then hightailed it out of there, never to be seen again.

Bean Me Up was in chaos.

Filthy mugs lined the counter, remnants of food lay on almost every available table, and there was what appeared to be a massive spill in the center of the floor. My eyes found Rory, her apron covered in coffee and a bewildered look on her face. When she saw me, she whispered "sorry" and snaked a wet rag off the counter. She rang it out, coffee dripping all over the freshly washed glass, and made her way to the front.

My jaw slacked and my breath caught in my throat. I coughed, the heat in my cheeks burning me alive as I watched Rory wipe the filthy rag over Joe Brooks's ocean-blue suit. A suit that was covered from lapel to waist in hot coffee.

# CHAPTER 2

When calculating the approximate level of embarrassment I felt watching Rory accost Joe with the rag, I took two things into consideration. The speed with which the stain on Joe's suit went from bad to you-need-to-burn-these-clothes bad, and his amused grin as Rory continued to slather him in more coffee. By my precise calculations, I was at level kill-me-now on the humiliation scale.

"I think I can take it from here," Joe finally said, reaching for the rag.

Looking him up and down, then glancing my way, Rory smirked. "Maybe my boss can help," she said. Then the kid winked at me.

Scratch that. We hit level pack-my-bags-and-move-to-another-country.

Cheeks burning like wildfire, I bit down on my tongue and walked over; my throat suddenly parched. I needed some strong coffee to deal with Joe on a good day, but today, I needed to dunk myself headfirst into an entire pot of espresso. Avoiding Joe's self-assured smile, I locked eyes with Rory. "Can you get the mop from the back and clean up the spill?" I asked. "We're due for another rush soon."

"Sure thing, boss!" The young witch lifted her hand in a salute, twirled on her heels, and strolled away so slowly, I wasn't sure I'd ever see her again.

When she disappeared into the office, I mustered the courage to face Joe. "Hey," I said. "Sorry about her. We're...training."

"Let's hope she's a better witch than she is a barista," Joe teased.

He kept his voice low despite us being the only two people in the cafe. You never knew who was listening in Orchard Hollow and if the last few months taught me anything, it was that this town hoarded secrets like they were its life juice. The last thing anyone wanted was for the truth about paranormals getting out, which was why most of us kept our mouths shut, even around our own kind. If you were a witch like me, or a vampire like Joe, you had to keep it under wraps. As history dictated, humans did not handle knowledge of magic very well, so if we wanted to hold the peace, we needed to blend in.

A shrill laugh sounded outside the window, and I glanced over Joe's broad shoulders to see Nancy Steeles walk by. Her hair was extra coiffed today and as she cast a side-glance through the glass, she pinned me with the death glare. Arm rising, she ran a manicured red nail over the charm bracelet on her wrist and pressed her lips into a taut line. Her family's talisman stared me in the face, a reminder of what I lost. *Shots fired.* I didn't know how Nancy found out about my gran's brooch getting destroyed, but she was definitely not above rubbing it in my face. I could feel Nancy's family magic even from where I stood and as she continued to play with the bracelet, the power within it only grew stronger. I was pretty sure the point Nancy was trying to make by rubbing her family talisman in my face was that she was better than me, but that wasn't what caught my attention.

How was I able to feel her magic from all the way inside?

The burst of energy I got from Nancy was dangerously close to what I felt when I handled Rosemary Hayes's pendant and the mystery of it made the hairs on my neck rise. As far as talismans went, your family's power was your own. It belonged to your bloodline, and no one else should have the ability to use it. Let alone feel it.

I growled under my breath, confusion threading through me.

"Are you okay?" Joe asked. His head swiveled to Nancy in the window. When she saw him, she flashed a row of pearly whites and stuck her butt out while simultaneously sucking in a breath. *What a fool.*

I stifled a laugh. "Yeah, all good. She's trying to get a rise out of me: it won't work."

Joe's eyes focused on the bracelet. "Any progress figuring out your little issue?"

The issue he was referring to was my weirdo magic, and it wasn't so little as it was a catastrophic disaster. Since first discovering I sported peculiar, non-witch powers, I hadn't been able to find anything to explain them. Every time I thought I had a lead, I hit a dead end. Aside from training Rory, it was the single most frustrating thing in my life. I turned my back to the window and gestured for Joe to follow me to one table, putting as much distance between us and Nancy as possible. "Nothing to report," I said, sitting down. "Either it was a fluke, and my magic is taking its sweet time leaving my system after the brooch broke, or I'm a freak of nature."

"Don't be so hard on yourself. You'll figure it out. As a matter of fact—" Joe reached into his suit pocket and produced a thin, worn-out book "—I brought you something to read."

I eyed the book with suspicion, uncertain if he was pulling my leg again. The last book Joe brought from his shop was a vintage copy of Dracula; an inside joke after I found out he was a vampire. This volume, however, was in terrible condition and had so much dust on it, I couldn't make out the title. It didn't help that Joe's giant hand was covering most of the cover and spine. Eager to find out the ruse the vampire put on; I stretched out an open palm. "Should I be worried?" I asked.

"Always," Joe said with a wink.

*Don't pass out. Breathe. Act cool.* Instead of doing any of that, I took a sip from the coffee cup on the table, quickly realizing it wasn't mine. It tasted of cold coffee beans, and I was pretty sure there was a piece of a ripped up sugar packet floating around in there somewhere. I gagged, spitting the abandoned coffee back into the cup. *Excellent.*

As though on cue, Rory popped her head out from behind Joe's shoulder and crinkled her nose at me. "That's been sitting there for like an hour," she said.

*Thanks, kid.* I shook my head, pushing the cup further away from me.

"Oh! Extraordinary Magic!" Rory exclaimed as she snatched the book from my fingers. I didn't fail to notice she made no move to clean up the table. "I read this last year."

"You did?"

"Yep! Fun read," the young witch said. "Far-fetched, but not bad."

I took the book from her and flipped through the pages, my eyes narrowing as I read. The majority of what I saw as I skimmed the chapter titles made me wonder why Joe thought this particular volume would be of interest to me. Manifesting Your Fae Spirit. Unicorns: Myth or Fact? Find Your Inner Demon. It all sounded like a book one might find in a human occult shop and not one a paranormal might take seriously. I could see why Rory held such a low opinion of the thing. Placing it on the table, I gazed at Joe and quirked a brow. "Really?"

"Hey," he said. "Don't knock it yet, it might prove to be helpful for your—"

Before he could spill the beans of my very personal, top secret magic problem, the door to the cafe swung open and loud laughter rang through the space. We turned simultaneously to watch three strangers, two women and a man, make their way inside. They were in their early twenties and, from the look of their attire, did not live in Orchard Hollow. If their fashionable clothes were not a dead giveaway, the awe with which they surveyed the cafe pegged the newcomers as tourists. Bean Me Up had that effect on people; something I attributed to its eclectic design and outer space paraphernalia. The man wore a tailored tweed jacket and jeans with more holes in them than actual fabric, while the two young ladies donned bright colored dresses much too thin for the cold weather. One girl had her hair up in two messy buns with several pens sticking out of each of them. She pulled one out, bringing it to her cotton candy-colored lips, and proceeded to chew the end off in the same fashion Harry often chewed the scones he stole. While the pen-eater made her way to the counter, her two friends found a table that was surprisingly not overflowing with cups and unloaded their bags.

I had never seen so many laptops in one spot.

Seriously, it looked like they were setting up a base of operations for world domination. Once all their gear was in place, the man reached into a large pack and proceeded to empty its contents. I counted two cameras, a microphone, and a stack of paperbacks, all with the same spine.

"What the..."

"No way!" Rory whisper-yelled beside me. "No freaking way!"

I peeled my attention away from the strangers to look at her, baffled. "Do you know them?"

"Are you kidding?" Rory's astonished face told me

she actually expected me to understand what was happening when I clearly very much did not. When I made no moves to talk, she rolled her eyes and said, "That has to be Archer Lee's crew."

"Who's Archer Lee?" Joe asked.

Rory's eyes rolled further into her head. I wondered if she could get stuck that way. "You guys are the worst," she said. Then, pointing to the book stack, "See those? Those are all Archer Lee books. He's like this super famous author and he's in town for a book tour. There's a signing and everything. It's all over social media. I can't believe they're here! This is the best thing that ever happened in this town. Do you think he'll show up, too?"

Neither Joe nor I had a chance to answer.

"Never mind! I'm going to go see what they want."

My witch assistant ran so fast, there was a Rory-shaped cloud of smoke lingering beside me when she left. I looked at Joe. "I've never seen her so excited about working before. This Archer Lee character must be a big deal."

"It says here he's the top paranormal investigator in the country," Joe said, scrolling through his phone. "A big deal indeed."

"Huh."

Everything about this situation rubbed me the wrong way. A paranormal investigator showing up in a town full of magic? Hiding our magic from the humans who lived in Orchard Hollow wasn't that difficult, mostly because everyone here paid little attention to others. There were a few people who loved to gossip, people like Nancy Steeles and apparently my new barista, but for the most part, everyone kept to themselves. Tourists were also easy to fool. Most of them came for the views and sightseeing; no one cared about noticing the paranormals in their midst. But a writer whose entire career depended on investigating my kind? I did not like the sound of that.

Before I could ask Joe what he thought of the book tour, Rory reappeared at my side. I glanced from her to Archer's entourage, shocked to see perfectly crafted lattes in their hands without so much as one spill. Rory could do her job well when she wanted to. Noted.

She pulled out a lip balm from her apron and applied what I counted as coat number forty-seven since she started her shift a few hours ago. "So?"

Words Rory refused to speak hung in the air. I waited for her to speak while Joe tapped his foot impatiently under the table. When Rory stayed silent, I nudged her with my elbow. "Spill it. You obviously have something you want to share."

"Well, it's not great," she said.

"We need more than that, Rory. Use your words like we talked about."

The witch pulled up a chair and settled in between Joe and me. Her large eyes narrowed to slits as she watched the table of strangers near to us. Lowering her voice, she whispered, "See the girl with the two laptops open?"

I nodded. Miss Cyber-chic was hard to miss.

"She's Archer's social media guru. All that stuff about him on the net, that's all her. And the guy playing with the camera? That's his personal assistant slash film crew. Apparently, they're here to film Archer's visit into town and it's going to be part of some big documentary they're working on."

"That doesn't sound all that terrible," Joe said.

At this, Rory's voice lowered a few octaves until we could barely hear her at all. I leaned in, my elbows sticking to the sticky table. Gross. When the three of us got close enough, we resembled a football huddle. Rory cleared her throat and nodded to the table. "The girl that ordered their drinks is Archer's research assistant," she said, quiet as a mouse. "And Archer isn't just here for a book signing. He's going to expose the paranormal activity in Orchard Hollow and he's going to plaster the proof all over social media."

Mouth dry, I reached for the coffee cup again, then slapped myself mentally, my hand dropping into my lap. I watched the table of strangers and tried to make out what they said, but I was too far away.

Hands fidgeting, I felt light sparks of electricity cover my skin and crammed my hands under my thighs instantly, worried I may be found out. The last thing I needed was for Archer Lee's crew to see me use magic out in the open.

As much as I tried to push it down, worry coated my stomach.

Paranormals stayed hidden for centuries and a part of me knew this was nothing more than a passing threat. People like Archer Lee had always been around; they always tried to out our existence, and they always failed. Humans did not want to know that the things hiding in the shadows were real.

Then why did I have a knot in my throat the size of a witch's cauldron?

I shoved my hands further under my legs and met Joe's concerned gaze. Archer Lee's arrival sent a very clear message—no matter what happened, until the author left town, magic was off limits.

Life in Orchard Hollow was about to become very, very interesting.

# CHAPTER 3

"Darling, when will you learn? Noses in books don't make for good social lives."

Not bothering to look at Stella, I finished the paragraph I was reading and closed the book. "I'm trying to find something, anything, to help me understand my magic. *You're* the one who suggested I get to the bottom of it!"

"I also suggested you donate your wardrobe and start fresh, but here we are."

"Ugh! Stella!" My hand slapped the table for emphasis, having little effect on the ghost. She didn't even flinch. If anything, Stella seemed to be impressed by my outburst, which should have worried me more.

"This is important," I said as calmly as I could manage. "If there was ever a time to get a grip on the situation, it's now. I can't risk my powers going haywire around Archer Lee. For all we know, I'll end up the lead character in his next book."

Stella's eyes twinkled. "Imagine the men lining up your door once you're famous!"

"I. Won't. Be. Famous," I said between clenched teeth. "I'll be a lab rat at best. Dead at worst. Have we learned nothing from the past? Humans don't take kindly to witches. I have no idea what to do."

Hanging my head low, I tried not to let the tears burning the back of my eyelids fall. I missed gran desperately. So much so, my entire body felt it. No matter what life dealt, she was level-headed and knew exactly what to do. She knew how to talk me down off a ledge and, right now, I was tiptoeing the edge and ready to hurl myself over. How did a witch with almost no magical abilities inherit such strange, powerful magic? And why did these powers wait until I was in my forties to manifest? It was as though someone was playing a joke on me and any second, a crew would jump out to tell me I'm being filmed for a gag reel.

I looked around the office. Waiting. "Nope, not a joke. This really is my life."

"Unfortunate, isn't it?"

Picking up a pen from the desk, I whipped it at Stella like a ninja star. It sliced through her arm and her ghostly body shimmered, becoming slightly more transparent than before. "Ouch!" Stella yelped. "Violence will not solve anything."

"According to you, neither will reading."

Stella arched an eyebrow. "Correct me if I'm wrong, but did you find your answers in that ridiculous tome Nerd Boy dropped off?"

She had me there. Not only did I not find what I was looking for, but I wasted precious time reading that nonsense. After skimming through it, I was pretty sure the book Joe dropped off had as much to do with actual magic as the Rose Hollow Hotel was haunted. Spoiler alert: there wasn't one ghost in the old hotel. Much like there wasn't one bit of truthful information about magic in this book.

I slid the ragged thing off the table and tossed it into my purse. "Keep an eye out on the place," I told Stella. "I'm going to give this back to Joe."

"You closed an hour ago," Stella reminded me. "While you're with the vampire, maybe you could give him a little—"

Shutting the office door before Stella could finish the sentence, I made an oat matcha to go and left the cafe, heading for Brooks Books. My eyes scanned the street as I walked, watching for Archer Lee. Despite it being later in the evening, Cliff Row was filled with people. Even the Orchard Hollow Royal Bank had a lineup outside. I couldn't recognize any familiar faces as I walked and by the third shoulder-bump, it was clear most were tourists. A group of teenage girls rushed by me, giggling as they ran into Ray's ice cream shop. I slowed my pace and peered inside. The girls shouted off their orders and asked for samples of almost every flavor behind the glass. My gaze met Ray's, and I snorted a laugh when the stocky old man mouthed "help me" before filling a tiny cup with an even tinier spoon.

Orchard Hollow was not scheduled for the holiday rush for another month or so. I glanced around again, noticing a similarity in the people crowding the street. Most were young and dressed in fashion not normally donned in our small town. Over here it was comfort before style and nothing about the tourists screamed comfort. I did a double take as a man in bright orange dress shoes and a red silk blazer crossed the street ahead of me. Nothing utilitarian about that.

The newcomers could only mean one thing: these were Archer Lee's groupies; and from the looks of it, the author was more popular than I realized.

By the time I made it to the bookshop, Joe was

already outside. He fumbled with his keys, catching them, only to have them make a break for it again and fall to the ground. When Joe bent down, I found a renewed interest in my shoelaces, so I didn't end up staring at his behind like...well, like Stella.

I seemed to have forgotten that I don't have eyes on top of my head because, in my urgency not to be a creep, I forgot to watch where I was going and ended up slamming my shoulder into a passerby. My body twisted around, the latte flying from hands and splattering all over the asphalt. I started to reach for it, but a hard object crashed into the top of my head, and I stumbled backward, slipping in the coffee and crashing down on the sidewalk. "Ow!" I yelped, rubbing my hip.

*If I need a hip replacement, Stella is never going to let me live it down.*

My eyes traveled up to see what leveled me, and horror crawled its way up my body. I slammed my head directly into Joe's behind. The very same behind I was trying to avoid.

*Maybe if I close my eyes, he won't see me.*

"Hey, Piper."

*Crap!* I peeled my lids apart and took Joe's extended hand, allowing him to pull me up. "Hi. Um, about that..." *Put your hand down! Why are you pointing at his butt?*

"I'm used to it," Joe said, waving me off. "The day you stop trying to run me over is when I'll start to worry. Did you need anything from the shop? I just locked up."

"I actually came by to return this."

Handing the book over, I took a couple of deep breaths and hoped the heat in my cheeks subsided before Joe noticed. His fingers locked around the book, and he tucked it into his jacket pocket, frowning. "Nothing useful, huh?"

"Nope," I admitted. "Fun read though."

"It was worth a shot, I guess. Hey, I was about to walk down to the beach. Care to join?"

I had no idea if I cared to join or not. After Joe revealed that he was a vampire, I had every intention of staying away from him. But I had to admit, he was not like any other vampire I met. Joe wasn't conceited, and he certainly didn't act like he was better than the humans we shared our town with. There was a lot of his past I didn't know, but from what I could see thus far, he was a stand-up guy. Aside from Stella liking him, I'd say Joe was a great candidate to get out of the dating dry spell I was under.

Then why was I having so much trouble accepting his invitations?

"Piper?"

My eyes blinked rapidly, snapping me out of my trance. "Sorry, I—"

"Have other plans," Joe finished for me. "Some other time."

"Definitely. I promised Stella we'd work on my magic again tonight and you know how she gets when I leave her hanging."

"Of course," Joe grudgingly agreed.

He most definitely did not know the full extent of my familiar's wrath. A few weeks ago, I made the choice to tell Joe everything, and I mean *everything*, about my magic. This included Stella, who, despite being useful when she wanted to be, was the oddest part of how my magic manifested. Having a ghost familiar was unheard of and only added to the confusion of my powers.

When I revealed my well-kept secret, Joe didn't even bat an eye. He asked no questions and since he found out, acted as though it was the most normal thing in the world: as though I was normal. While I loved how easy it was to be with Joe, I had my reservations. He was still a vampire, and no one knew how those guys would react if you struck them the wrong way. Even someone as easygoing as Joe could have a short fuse, and as a vampire, he'd be better at hiding it. They were a smooth-talking bunch. So, considering my less than stellar dating history, I left a couple of things out when introducing Joe to the idea of Stella.

Things like her mysterious murder which she refused to talk about, even though she miraculously started regaining her memory of the horrific event.

As it turned out, Stella may or may not have died on her own terms.

Each time I brought it up, the ghost brushed me off. Out of respect for her, I stayed out of it until she was ready. I extended that respect to Joe and how much I was willing to share. If Stella felt her death was none of my business, it was definitely none of Joe's.

Which was why all Joe knew of Stella was that a: she was dead; b: she was my familiar; and c: she was the most opinionated person on the planet.

Joe cleared his throat, and I shook my head, realizing I drifted off again. "Anyway," I said. "I should probably get going. Thank you for the book."

"I wish it was more helpful. Have you thought maybe—" His words cut away, and I noticed discomfort cover his features. "Never mind."

"Oh, come on! I walked into your butt. No need to hold back with me."

The vampire laughed, and I tried not to think about how the sound made me shiver. "In that case," Joe said, chuckling, "I was thinking about what I saw when I was a kid."

My eyes bulged. "You mean when you saw me bring a squirrel back to life?" I asked. "Allegedly."

"It happened, trust me. And yes, about that. Have you considered that you had this magic your entire life?"

I seriously have not considered it. At all.

Why would I? I was a witch. My mother is a witch. Gran was a witch. I could keep going, but the point stayed the same. Every woman in our family line was born a witch. It was the paranormal gene my family carried and while some did not have their gene activated, it didn't change the magic in their blood. The Addisons were witches. It was what defined us, what made us whole. Until me. For most of my life, I was pretty useless as a witch, and now—now I was something else.

Except, what if Joe was right? What if I was no good at being a witch because it wasn't what I was?

"That doesn't make any sense," I said, unsure if I was answering Joe or myself. "If I was born with this magic, why did it wait so long to manifest? Why now, halfway through my life? And how does it explain what you think you saw when we were kids?"

Joe worked his jaw while I attempted not to think about how chiseled it was. "I'm not sure. But it's worth considering. Any way you can find out your family history? See if anyone else might have had the same powers?"

*Doubtful.* "I'll see what I can do," I lied. "Rain check on the walk?"

As we said our goodbyes and I made my way back to the old, rust-bucket of a car I parked near the cafe, my thoughts ran miles in my head. The Addison family tree was not exactly well-researched. Most of what I knew of my lineage came from gran's stories and since she was a powerful, well-known witch around these parts, I took her words for what they were worth. I took them for the truth. It never occurred to me to research the history of our family. Even if it did, where would I start? The one person who could answer my questions was long gone; mom ran off to join a dark magic coven and left gran and I in the dust.

*Could I?*

"No!" I told myself. "Absolutely not."

I wasn't contacting my mom for anything. Even if the woman knew how to explain what was happening to me, no amount of information would be worth having her back in my life. I was finally on my feet, and I wasn't about to let Sylvie Addison ruin it. There were other ways to get to the bottom of my family's background, and I would exhaust every route before I invited trouble back into my life.

My steps sped up, the sun setting at my back and casting Cliff Row in a shade of orange. I squinted my eyes, about to open the beetle, when something stopped me dead in my tracks. My heart gave a jolt and sweat pooled at the base of my spine as a blood-curdling scream sounded from the narrow side-street I parked the beetle on.

*Oh, no. Not again.*

# CHAPTER 4

Panic blurred my vision, and I stutter-stepped backward, the pitch of the scream knocking me down. It sounded so close. I reached for my phone, ready to call the police, then paused. The sheriff and I had only recently gotten back on good terms, and I didn't want to waste his time unless I was absolutely sure there was something to report. Slipping the phone back into my purse, I started for the side street.

"Ah!"

Goosebumps covered my flesh and my pace quickened as I darted left toward the voice. My body wracked with nerves and the beads of sweat at the base of my back froze in the cool air. Footsteps landing hard on the rough gravel of the small street, I rounded the corner. My hands reached into my bag, searching for a weapon I could defend myself with.

Nothing.

Unless you counted the half-eaten, soggy bagel; my means of self-defense were slim to none. *Perhaps the attacker is allergic to sesame seeds?* I shook my head and reached deep down to call on my magic. Electricity sparked on my fingertips and my entire body shivered with the energy I felt within me. My skin was on fire, and I loved it.

Eyes darting left and right, I made sure no one was around to see me use magic and crept closer to where I heard the screams.

"Ew! Shoo!"

My legs dug into the ground. That did not sound like someone in trouble.

Crouching, I spotted the beetle a few feet away and crawled toward it, making sure to stay out of sight. The streetlights have not yet been turned on despite the sun having set and it was dark enough that I could hide easily. Slowing my breathing, I dared to poke my head out from behind the beetle's wide back.

"Get out of here!" a girl's high-pitched voice exclaimed.

I recognized that voice. Without a doubt, it belonged to one of the girls Rory identified as Archer

Lee's employees. My eyes narrowed to make out her shape in the dimness and sure enough, I spotted the two buns in her hair: pens and all. The girl stomped her feet a few times and made a waving motion with her arm. I followed her gaze to another parked car and stifled a laugh. At the base of the front wheel crouched Harry Houdini. His back arched and his bushy tail vibrated, indicating this girl had something he wanted. Harry hissed, and the girl tossed a wrapper his way, yelling, "Fine! Take it!"

Harry's grabby paws wrapped around the bar of candy on the floor, and he hissed once more before ducking under the car. Not to be seen again.

Feeling foolish, I was about to crawl my stalker butt away when the girl spoke.

"Seriously, this town is the worst! I don't know why you like it." My breath caught in my throat, and I pressed my palms to the ground, peeking out into the street. "A damn raccoon just stole my chocolate. Everything here sucks."

At least her main complaint for Orchard Hollow was Harry's crime and not the magic we hid from humans. If his research assistant didn't know about paranormals, there was a chance Archer Lee didn't have a leg to stand on when it came to exposing our town's dirty secret. I was pulling at strings, and I knew it. But hey, a woman could hope.

"Don't Zeta me!" the assistant yelled into the phone. "I wasn't even supposed to be here. We had a deal, and you blew it. I told you a million times I want to be as far away from this place as possible, especially this week. But here I am!"

She turned toward me, and I ducked behind the beetle so fast, I saw stars. My lungs refused to work, and I swallowed the air I held in my cheeks like a freaking hamster, hoping I didn't pass out. Feet shuffled back and forth as the assistant, Zeta, paced the width of the street and back again. Whoever she was talking to, she was nervous. I wondered why Archer's research assistant would want to be away from Orchard Hollow during this particular week. From what Rory told me, the tour was a pretty big deal to the author. Shouldn't his assistant be at least somewhat excited?

From the sounds of it, Zeta wanted nothing to do with the entire event.

Ears perked, I pursed my lips and continued to listen.

"I don't care," she ground out through clenched teeth. "This is getting out of control. You have this week to dig up what you need or I'm out." She took a breath in, then added, "And I swear, if I go down for this because of you, you'll be sorry."

*Wait, what?* My hand slipped, and I toppled over, shoulder hitting the rear bumper with a thud. *Crap!*

"Hang on," Zeta said. I heard her steps shuffle nearer to me. "I think there's someone here."

I pressed my back to the car so tight; I became one with the beetle. Grime and dirt coated my jacket, and I gagged in my mouth. I really needed to wash the dumpster on wheels one of these days. I was about to come clean and explain why I was spying on Zeta when another noise stopped me in my tracks. Familiar chitters echoed down the street and I heard Zeta yell out again. "Ugh! The damn raccoon is back! I have to go. Get your act together. I mean it!"

With that, she hung up. Letting go of a loud huff, Zeta shoved her phone into her pocket and sped down the street, away from me and Harry, who climbed out from under the car to demand more chocolate. When I was sure the coast was clear, I stood up and walked toward the rascal, pulling out my leftover sandwich. "Here you go, Harry," I said, dropping it next to his outstretched paw. "You earned it."

Heart racing, I fumbled for the car keys and poured myself into the beetle. It took forever to warm up and while I sat there, shivering, I recounted Zeta's conversation. Without context, I had no idea what I overheard. No matter how I tried to piece it together, the experience left a strange taste in my mouth. I groaned, bringing my hands to the vent to soak up some of the heat. It seemed even the tourists in Orchard Hollow had secrets.

Maybe Zeta was right. Maybe this place did suck.

Suddenly, her words sharpened in my mind and my lips curled at the edges. Zeta mentioned digging and while I didn't know what she referred to, it gave me an idea for my own problem.

I was also in need of some digging. When it came to buried family secrets, there was only one place I could think of to look. Gran's mountain of useless junk in the attic. I hadn't stepped foot in the hazardous dust-collecting tomb since she passed, but it might hold something that could point me in the right direc-tion. It was worth checking out since my other option was to track down mom and there was no way in fresh hell would I be doing that any time soon.

My spirits uplifted, I started the car and headed home, leaving Zeta's odd conversation, Harry Houdini, and the wrapper from a soggy sandwich behind.

# CHAPTER 5

"The key to finding the correct angle to approach paranormal activity is in the timing."

Archer Lee adjusted his burgundy, thick-rimmed glasses and ran his fingers through his hair. His index finger got stuck in a clump of hair gel and he grimaced, yanking it out. "Cut! Let's do this again. By the window this time."

At his words, the man holding what I assumed was a very expensive camera pressed a button and followed the author to Bean Me Up's front window. The two tested filming positions, then proceeded to move on with the charade. Archer drawled on and on about some nonsense I couldn't quite make out while the cameraman stared at him attentively, occasionally interrupting to readjust the microphone attached to the author's necktie.

This had been my entire morning at the cafe.

When Rory approached me to ask for a favor, I assumed it involved her skipping out early. What I didn't realize was the favor had nothing to do with my employee at all. It turned out Rory ran into Archer's crew last night and suggested they film their ridiculous spectacle of an interview at Bean Me Up. She pitched it as a quid pro quo: Archer would capture a true experience of Orchard Hollow on film for his marketing videos and the cafe would receive free exposure.

I looked around at the wires and lights spilling around three of the four available tables.

Archer Lee was definitely getting the better end of the quid.

Not only did he and his three lackeys completely overrun the cafe, but to put me through having to listen to the man speak for hours was unforgivable. It was a punishable crime, as far as I was concerned. Even before Archer opened his mouth to introduce himself when he arrived, I could tell the man was a pompous wannabe. The entire time he spoke to me, he barely made eye contact, his hazel eyes darting around the cafe while he acted as though he was so above me, I wasn't worth his time. Then he asked Rory to remake his stupid double Americano four times because apparently, the temperature had to be just right, or his precious head would explode. I was surprised the teenager complied without complaint; she had it bad for the stuffy idiot. I, on the other hand, could not stand Archer Lee. For heaven's sake, even the glasses he kept rearranging weren't real! Pathetic.

"Most people don't have what it takes to grasp the reality of the paranormal," I heard the author say.

I rolled my eyes, turning to face Rory, the two of us watching the extravaganza. "Still admire this clown?"

"He's not so bad." Rory shrugged. "Ray says this documentary might make it to a streaming network. Pretty cool, huh?"

Brow furrowing, I surveyed the group. "Which one is Ray, again?"

"Camera guy."

"Right," I said. Curly hair, eyebrows for days, hipster vest. Got it. Pouring myself a second triple espresso, I topped it up with a dollop of cream and sprinkled cinnamon on top. My eyes found Zeta, Archer's research assistant, in the corner with the backend of a pen in her mouth. She seemed to be absorbed in her laptop and I wondered if whatever she was reading had anything to do with the strange conversation I heard last night. The girl stopped reading and shot her head up, meeting my widened eyes. Cheeks burning, I investigated my coffee cup, pretending to mix the cream in over and over until I couldn't feel her eyes on me.

I wasn't sure why I was acting bizarre around Zeta. She didn't see me, didn't catch me in the act of army-crawling behind my car to eavesdrop on her. Still, the embarrassment of my pathetic behavior weighed heavily on me. I was worse than Nancy Steeles; at least the witch didn't stoop so low as to spy on people to fill her gossiping needs.

Daring to look up again, I eyed the girl sitting beside Zeta at their table. Unlike Zeta, who was fidgeting and appeared somewhat distracted, this girl was all business. Her hazel eyes glimmered in the light of the open screen, and she tapped her sharp, pointed nose with one finger while typing one-handed. "That's Vivien, then?" I asked Rory.

"Yep! Marketing Guru Extraordinaire," Rory announced. "Or so Zeta says. Apparently, Archer was a nobody on social media until she took over. But now he's like super famous, so she's magic."

I nudged her with my elbow. "What did we say about that word while they're in town?"

Lips puckering, Rory waved me off nonchalantly.

"I'm serious," I warned. "We can't draw added attention to ourselves. If this guy is half as good as he pretends to be, we need to lie low. You could cause some serious damage, so please, keep the conversation with Archer and his crew to a minimum."

As I finished speaking, the bell over the front door rang out and a group of teenagers strolled into the cafe. They took one look at Archer and whispers circulated, followed by a few excited giggles. To say I was done with the Archer Lee fanbase was an understatement. Rory, on the other hand, seemed to be sucked right into the craze and before I could ask her for help in the back, she announced, "I'm going to see what they want for drinks."

Then she rushed off to join the teens while they circled Archer like hungry hyenas.

"Excuse me?"

The voice, soft and melodic, startled me from my frustrated inner rant. I tore my attention from the front window and choked on my own saliva. *Shoot!* Before me, Zeta's nose scrunched, and she appraised me with a careful look. "Are you alright?"

"Stellar," I coughed out.

"He's almost done," Zeta told me, even though I didn't ask. "I know it's a lot to handle, but he means well for the most part."

Shakily, I put down my espresso cup. "Sorry?"

"Archer," she explained. "He shouldn't have taken over your business like this. But hey, free publicity, right?"

The way Zeta spoke painted her in a completely different light from the person I overheard on the phone yesterday. Gone was the commanding tone and bossy language. Instead, it was replaced by the voice of someone who'd had enough. It made me wonder if perhaps Zeta didn't agree with her boss's way of operating. Could that be why she didn't want to be here during the tour?

Before I could stop myself, I said, "I'm not sure the crowd this will bring is what we need in Orchard Hollow."

"You mean the occult crowd?"

I mean the burn-you-at-the-stake-you-witch crowd. My shoulders stiffened. "Sure."

"Look, I'll be honest with you," Zeta said, her voice lowered. "Archer can be a lot. If anyone knows that it's the three of us. If you only knew the things Viv had to deal with daily. His Twitter account alone.... Anyway, what I mean is, he's a handful."

"Um, okay."

"But the guy gets followers like you wouldn't believe," she added as though it explained anything. "Especially when he's hunting."

The way she said the word made the hairs rise on the back of my neck. "Hunting?"

"Hunting for paranormals," Zeta answered. "It's what he calls it when he's about to expose supernatural phenomena."

"Ahh," I whispered. My blood froze in my veins and there was a lump the size of a school bus lodged in my throat. "Can I ask you a question?"

Zeta smiled. "Sure thing."

"Do you believe any of the stuff he writes about?"

This earned me another smile, this one wider. "What I believe doesn't matter. It matters what they believe." She pointed to the teenagers who crept so close to the window, I was pretty sure one of them was in the shot. "But if there is magic out there, Archer will find it. He's like a truffle pig when it comes to sniffing out this stuff." Her face dropped. "Anyway, I have to go. They're about to wrap up and if he catches me slacking, I'll never hear the end of it."

With that, Zeta rushed back to their table; her nose buried in the laptop once more.

My shoulders hurt from the weight of her words. While Zeta meant to put me at ease about their takeover, all she did was cause more anxiety to settle in my gut. Despite her apparent distaste for Archer's public behavior, she seemed convinced he excelled at spotting paranormal activity. A wonderful trait for an author who built his empire on the business of "hunting paranormals" and horrible news for Orchard Hollow. Panic racked my body as I considered the ramifications of Archer keeping his word and exposing our town and its secrets. It wasn't only me who stood to be damaged by the truth coming into the light. Everyone was in danger.

"It is the sole reason we are here, in this quaint town," Archer's voice boomed in the background. "Mark my words, folks. This will be the book tour of a lifetime!"

"And cut!" Ray yelled out.

As he put the camera down, I heard Archer say, "Let's do it again, this time across the street. I want to get the hotel in the shot."

*Hmm. Is the Rose Hollow a big deal for you, Archer? Are you here to unearth the ghosts roaming the halls?* How I wished that was the case. I needed to find out what the next book the author was writing was about; it was the key to gauging how big of a threat he was. The way I saw it, if Archer fell for the fake news of a haunted hotel, the rest of us were in the safe zone. We'd have to be careful until he left, but at least we wouldn't be in any immediate danger.

A sudden realization hit me like a brick in the head. My eyes found Rory, and I waved her over, waiting until we were out of earshot to speak. "We need to get the word out about the tour," I said, feeling foolish for only now thinking about it. "Every paranormal must be on their best behavior. If we all have to stay home until the coast is clear, then that's what we do."

"Oh, it's taken care of already," the teenager said.

"Huh? How?"

Rory's eyebrows wiggled mischievously. "I may or may not have let my aunt know about him and she may or may not have told Miss Steeles."

Of course. This may have been the only time I was glad to have Nancy Steeles and her big mouth around. If the witch and her coven got wind of the reason for Archer's visit, there was a good chance every paranormal in town would know of it come morning. Gossip traveled faster than a witch on a broom where Nancy was involved.

I watched Rory stalk toward the espresso machine to make lattes for the group of teenagers she befriended. Though I doubted any of them would pay for their drinks, it was refreshing to see her work for a change. I was about to compliment the leaf she drew in the foam of one latte when the bell rang again.

"Hi, auntie!" Rory yelled out. "We were just talking about you."

Cilia Craven cast an annoyed glance at Archer as she passed, huffing out a breath that reached the front counter. "All good things I hope," she said. I didn't fail to notice she was looking at me when she spoke.

In the last few weeks, Cilia and I got closer, or as close as we could, considering she was part of the coven that hated my guts. Until recently, Cilia and Nancy had been attached at the hip, but things shifted after I found out about her relationship with Sebastian Tse, our resident warlock. I wasn't sure if it was because I helped solve the murder of Sebastian's cousin or if Cilia was finally seeing Nancy for who she was. Whatever it was, she wasn't such a wretched witch towards me. It was a breath of fresh air.

"Nothing to worry about," I told her. "Are you working today?"

Cilia's eyes darted to the hotel across the street. "Not until evening. I thought I'd stop by to see how Rory is doing."

"I'm fabulous," Rory announced. "Right, Piper?"

Fabulous was not the word I'd use to describe her work ethic, but I swallowed my disdain. "You're learning fast," I offered. "Can I get you a drink?"

Studying the menu on the board behind us, Cilia tapped a long, polished nail on the counter. "Why not? How about the oat—"

BAM!

Her words were cut out by the sound of a crash, followed by a scream. My head jerked toward the front window, thinking Archer broke something while filming. When I saw the man's stunned expression, I knew he wasn't the problem. I followed his gaze to the table Zeta and Vivien sat at, my heart sinking to my boots. At the base of the table lay Zeta, her face covered with her hand so I couldn't see her eyes. Above her, Vivien crouched and yelled words I couldn't make out.

"Is there a doctor here?" she yelled again; this time clearer.

I looked from Rory to Cilia, whose eyes were so wide they resembled big, bulging orbs. Rounding the counter, I rushed toward Zeta. I ducked beside her, my instinct urging me to move her hand away.

When I did, I wish I hadn't.

Zeta's face was ashen and as I brought my ear to her parted lips, I couldn't hear her breathe. Her eyes, wide open and blank, stared back at me as I turned around and yelled, "Someone called an ambulance!"

Several people got on their phones instantly. I saw two teens fumble with the keys, but it was Cilia who finally got through. "They're on their way," she said, shielding Rory with her body. "They want to know what happened."

My gaze traveled up and down Zeta's body. Her legs buckled under her from when she fell and there was foam dripping from the corner of her lips. Under her hair, the coffee she spilled going down spread in an oozing puddle. Her lips were blue and the buns she had secured atop her head had come undone, messy waves laying behind her like spilled ink.

Stifling a cry, I backed away from Zeta. "I'm not sure," I said. "But this girl is dead."

# CHAPTER 6

While we waited for the sheriff to arrive, silence covered the cafe in its icy dome. When I got a hold of Romero, he instructed us to stay put and we did just that; no one moved an inch since the truth of the situation daunted on us.

Zeta was dead.

I huddled near the front counter beside Cilia and Rory, occasionally making eye contact with the few patrons in front. Everyone divided into their respective groups, and it made the cafe feel like solitary confinement. Archer, Ray, and Vivien stayed near the window; their equipment gathered into several neat piles on the floor. The teenagers hovered by the display wall nearest the restroom. Four of the five called their families at Romero's instructions and sat diligently next to their parents while we waited.

One thing was for certain: we all kept as far away from Zeta's lifeless body as possible.

"Well, will you look at that?"

Head straight and eyes on the door, I struggled to wave Stella off, but she wouldn't get the clue. The ghost floated to Zeta's body, hovering over her for a few seconds before whooshing down and shoving her pointy nose into the girl's mouth. *Ew, gross. Why, Stella? Why?* If she could hear my thoughts, she made no motion to acknowledge me. My familiar took another whiff, then bolted up and vanished, reappearing beside me. Her shoulder was only an inch away from mine and shivers broke down my arms.

I stood up and pretended to stretch. "I think I need another coffee," I announced. "Does anyone want anything?"

Most didn't answer, though I did get a request for an oat matcha latte from one mom. Her cheeks had sunken in since she arrived, and she kept glancing at her phone while comforting her daughter. The woman was a ball of nerves, and I was certain caffeine would not help. I made a note to opt for a decaf when making her drink and started up the espresso machine. The whirring of the grinder masked my hushed words as I began to grill Stella. "What are you doing? Leave the girl alone."

"Not sure if you noticed," Stella rebutted, "but I don't think she minds. On account of being dead and all."

I untwisted the portafilter and banged out soggy grinds. "Why are you smelling a corpse? That's weird even for you."

"If you must know, I was confirming a suspicion."

"Which was?"

Stella opened her mouth to speak, but the sound of the bell ringing cut her off. She sneered deviously and waved her slender fingers in my face. "Toodles," she sing-songed. "Good luck with all of this."

"Ugh!" I yelped, a little too loud.

Archer and Ray both shot their heads up to look at me and I coughed, covering my outburst as best as I could. Luckily, it was the exact moment that Romero burst inside with his team. All eyes turned to the door. The sheriff stalked into the cafe with two deputies on his tail and a third man—one I vividly recalled— behind them. The coroner's gaze drifted over the scene and landed on me, his brow furrowing.

*Trust me, buddy. I'm as shocked as you are.*

With a nod, he veered off from the rest and made a beeline for Zeta, his large case banging on the floor beside her. The sound of locks clicking open echoed through the cafe. We stood frozen, watching the coroner as he examined the body. His hands moved quickly, checking for a pulse, then nodding at Romero to confirm what I already knew. Zeta was gone and nothing was bringing her back.

The coroner—I really should learn the man's name—swabbed Zeta's lips and deposited the swab in a plastic container. He repeated the same motion on the lip of the broken coffee cup on the floor and handed both packages to one officer. Then he pinned Romero with a serious glare. "You can rule out a natural death," he announced. "This woman was poisoned."

"I could have told you that," Stella said beside me.

Ignoring her, I kept my focus on Romero and the coroner, who now hung close to the body and exchanged words I couldn't make out. I wondered why they bothered speaking discreetly when the coroner already announced to the entire cafe that Zeta was murdered. If the sheriff planned to get a confession out of someone, wouldn't it make sense to hide his hand? Or at least bluff until the killer got scared enough to talk?

My knees buckled.

Another death in Orchard Hollow.

What was up with our town lately? Were the ley lines acting out and causing people to lose their sense of right and wrong? I never knew of ley line energy interfering with humans, but it wasn't out of the question. Magic constantly grew; it evolved. Perhaps it changed enough to affect the entire population of Orchard Hollow. Or maybe a town full of secrets was always going to combust? A ticking time bomb waiting to go off when we least expected it. My gaze traveled over the people in the cafe, landing on Archer. All his self-assured demeanor evaporated and his face paled until he was almost as gray as Stella. The fake glasses sat so low on his pointed nose, I thought they might drop at any moment. Archer must have felt so too because he removed them carefully and slid them across the window table. My teeth split open. It was surprising to see his act collapse, but I supposed finding out someone killed your assistant would do that to a man.

Next to Archer, Vivien stood with hunched shoulders and puffy, red eyes. Occasionally, she sniffled loudly and wiped her nose with a napkin Archer handed her earlier. I had half the mind to get her an entire pack from the back, but I didn't dare leave my spot.

Giving the cafe one more glance, I inched closer to Cilia and Rory. I was about to check on the two when a throat cleared behind me. "A word, Miss Addison?"

Turning slowly, I smiled meekly at the sheriff and nodded, gesturing for the back office. He stalked off, and I followed, closing the door behind us. When it was only the two of us and I was certain I couldn't be overheard, I sucked in a breath and faced Romero.

"Look, it wasn't me, okay? I didn't even know the girl until yesterday."

The sheriff held up a hand. "Relax. I'm not accusing you of anything." Then added, "Yet."

My blood froze in my veins and my head spun. I steadied myself with a hand on the wall, trying to appear more like someone who wasn't about to pass out. Somehow, the reality of what happened waited to sink in until this very moment, with Romero watching my every move. My thoughts raced. Not only did someone else die in Orchard Hollow, but they died on my turf. Again. This time even closer.

As though on cue, the rear door slid slowly open, and I rolled my eyes, waiting for the sheriff to notice the thief amongst us. It took Romero a second to spot Harry's clumsy behind, and when he did, he had to do a double take to make sure he was seeing correctly.

"Is that a—"

"Raccoon," I said, nodding. "Correct. Meet Harry Houdini."

"I'd much rather not," the sheriff replied.

Frowning, I walked to the desk and reached for the broom I kept there. These days, I didn't even need to use the stupid thing. Harry hated the broom almost as much as he hated Stella, so all I had to do was show him my weapon of choice and he'd go running. Wrapping my fingers around the handle, I glanced at the sheriff. "Give me a moment."

Not bothering to explain further, I leapt into Harry's path, the broom in clear view. The beast slowed his already snail-like stride and his vision narrowed with a singular purpose. Teeth gleamed in the overhead lights as the raccoon stood on his hind legs and hissed.

*Not today, Harry!*

I lifted the broom in the air and made a sweeping motion. "Out you go!" I bit out, pointing to the exit. "No treats today!"

Catching my drift, Harry hissed three times in a row, drummed his front paws in the air, then dropped on all fours and scurried away. His big butt pushed the back door wide open when he left, and I had to follow the monster outside to lock up. With Bean Me Up's nuisance out of the way, I placed the broom by the door and sighed, turning back to the sheriff.

His bulging eyes widened, and he opened his mouth, then closed it again.

"Don't ask," I said.

Romero nudged his chin to the broom. "Not how I thought witches used those."

"Are you serious? We don't actually ride them!" I scoffed. "You're worse than..."

I nearly said Stella's name but stopped myself. Now was not the time to reveal to the sheriff that I had a certain ghost of the annoying variety following me around. Not when there was a dead body fifty feet from us, and definitely not after he watched me chase a raccoon out of my place of business with a broom. Romero distrusted paranormals enough without me unleashing the crazy. I brushed a loose strand of red hair off my face and leaned against the desk. "Anyway, you were saying?"

The sheriff cleared his throat again and rubbed his eyes as though he could scrub them clean of the last five minutes.

"Right," he said. "I need to know who had access to Miss Huxley's coffee since this morning."

Back ramrod straight, I asked, "You think someone poisoned her coffee?"

"It is the most reasonable explanation," was all the sheriff said.

I got the sense I wasn't going to get any more infor-mation out of him, considering we were back here again. Him, me, and a corpse between us. *Stay out of it,* I told myself. *Answer his questions and call it a day.* The last thing I needed was to get myself wrapped up in another murder investigation, so whatever got Romero off my back and out of the cafe was what I had to concentrate on. Just because Zeta died right in front of me, didn't mean I had to place myself knee-deep in police business.

Forcing a meek smile, I straightened my curled spine and rolled my shoulders. "I didn't pay much attention to their table," I answered. "Rory made her coffee about twenty minutes before she collapsed. After that, I tried to stay out of their way for the most part."

"You didn't speak to the victim?"

"Not for long," I admitted. "We chatted for a bit, but it wasn't anything notable."

The sheriff's favorite notepad was out again, and he was writing down what I said word for word. He underlined a sentence, looking at me. "What did you talk about?"

"Like I said, nothing important. She came by to apologize for her boss, said they'd be done soon and out of our hair."

"Hmm. Why did she feel the need to apologize? Did something happen?"

I shook my head. "No, no. I think she felt she needed to because Archer Lee is, well, unbearable.

And a bit of an ass." My fingers instinctively reached for the spot on my sweater once holding gran's brooch. "Other than that, we didn't speak. This morning was the first time Zeta said a word to me and I'm pretty certain she only came by because Rory must have mentioned I was over their spectacle."

Waiting until the sheriff finished writing, I looked around the office. Was I forgetting anything? I tried to work through the morning, recounting my exact steps and piecing together what I could of Zeta's time at Bean Me Up. Their crew arrived shortly after we opened and I busied myself stalking the displays, avoiding getting in the way. I vaguely recalled Zeta and Vivien arguing over a social media post and Archer breaking it up. After that, filming commenced, and the girls stayed glued to their respective laptops. Vivien couldn't have killed Zeta over a post, could she?

I ground my teeth. That theory seemed too far-fetched even for me. Muffled words filled my ears, and I snapped back to reality in time to hear Romero ask, "Was Rory the only one near the cup?"

"Yes," I answered. Then quickly added, "But she didn't do it. Like me, Rory has no reason to want Zeta dead."

"I never implied that."

"I know how you roll by now," I countered.

The sheriff deadpanned, and I buckled back, my

butt hitting the desk. "Then you know what our next steps are," he growled out. "If you are sure no one else had access to Miss Huxley's coffee, I'll need to question everyone here before we can clear the scene. And," he added, "since you know our police procedures so well, I don't need to remind you the cafe is to remain closed until I confirm otherwise. Again."

"Again. Of course."

Mind spinning, my jaw snapped shut as I recalled last night. "Actually," I told Romero. "There is one thing you might find interesting."

Slowly, and in great detail, I recounted everything that happened the night before. I told the sheriff about the phone call I overheard Zeta take, about her reaction. I even told him about Harry and the dirty stains on my jacket from the back of the beetle. The way I saw it, no detail was too small, and I'd preferred for Romero to have too much information than not enough of it. The last time I kept things to myself, I ended up almost getting killed, so I wasn't taking any chances. The more I could tell Romero now, the less he'd bother me later.

And the faster I could get the police, and Zeta's body, out of the cafe.

When I finished speaking, I asked, "What happens now?"

Romero looked me up and down as he pocketed

the notebook. The hat he wore today slipped low on his brow and half his face darkened in its shadow. "Now my deputies and I get to work," he said. "I'd power up that espresso machine if I were you, Miss Addison. It's going to be a long day."

# CHAPTER 7

Romero wasn't kidding about it being a long day. My back ached from standing for hours while he and his deputies conducted interviews with everyone in the cafe. It being an active crime scene and the suspect pool narrowed to those of us present meant no one could leave. Not even for a second. At one point, Ray tried to sneak out for a cigarette break and one deputy actually threatened to cuff the guy. But it wasn't all bad; at least they took the body away.

The scent of death permeated the cafe long after the coroner wheeled Zeta out in a body bag. It clung to every surface and tainted the space, making me wonder if Bean Me Up will forever be known as the place people die in.

It wasn't too far off the mark.

I frowned, biting my nails as the last of the interviews wrapped up. It was with one of the girls in the group of teens and I watched her squirm in her seat as Romero's deputy grilled her. Behind her, the girl's father stood with broad shoulders and a grim look on his face.

"She's going to cry for sure," Rory whispered.

Beside my employee, Cilia's stoic expression faltered as she flinched at her niece's crass attitude. The witch pulled Rory's elbow and yanked her down to sit. "Have some respect," she snapped.

"And eat your croissant," I added. "You haven't eaten all day."

The comment earned me a satisfied glare from Cilia, and I nodded, sliding a plate with a second croissant her way. "You should eat too. It's getting late."

"Do you think we'll get out of here soon?" Cilia asked, checking her watch. "I need to get Rory home before her dad rips me a new one."

"Looks like they might be wrapping up. I'm sorry you two got roped into this," I said. Then added, "I can't believe this is happening again."

The three of us exchanged solemn looks, and I fidgeted nervously, craning my neck to take a mental inventory of the cafe. Everyone appeared to be abso-lutely wrecked. The teenagers and their parents slumped in the few chairs available, and several rested their heads on the table, their eyes shut in deep sleep. I noticed two boys cling together, whispering softly and occasionally glancing around. They were probably taking guesses at which one of us was the cold-blooded murderer of the group. I couldn't blame them; I was doing the same thing.

My eyes narrowed as I surveyed Archer Lee and his remaining team members. Each of them sported similar looks of worry with creased brows, red eyes, and quivering lips. The egocentric air around the author dissipated with Zeta's death and it depressed me to know this was what it took for him to get over himself. As pompous as Archer was, he really did seem genuinely upset. Though not quite as destroyed as Vivien.

The girl was unrecognizable.

Her dark, long hair was matted from her constant pulling of it and her nose was as red as blood, worn out from too many blows. She brought another napkin to her face, dabbing it under her watery eyes, and let out a quiet whimper. Next to her, Ray reached an arm over and squeezed her shoulder, a gesture which didn't do much to relax his distressed co-worker. She turned her nose up, looking at him through wet lashes. "How did this happen?" I heard her ask.

Ray shrugged and shook his head, staying silent.

What a strange question to ask. Their co-worker collapsed in front of them, dying instantly, and all Vivien wanted to know was how it came to be. Not why or who—how.

I rubbed my temples.

*Don't get involved.*

Romero must have sensed me inserting myself into yet another investigation with his freaky third eye because he chose that moment to say, "We got what we needed here. You folks can go home."

As people cleared out, I kept my eye on the sheriff to see if I could read his demeanor. He kept a straight face, his attitude solid despite what happened. Somehow Romero was used to this by now, though we both knew what it meant for the town. Orchard Hollow was no longer the quiet, peaceful place we once lived in. People died here. The plural was key. I thought about gran and what she might have thought of the last few months. I'd bet she'd have spells exactly for this occasion.

My chest tightened.

With the craziness of the day, I completely forgot I promised Stella I'd be home early to snoop out the attic. Leaving the cafe in a hot mess, I vowed to clean up in the morning and followed the crowd outside. No one lingered, and I was glad to have a moment of peace as I locked up for the night. My steps quickened on the way to the car, and I tried to swallow the awful taste in my mouth the day left behind. More than anything, I wanted to follow the sheriff to the police station and find out what his thoughts were on the matter, but I couldn't risk it. Romero had the situation handled, and I had problems of my own to get home to.

I needed to trust the cops to do their jobs so I could get back to Stella. If there was one thing the dead snob liked less than bad fashion sense, it was tardiness.

Breaths coming quick, I started the beetle and drove home, readying for a fight.

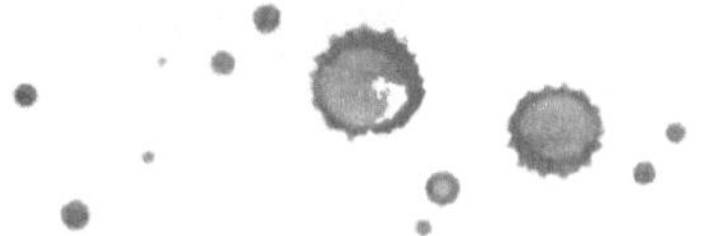

"Stella! Don't!" I yelled, ducking out of the way as a day-old dinner roll zoomed by. In the last few months, my familiar was hard at work trying different ways to have a physical presence in our world. She couldn't do much, but her moving objects game was on point. Unfortunately. "Seriously?" I bellowed. "You finally learn to interact with the living, and this is what you choose to do?"

The remark earned me a date with the dinner roll's moldy cousin. This time, I didn't swerve fast enough and got forehead-slapped by mildew and what appeared to be room-temperature butter. I gagged in my mouth, wiping myself down with a kitchen towel.

On the other side of the counter, my ghost familiar ground her unnaturally white teeth. "One: I will do what I please with my talents. Two: serves you right for leaving me to rot all night."

"I was only an hour late. Will you get a grip?"

"Grip this!" Stella yelled, catapulting another roll.

Unfortunately, I did grip that. My fingers closed around the roll and a squishy sound echoed through the kitchen as I squeezed the life out of the pastry. Why, in the name of all that is good, did I not throw these out? I really needed to get a handle on cleaning up. The farmhouse was starting to look worse for wear and I shuddered to think of what gran would have said if she saw it in this condition. Groaning, I threw the roll into the garbage and rinsed my hand in the sink, though it would be days before the stench of old bread would leave my fingers. "Are you quite finished?" I asked Stella. "Someone died. I couldn't very well leave without being arrested and last I checked, telling the sheriff a ghost is waiting on me wasn't on the excuses-for-disobeying-his-orders list. Now, can we PLEASE get back to what's important?"

"Oh, good," Stella said with a huff. "You're finally going to get a haircut."

I rolled my eyes. "Not that! The attic. Or did you forget the plan already?"

Not missing a beat, Stella vanished, only to materialize a second later at the top landing of the stairs. "Darling, there are two things I would never forget," she said. "The summer I met Lagerfeld in Paris and plans to find a witch's gold."

"For the last time, there is not gold!" I stalked up the stairs after her. "We're going to go through gran's things and see if we can find anything to help me piece together my magic. Magic—yes. Gold—no."

"Whatever you say," Stella whispered. In her eyes, I saw the glimmer of mischief, which usually meant she didn't hear a word I said.

The evening was off to a stellar start.

Mumbling under my breath, I followed the spoiled-brat-of-a-ghost up the stairs and to the pull-down ladder. It had been so long since I stepped foot up here—not since long before gran passed—when I dropped the ladder, a pile of dust fell from the attic and covered me head to toe. I coughed, clearing the air with my hand before venturing up. At the edge of the opening, Stella waited with her arms crossed and her eyes wide. My palms spread on the creaky wood floor, and I pulled myself up, eyes watering from the smell of mildew filling the tight space.

Fumbling in the dark, I found the rope for the overhead light and clicked it on. The bulb swung from side to side, revealing the disaster that was the attic in fractions.

"Yikes," Stella breathed out. "This is worse than your bedroom closet."

My head snapped to her. "Stay out of my closet!"

"Trust me, it's not as riveting as you may think," she retorted, looking around. "Where do you want to start?"

"I guess we can try the boxes in the corner."

Taking a few long strides to get across, I pulled out one of the five dust-covered boxes and opened the lid. A putrid scent permeated my nostrils, and I sniffled, fighting the urge to sneeze as more dust settled into the rear of my throat. I wasn't sure how long gran kept things up here, but from the looks of it, this was generations' worth of stuff no one wanted. No wonder we barely came up here. The last time I was in the attic was when gran asked me to put away mom's belongings. I glanced at the single small suitcase at the opposite wall, my stomach turning. Yet another reminder of the woman who walked out on her family without looking back.

Turning my back to mom's crap, I settled in and started sorting through the boxes. As I brought things out, I showed them to Stella, who made continuous remarks about the ancient state of each item. We made three piles: one for junk, one for possible clues on our family magic, and one for things Stella thought deserved to leave the attic. When we finished with the last box, I took note of the piles. It seemed the garbage pile had an unfair advantage because it was the biggest of the three.

I made for an old, leather-bound journal, flipping it open. "I'm going to need a bit of time to get through all the entries."

"And to decipher that handwriting," Stella added. "Was your ancestor a doctor, by any chance?"

Fingers flipping through the pages, I read the inscription in the tail of the journal. Daphne Margaret Addison. Gran's great-great grandmother. The concept of that much history lying in my hands hit me like a brick and I wobbled, wiping rogue tears. With mom gone and gran dead, I wished we had more family around. Addison women didn't marry, and if they did, the marriages didn't last. The thing about being a paranormal was unless you got together with another of our kind, you had to spend your entire life built on lies. Marriages between humans and paranormals rarely worked out. I thought back to Jen, a werewolf, and Tristan, a human. Their marriage was done even before Tristan turned out to be a murderer. Sure, it was due to his philandering ways—the cheating scumbag—but I was certain the secrets Jen had to keep on the daily didn't help. Hard to form lasting commitments when you're constantly looking over your shoulder.

Thoughts of my mom rushed through me, and my heart sank to my toes. *Did you love my father, Sylvie? Or was he a means to an end?*

Knowing mom and considering I knew next to nothing of the man, she probably never even told him she was pregnant. Which was mostly fine except for nights like tonight when I wanted nothing more than to not feel so alone.

"If you're quite done with the self-pity train, I'd like to get this over with," Stella said over my shoulder.

I laughed. Leave it to my familiar to make sure I remembered I was never on my own. Not even when I wanted to be. My eyes darted around the journal passage, and I closed the book, tossing it back into the pile on the floor. "Nothing here," I announced. "It's a diary of sorts. Some spells and a lot of self-reflection. If there's anything about non-witch magic, I'll need time to find it."

"How about this thing?" Stella asked.

I followed her pointing finger to mom's suitcase

and cringed. "I doubt there's anything there. Gran packed the thing herself and I'm sure if there was something of note to be found, she'd have told me about it. Probably a bunch of stuff from when mom was a teenager."

"Only one way to find out," Stella said.

Body heavy with nerves, I walked to the suitcase and laid it carefully on its side. The electric spark of my uncontrolled magic thrummed at my fingertips as I snapped the lock and opened the top. Inside, clothes and knick-knacks filled the case and my throat closed up when I realized this was the closest I'd been to mom since she left. My hands shaking, I reached for the first item and yanked it out. A floral dress with a thin lace hem and a low neckline. I placed it on the floor beside me, straightening it out until it resembled a flattened body.

"Put that in the keep pile," Stella instructed. "You'll look good in it."

I forced a smile, shocked at the rare compliment. Not that I had any intention of wearing mom's old clothes, but it would be nice to have a piece of her back in the main part of the house. After she left and gran made me get rid of all things Sylvie, I felt like we buried her somehow. Like she was gone forever despite the few postcards we received yearly. Having reminders couldn't hurt, could it?

One by one, we went through the suitcase with a fine-toothed comb. It was mostly more dresses and the occasional book with dog-eared pages. I kept a copy of an Archie comic to stash on my bedside table, an old polaroid camera, and two silk scarves that still had mom's violet perfume all over them.

When the case was emptied out, I looked up at Stella. "See? Nothing."

My familiar wasn't convinced. Kneeling beside me, she pointed to the bottom of the empty suitcase and said, "Check inside the lining. If I was hiding things, I'd put them there."

"Stella, really? My mom is not some criminal mastermind! She's not going around stitching things into—"

My body froze. As I felt my way around the silk lining of the suitcase, I caught on something hard beneath the fabric. The hairs on the back of my neck stood straight, and I shot Stella a surprised look before reaching for the top corner where the stitching had come slightly undone. Wincing, I pulled at the seam, revealing an opening large enough to slide a hand through. "Holy mothballs," I whispered, pulling out a stack of envelopes tied with a ragged old rope.

"Told you," Stella said. "It's always in the lining."

Carefully, I undid the rope and took out the first envelope. It was addressed to my mom, but there was no return address and no name. The stamp had been torn off in a hurry, like someone tried to dispose of evidence. My eyes narrowed as I opened the envelope and pulled out a folded piece of cream-colored paper.

"What does it say?"

I ran my fingers over the ink, not recognizing the handwriting, and read.

"My dearest Sylvie.

I apologize for the delay, but know you are on my mind. Though it had been years, it feels like it was only yesterday since I saw you. I truly cannot wait for summer. Are you certain you can get away without your mother finding out?

I have secured a small apartment in the city for your visit, and we have everything we need for the ritual.

Meet me at the spear tonight.

Stay safe.

Yours always,

M."

Mouth dry, I reread the letter, then folded it back up. "What the heck does that mean? What's The Spear? A bar perhaps?"

"And who is M?" Stella added.

I reached for another envelope but was interrupted by the incessant vibrating of a cellphone in my back pocket. Growling, I pulled it out, sweat breaking out on my forehead when I saw the caller ID. "It's Romero," I told Stella.

"Better clean up before they get you in an orange jumper," my familiar teased, then vanished. Clearly, she didn't care to hear my conversation with the sheriff.

Placing the stack of mysterious envelopes into the clue pile on the floor, I clicked the phone on. "Sheriff? How can I help you?"

There was a long pause on the other line, followed by the sound of the elevator music the police station loved to blare. I heard Romero cough and mumble a few choice words. "Miss Addison," he finally said. "I'm glad I caught you."

"Is everything alright?"

"Not quite," the sheriff answered, making my blood run cold in my veins. I so did not look good in orange. "We uncovered some things on Zeta Huxley's laptop; things that, if they come to light, will not look good for the paranormals in this town."

I blanched. "Oh?"

"I'll cut to the chase," the sheriff said. "The running theory right now is that the victim found indefinite proof of magic, and someone killed her to keep the truth from coming out. I am amid gathering evidence, but that seems to be the most plausible explanation. And I'm sure you know I must keep things under the radar, subject matter considering."

"Of course. But what does this have to do with me?"

I genuinely did not know where the sheriff was heading with this. Why bother telling me all that information when I wasn't the one who killed Zeta? I didn't even know they had actual proof of paranormals. Up until this very moment, I assumed Archer Lee was talking out of one side of his mouth.

"Miss Addison?"

*And I zoned again.* I collected myself and pressed the phone closer to my ear. "Sorry, you were saying?"

"I said I'm calling in the agreement we have. I need you to find out whatever you can about who in the paranormal community had dealings with Zeta Huxley since she'd been in town."

My body tensed and shivers broke down my arms. "Sheriff, I'm not sure that's the best idea. If I go snooping around, whoever killed Zeta might make a run for it."

"I have deputies stationed at every exit from town," Romero said. "Trust me when I tell you, I do not want to do this, but I don't have a choice. I can't send my deputies to question people without telling them the truth of your kind. You're our best resource on this." He breathed in long and deep, as though admitting he needed me physically hurt him. "Can I count on your help?"

Head spinning, I ran a finger over mom's open suitcase, glancing around the attic. My mission to find out more about the past would have to wait. Romero needed me and I couldn't very well leave him hanging, and not only because he could lock me up or pin the murder on me. Not that he would; Romero was one of the good guys. But I knew how it looked. A second body at Bean Me Up? Not exactly great marketing. The faster the cops could figure out what happened to Zeta, the faster this entire mess would go away. And who knew? Maybe this would get Archer Lee to drop his book idea and leave Orchard Hollow. A win-win for everyone if you asked me.

"I'll do it," I said, hesitantly.

The sheriff breathed out the breath he was holding. "Wonderful. I appreciate the assist." I was about to hang up when he added, "And please keep it to yourself. No one can know you're working with me on this."

"Ten-four," I said, saluting the empty attic.

"Don't say that again," the sheriff said grimly. "Be careful, Miss Addison. Find out what you can, but don't get involved. This is research only. Anything you find, you bring to me. I'll take it from there."

As the sheriff hung up, my shoulders hiked so high

they grazed my earlobes. Somehow, I was in the middle of yet another murder investigation, and this time, I wasn't even trying to butt in. Super awesome.

I picked up the few items going downstairs and climbed down the rickety steps, gran's words running through my mind. *There is no rest for the witches.* Sucking in a breath, I headed for the kitchen, convinced a coffee was exactly what I needed. "No rest for the witches, indeed, gran."

# CHAPTER 8

Step one of getting information from people without having a mark on your back, or ending up in a ditch, was to show up where you were least expected. If people didn't see you coming, there was a chance they wouldn't stab you in the face or something equally morbid. At least that's what I told myself as I made a list of suspects over my morning coffee. When my cup emptied and I looked over my work, disappointment racked my bones.

Not only did I know nothing about Zeta Huxley, but I knew even less about anyone who might want to harm her. At least not anyone in the paranormal community.

Considering how low-key my kind stayed, it was

impossible to figure out who may have been desperate enough to kill to keep the truth about magic from seeping out into the world. And if I was being honest, pretty much every paranormal would want our secret buried. Even me.

If only there was a way to retrace Zeta's steps since she arrived at Orchard Hollow without kicking up dust.

My head swiveled to the stack of envelopes on the table and for a second, my mind slipped to another matter. "Who were you talking to, Sylvie?"

Looking around, I half expected Stella to pop up and answer the question for me. The ghost was often nearby when I least needed her to be and yet today, when I actually wanted to brainstorm my dilemma, she was nowhere to be found. Leave it to Stella to disappear at the most inopportune time. I wished she would take the same liberty when I was in the shower.

I gave my familiar a few more minutes to make a dramatic entrance, then gave up, my focus back on the piece of scrap paper before me. All I managed to jot down was Zeta's name, and a line drawn down the center: one for immediate suspects and one for anyone who might offer some clues. The problem was that both columns were as empty as my drained cup. There simply wasn't anyone I could think of who had the motive to kill.

Granted, my friend list was short—or nonexistent as Stella continued to remind me—and my presence in the paranormal community was even less eventful. What I needed was someone with a finger on the pulse of magic, which was ironic since the sheriff counted on me to be that someone. My head started to pound, and I stretched over the table for the coffeepot, refilling my mug. Gaze blank, I placed my palm over the chicken scratch on the paper and sighed. Maybe I was going about this all wrong.

Considering the assumption that someone killed Zeta to keep magic under wraps, it was fair to start with paranormals as my main suspects. But that was much too difficult a task and clearly, I was on a fast track to getting nowhere.

What if I began my search with someone closer to Zeta than a stranger in our town?

Hope renewed, I pushed the paper aside and pulled out my laptop, pulling up a search bar. In it, I typed Archer Lee's name and scrolled through page after page of interviews and book blog reviews, all dedicated to the author. It wasn't until I got to page seven of the results that I found what I was looking for.

"Aha!" I yelled out. "Here we go."

Clicking on the link, I pulled up Archer's contact information and found a directory with several emails attached to each type of inquiry. I briefly wondered why the author wouldn't have this readily available, then realized that the nature of his work likely dragged in lunatics, and I doubted he had the time to answer every oddball email hitting his inbox. I read through the list, finding an email for marketing and promotion appeals. There, listed clear as day, was the word "contact" followed by Vivien's name. Vivien Blythe, the author's marketing guru.

My heart raced as I dialed the number on the screen. I may not have knowledge of who Zeta saw in town, but I knew she spent a lot of her time with her co-workers. It was a safe bet one of them could point me in the right direction. The line rang, and a rogue thought shattered my excitement. I pressed a button, ending the call immediately.

What if it wasn't a paranormal who killed Zeta? What if it was someone she already knew before coming to Orchard Hollow?

With the contact tab open, I searched for Vivien's name. I didn't have a chance to look far when my phone vibrated with a message. Turning it over, I looked at the screen, my pulse rising.

"I heard what happened. Are you alright?" Joe wrote.

I grinned like an idiot. "Fine. Romero tapped me in to help find out who the victim crossed paths with in the community. He thinks one of us killed her to bury her research."

Three dots flashed a few seconds after I pressed send, followed by another text from Joe. "Tell him no. It sounds dangerous."

He was right. Of course, he was right. I should walk away; tell Romero I'm not interested and hope he doesn't make my life a living hell. Or.... My fingers typed quickly, and I swallowed hard. "I know. But I think I can be helpful, and I can't risk the cops messing this up. It could be bad for every paranormal in town if they go in guns blazing without all the information."

Sipping my coffee, I continued to look for clues about Vivien while I waited for Joe to reply. My brain started to fog after scrolling through what seemed like an eternity, and I was close to shutting it down when a website caught my eye. It was a page for a PhD candidacy program at a college in King City, one that sounded like a big deal. I clicked on the link and read the description. The program described a doctorate degree in English with a creative writing dissertation and, from what I gathered, spaces were limited. It took me a second to understand why this particular degree came up in my search for Vivien; then I saw the comments section under the school's blog post. Vivien's name was the last one at the top.

"@user53964 Don't get your hopes up."

My brow creased, and I bit my lower lip, scrolling down the comments feed to see who Vivien targeted. Not far down, I found the person's original statement.

"Thank you for this opportunity! This program is the culmination of my life's work, and I am pleased to say I am the perfect candidate for the degree."

Jaw snapping shut, I clicked on the small image next to the user's name. It enlarged and the coffee in my mouth shot down my throat. I coughed, wiping my chin with my sleeve, and staring at the image on my laptop.

It was Zeta Huxley who stared back at me.

Despite the sheriff's implication that the girl's death had to do with magic, I had another lead. Zeta and Vivien were competing for the same doctorate degree. I glanced at the picture on the screen again. It could be a stretch, or I could be onto something big. Could Vivien have wanted to get in bad enough to hurt Zeta? As my annoying familiar said a million times; there was only one way to find out.

Grabbing my phone, I typed a final message to Joe. "Don't worry," I wrote. "I'll be careful. And I have a lead!"

Then I dialed Vivien's number.

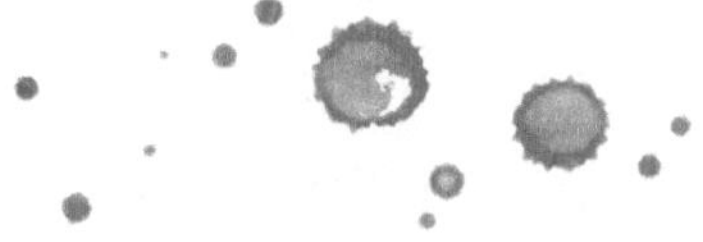

Parking in front of Miss Roland's Bed and Breakfast was like stepping into a fairy tale. When Vivien suggested I meet her where she stayed while in town, I half expected it to be at the hotel across from Bean Me Up. Instead, Archer's employee chose the most eccentric place for her trip to our small town. I shut the car door, careful not to slam it in case I awoke some fairy creature hidden in the garden.

Eyes traveling up and down the over-the-top cottage, I sucked in a breath and marveled at the building before me.

The house hid behind a lush garden contained only by a white picket fence, which appeared to be freshly painted. As I approached, I noticed a winding cobblestone path leading to the entrance. A massive round door made from wooden beams with intricately carved iron handles took over most of the porch. Above the door, a shingled awning protected all those who entered from the overhead sun. My gaze moved up, noting the small windows with pink shutters and flower beds under each one. Ivy trailed up the side of the home all the way to the roof; painted the same shade of pink as the shutters.

My finger reached for the doorbell, above which a sign read "Welcome one, welcome all."

I didn't feel the least bit welcome.

A latch undid on the other side of the door, and it swung open, revealing a red-eyed Vivien. Her cheeks sucked in when she saw me, and she brushed a hand over her unruly mane of hair in a failed attempt to appear presentable. My heart jolted. The young woman looked like she hadn't slept or ate since yesterday morning.

She definitely resembled someone who poisoned a co-worker.

Vivien smiled, though it never reached her eyes. "Come in," she said. "Rebecca arranged for a tour to the lighthouse, so it's only us here."

I slid inside, grateful for Rebecca Roland's hostess abilities. The conversation I was about to have with Vivien did not require an audience. I glanced at the door over my shoulder as Vivien shut it. Unless I was way off and walking straight into a killer's trap. Note to self: do not drink anything Vivien offers.

"Coffee?" she asked, heading into the small kitchen to the right of us.

"Sure."

*What did we just talk about?* I could have slapped myself. But come on! Who could deny a cup of coffee? I followed Vivien and watched her put on a fresh pot, then pour out two cups. My gaze stayed glued to her heaping mug and my shoulders didn't relax until I saw Vivien take a sip without collapsing on the floor.

Good. Not poisoned.

After I had a chance to dress my coffee with a dollop of cream, Vivien shepherded us into the dining room and sat on one end of a long mahogany table. I noticed a bowl of fresh fruit in the center, which Vivien eyed hungrily but didn't reach for. It was as though she was punishing herself by refusing to eat when she clearly needed the sustenance. I briefly wondered if what Vivien was eating instead was her guilt.

"Thank you for meeting with me," I finally said, breaking the uncomfortable silence between us. "I know it's probably not the best time."

Vivien's eyes watered. "No problem. On the phone you said you had questions about Zeta?"

*Straight to business.* I bit down on the inside of my cheek, swallowing my nerves.

"I have a couple questions," I said, truthfully. "But I also wanted to see how you were doing. I'm sorry about your friend, in case I haven't said it before."

"Oh." Vivien's eyebrows met in the center of her forehead. "Zeta wasn't really a friend. I mean, we were friendly, but it was mostly all work related. She was—"

Her words trailed off, and an alarm sounded inside my head. "She was what?"

"Zeta wasn't exactly a nice person, for the most part." The girl wilted in front of me, her fingers inching closer to the fruit bowl. "I feel awful saying it, considering what happened. But it's the truth. Although maybe I'm being too harsh. It wasn't that she wasn't nice, she wasn't someone who let you in. You know?"

Flashes of Stella's face rushed before me, and I nodded. I knew exactly what she meant.

"It's not her fault," Vivien quickly added. "Zeta didn't really have a family growing up, and she didn't talk about it much, but I think she had a pretty tough life. After my mom died, I thought it might change our relationship. You know...because we were both orphans now. My dad was, well, let's just say he was never in the picture. I figured that's something we had in common, but Zeta closed herself off too much. It was impossible to get to know her." Tears rolled down her cheeks, and she swiped at them clumsily with the palms of her hands. "Sorry. I probably look insane right now. I can't believe someone did that to her. Why would anyone want to hurt Zeta?"

The way Vivien looked at me made me wish I had answers for her. She was so destroyed, I almost completely forgot why I was here. I vaguely recalled the act Patty Nolan put on in her antique shop when I questioned her about Rosemary's murder. My heart stopped beating. Even killers shed tears. Steeling my spine, I looked past Vivien's wet eyes and said, "That's what I wanted to ask you about."

"Me?"

"Yes," I answered. My mind raced, thinking of how I should phrase my next question without making Vivien shut down. Or worse, decide to kill me like she may have killed Zeta. "Can you think of anyone Zeta was talking to in Orchard Hollow? Someone outside the three of you?"

The girl shook her head. "No. Like I said, Zeta kept to herself. Unless she wanted you to do something, then she was all talk."

My one eyebrow jumped. "You're saying she was bossy?"

"Kind of," Vivien admitted. "And competitive. She was one of those people that had to be number one. When Archer first hired me, it was a turf war between the two of us. I don't know what made Zeta act like we weren't on the same team, but no matter what ideas I came up with, she shut them down. And she tried to make Archer fire me. She was a lot."

*Interesting.*

"Did Archer usually do what she suggested?"

Vivien laughed, then straightened her crooked

lips. "Not sure how much you gathered from the short time you spent with the guy, but Archer only listens to Archer. He did respect Zeta a lot, though. But that was probably because he'd be nothing without her."

The odd dynamic between Archer and his co-workers was making the hairs rise on my arms. It seemed even the man's own employees thought poorly of him, but then why bother staying on? Why not quit and find another job? Well-known author or not, Zeta and Vivien struck me as intelligent, successful women; why would they work for a pompous ass like Archer?

I was about to ask her about it when what Rory mentioned on the first day the group came in ruffled my memory.

"I heard it was you who made Archer successful. My employee told me you're a bit of a marketing genius and Archer has your brilliant promotional strategies to thank for his fame."

Buttering her up must have worked, because Vivien smiled genuinely for the first time since I arrived. "I wouldn't say brilliant," she said humbly. "I painted a picture of him others wanted to see more of, that's all. If he had anyone to thank, it was Zeta. He wouldn't have half the material he writes about without her."

"How so?"

Vivien frowned. "She was a really, really good research assistant."

Stomach dropping, I searched her face for more, but that was all the information I got. This whole time I was worried Archer Lee would expose our town's secret, but perhaps it was his assistant I should have been watching out for.

I fixed Vivien with a serious glare.

"Since you mentioned Zeta's competitiveness," I said. "Mind if I ask another question?"

She nodded.

"I heard you two were in line for a PhD program. I'm assuming Zeta was serious about it since she liked to win, huh?"

Before me, Vivien's body straightened, and she crossed her arms. "Who told you that? Ray?"

Since no one actually told me anything and I found out about the program by my own stubborn digging, I only shrugged. I hoped it was enough to make Vivien keep talking and not lock up and kick me out. When she spoke again, relief washed over me.

"That guy needs to mind his own business," she said. "But yes, we were going for the same program. And yes, Zeta did enjoy taunting me about how she's a shoe in for the spot."

"That must have been frustrating."

"Not really," Vivien said, shrugging. "I mean, I guess a bit. Except...never mind."

My ears burnt a fiery red. "It's okay, I won't repeat any of this," I told her.

"Well, the thing was that I kind of already got the spot." Vivien explained. It shocked me to hear this and there was a ping of disappointment since the competition was why I was here talking to Vivien in the first place. If Zeta was out of the running, there was no reason to kill her. My theory was thin at best before and now, it was nonexistent. While I spun out of control in my head, Vivien continued. "I didn't tell anyone about it because I didn't want any drama during the tour. It was a big deal to Archer, and I wanted everything to go smoothly. The last thing anyone needed was for Zeta to wallow in pity instead of doing her job."

That actually made sense. *Crap*.

I pinched the backs of my thighs and shifted my weight in the chair. "Yesterday in the video they filmed, Archer mentioned having a big revelation. A surprise to make this book tour the most memorable yet. Any idea what it was?"

The straws I grasped were dust in my hands. The entire morning was a disappointment, and I was no closer to finding out who may have wanted to harm Zeta. From what Vivien described, she was a bit of a problematic person, though not so much so she deserved to die.

"Archer never shared it with the rest of us," Vivien said, jarring me back to the dining room. "I had the feeling Zeta hit a big break because he organized this trip quickly. To be honest, I didn't care to know. The mystery of not knowing made for good marketing. Archer's followers doubled in the last month alone, so my job was safe."

How great for Archer.

I battled the urge to roll my eyes into the back of my head.

Luckily, Vivien spoke again to stop me from making a fool of myself. "Look, I should probably take a shower," she said. "Thanks for checking in on me."

"No problem. If you think of anything else, you have my number."

Pushing the chair away, I stood up when Vivien stopped me, saying, "Actually, you might want to talk to Ray."

"Oh? Why?"

She bit her bottom lip so hard, I thought she would chew it right off. At least she'd be eating. Tension built between her brows and her eyes jerked from side to side, as though she wanted to stop herself from talking. Finally, she said, "I'm not saying he would ever...you know. A few months ago, Zeta caught him stealing money from Archer's business accounts. It wasn't much and I'm certain it was a big misunderstanding, but their relationship has been strained since."

Interesting.

Thanking Vivien for her time, I walked down the hallway toward the front door. Before leaving, I made sure Vivien knew she could call me if she needed to talk to someone. Despite having come here to accuse her of the worst possible act, I felt sorry for the girl. For all her big talk, she clearly cared for Zeta, enough to cry her eyes out for the last twenty-four hours.

My fingers clutched over the handle as I closed the door behind me, leaving a wet sweat mark on the iron.

This morning's theory was a bust, though not entirely. I had another lead. Briefly considering telling the sheriff what I found out, I forced myself to wait. Romero was stuck on a paranormal suspect and before I gave him anything, I had to see if what Vivien said about Ray was true. For all I knew, Ray was a paranormal himself. I highly doubted it since he worked directly for a man who hunted our kind, but I couldn't rule anything out.

I walked along the garden pathway, taking my phone out when I reached the fence's gate. Pulling up the message thread with Joe, I grinned, typing, "Want to play detective again?"

A t Joe's adamant suggestion, we met for a coffee and to discuss my half-cocked plan before I rushed into yet another tragic situation. With Bean Me Up closed due to it being a portal to the land of the dead, it was easy enough to get the privacy we needed. Driving down Cliff Row, I found myself releasing the gas pedal and cruising slower while my nerves kicked into fifth gear.

I was desperately trying to prolong the meeting with the bookstore owner.

Normally, I wouldn't mind spending time with Joe, cherished it even, but today was different somehow. Likely because of a certain stubborn ghost who thought it was a great idea to give me a pep talk. I didn't even think it a big deal for Joe and me to be alone in the cafe until Stella put it in my head. In her defense, she wanted to make sure I at least brushed my hair before showing up. But then the word "date" got thrown around and here I was, chewing on my tongue and slowly creeping down the street like it was my first time alone with a boy.

Why did I have to listen to her?

Oh, right. It was because there was no such thing as blocking out Stella Rutherford. The woman would get in your face to say her piece, whether you let her or not. Which was exactly what she did after I texted Joe. Leave it to Stella to vanish when I was interviewing a possible murderer then materialize with dating advice.

Sweat beaded on my brow. *Not a date. Not a date. Not a date.*

Painstakingly, I parked the beetle as far from the cafe as possible and crawled to the front door. When I arrived, Joe was already waiting, a stack of books in his hands. He wore a wool sweater and a pair of dark gray pants that were a little on the tight side and thus made my knees lock up. Swallowing the sea of saliva in my pathetic mouth, I looked down at my leggings, frowning at the ketchup stain from this morning's eggs I forgot to wash out. I wanted to duck into the back alley and spend the rest of the afternoon eating garbage with Harry Houdini.

*Not. A. Date.*

Joe grinned as I approached, his eyes traveling over my body until they reached the dreaded stain. He grinned wider over the book stack. "Condiment fight?"

"You should see the other guy," I said sheepishly, and pulled my sweater down. "Ready to start?"

As we walked in, I found my body relaxing. Bean Me Up was my happy place and nothing could take that away. Not even the murders the cafe seemed to attract like ships to a lighthouse. Once the sheriff had whoever killed Zeta in custody, I needed to speak to Rory about a plan to revive the town's trust in the business. Maybe if I was lucky, I could pick Vivien's brain before she left Orchard Hollow.

Guilt scraped the edges of my mind.

Zeta's body was barely cold, and I was thinking of my cafe instead of concentrating on finding out who did this to her. Every moment, the sheriff's belief in my abilities dwindled, and I was certain if Stella was here, she'd agree. The ghost was an expert in seeing through people's falsities.

Another thought racked my crowded brain.

If Stella was so great at reading situations, how did she get herself into one that ended her life?

"I brought these," Joe said, making my head spin as I fought my wayward thoughts.

Scanning the books in his hands, I read the titles

on the spine, eyes narrowing on the author's name. "Archer Lee's books," I whispered. "Is this all of them?"

"All the ones we had in the shop. I think my uncle was a fan."

I frowned. "Either that or he was keeping tabs on the man," I said. "Do you think your uncle believed there was truth to anything Archer wrote?"

Joe shrugged. His chest rose and fell with deep breaths, and I tried hard not to concentrate on his thick build. Instead, I focused on making two coffees—both for me, since vampires didn't drink or eat human foods. What they did eat made my stomach turn, and I had to remind myself that Joe abstained from drinking human blood, unlike most of the other vampires I knew.

While I was busy putting the final touches on the drinks and trying not to think of vampires feeding, Joe asked, "Where should we start?"

"Why don't you gauge what Archer actually knows of the paranormal world based on his books?" I suggested. "I'll scour Zeta's social media accounts when I finish up here."

Two hours, fifteen minutes, and four coffees later, and we barely made a dent in our research. Zeta's social media was basically non-existent and not only was it impossible to see who she may have had contact with in Orchard Hollow, it was even less possible to figure out if she knew any paranormals. I went over her friends and followers several times, hoping a name I recognized would spark some interest, but nothing rang a bell. Either Zeta didn't know anyone from town, or whoever she knew stayed off the radar.

I briefly recalled the conversation I overheard Zeta have the night before she died. *Who were you talking to?*

Beside me, Joe sighed and closed the last of Archer Lee's novels. "I can't get a read on this guy."

My lips tightened together. "You think he's the real deal?"

"Not sure," Joe admitted. "There are some things he mentions that hit a little too close to home. He talks about amulets, which could be a reference to our family talismans. But then he goes off on a tangent so far off the mark; I'm not sure he even understands how magic works. Honestly, I don't get what all the hype is. It's a bit like reading someone's private journal. A lot of rambling and thoughts that jump from place to place."

Sliding a book toward me, I read out the title. "Afterlife as We Know It." I snickered. "This is brutal."

"Try reading more than one page," Joe said. "I dare you."

Considering how little we discovered of Zeta's personal life, I had no choice but to oblige. Perhaps another look into Archer Lee's wild paranormal accusations could help. It certainly couldn't hurt to have another pair of eyes on them since I got the distinct impression Joe would have preferred to wrestle Harry for the last muffin than read anything Archer wrote again. I opened the book in front of me and started to read. I managed to get only a sentence in when there was a knock on the door, followed by another rapping of the knuckles, this time faster.

I glanced at Joe, then got up.

Curiosity hiking, I slid the lock out and opened the door, my mouth hanging open. "Archer," I said, noting the author in my sightline. "How can I help you?"

"A double-shot, skim milk, extra foam latte, please," the man announced. The petticoat he wore today flung open, and I noticed bright-red suspenders peeking out. Even his outfit was obnoxious.

Casting a solemn glance in Joe's direction, I turned back to Archer. "I'm sorry, but we're closed. Because of the active murder investigation." I knew I should have stopped there, but added, "Of your assistant."

I might as well have been speaking in tongues because the look the author gave me implied we were from different planets.

"What am I supposed to do for coffee in this

town?"

Wow. Just wow. *Step aside ladies and gentlemen, our winner for Most Compassionate Human of the Year has arrived! What a tool.* Clearing the angry lump in my throat, I gestured to the hotel across the street with my chin. "You're staying at the Rose Hollow, right? I'm sure they can get you a coffee. I hear the breakfast is fantastic there."

"They have drip coffee," Archer said as though it explained anything. "I don't drink drip coffee."

It took everything I had in me not to zap the buffoon with my magic. In fact, I was so close to letting my emotions overcome me that I could feel the energy inside me building. Before I could do something I would regret, and something that would land me in one of Archer's ridiculous books, I slid the door shut to an inch of an opening. "As I said, the cafe is closed so I'm afraid drip coffee is your best solution. Unless you're willing to venture to the coast. Cliffside Diner is a great option, and I can personally vouch for their lunch menu." I remembered the overpriced burger I had there a few months ago. "Sorry again."

Archer's face scrunched, and I started to close the door, eager to free myself from the man's vapid attitude. I paused, realizing an opportunity quite literally knocked on my door. ", I said. "Do you mind if I ask you a question before you leave? It's about Zeta."

"What about her?" Archer asked, his expression souring. The gold specks in his eyes darkened to a deep brown, and he scratched his sharp nose, pushing up those stupid fake glasses.

Refusing to back down, I forced myself through the doorway. "I was wondering if you knew anyone she might have met with in town. Maybe about the tour? Or for research?"

"In this town?"

*No, genius. In the other town your assistant died in. Geez.* I nodded, smiling as warmly as I could manage. "Uh-huh. You see, we're a peaceful community—" pure lies "—and it alarmed everyone to have this happen. I was hoping to see if Zeta had close friends in the area so I could offer my condolences. We stick together in Orchard Hollow."

I was laying it on so thick, I nearly gagged. Luckily, Archer was too into himself to notice. "I'm still in shock over what happened," he stated. "But I can tell you without a doubt that Zeta had no friends here. My team is only visiting for the tour and for—"

"For?"

"Never mind," Archer brushed me off. "I'm sorry I can't be of more help. Please let someone on my team know when you reopen."

With that, he turned on his heel and marched into the hotel where I was certain he would choke down a cup of drip coffee and curse my name for all of eternity. He moved so fast; he left an Archer Lee-shaped cloud of dust in the doorway.

"What was that about?" Joe asked.

I wiggled my nose. "I think he was about to spill the beans on the proof of magic Zeta discovered."

"Speaking of, did the sheriff ever tell you what it was she found?"

It was a wonderful question and one I should have thought of sooner. Romero never mentioned what made him so adamant to blame Zeta's death on a paranormal. Whatever he found on her laptop solidified his hunch that the girl died because of proof she found of my kind's existence. Proof she was going to give to Archer. I wondered if she had a chance to do it before she was killed, though judging by Archer's behavior, I doubted it. Someone as self-centered and obsessed with his image as Archer Lee would not sit on the discovery of a lifetime. If Zeta showed the author her cards, there would already be media outside our doors demanding to see the paranormal freaks living here.

No, Archer didn't have his smoking gun. At least, not yet.

I started back for the table in hopes of finding anything we may have missed when a figure materialized in front of me. Not having enough time to stop my forward momentum, I stumbled, crashing right through Stella's ghostly body. Shivers ran up and down my arms, and my lungs felt like someone punched me in the chest repeatedly. Clambering to right myself, I sucked in a frigid breath and waited until my familiar reformed.

"Do we need to have another talk about personal space?" Stella bellowed, her gray body shimmering back into existence.

"You're the one that popped up in my path," I snapped back.

The ghost brushed her hand down over her tennis skirt and flipped her long ponytail, her overstuffed lips puckering. "I have no time to do this with you," she barked. "You need to get home. Now! We have an emergency."

"What happened?"

"Not now," Stella repeated. "Get home quick. There's been a break-in."

Her warning hung in the air between us long after she disappeared, and my heart sank into my boots as I rushed to get my purse and hurry Joe outside. Someone broke into my house. My safe place.

Fear gripped my every bone. What if whoever Stella warned me about wasn't gone? What if they were waiting for me to return?

My eyes widened until they resembled large orbs.

What if it was the same person who killed Zeta?

# CHAPTER 10

One hand covered in electric blue magic and one gripping an old, busted tire iron I found in the trunk of the beetle; I tiptoed into the farmhouse, Stella floating a few feet behind me. The porch steps creaked as I clumsily placed a boot atop them and I cringed, casting a quick glance at Stella. Her gray index finger pointed to the front door.

I froze in my place.

The door was slightly ajar and there was a trail of mud all the way down the porch and heading inside. As though someone had dragged a dead body in.

"It's not another corpse," Stella whispered.

My brow furrowed. "How did you know I was thinking that?"

The ghost scrunched her nose and waved a hand in front of my face.

"You have the worst poker face," she said. "That and the chances of someone planting another body to frame you are slim to none."

Somehow, I doubted that. Orchard Hollow was far from the serene, sleepy town I grew up in. These days, coming home to find a dead body stashed in my living room seemed more probable than not. "I'm not taking any chances," I told Stella, my fingers winding tighter around the tire iron.

"You sure are gambling with that eyeshadow choice," she sniped.

Shooing her off, I prodded the door's opening with my sad little weapon, pushing it wider. One shaky step after another, I made my way into the house, the knot in my stomach growing by the second. What was I thinking telling Joe I got this handled? I did not have anything handled. At all. My back scraped the doorframe and my sweater caught in the lock, causing me to knock my hip into the wood with a thud.

*Oh, yeah. I got this.*

Ignoring Stella's disapproving stare, I pushed my body inside and yelled, "Whoever you are, I have a weapon!" Then, looking at the bent tire iron, added, "And I called the cops!"

A shuffle sounded upstairs, and I bit down on my

tongue, the taste of blood filling my mouth. I glanced at Stella over my shoulder, motioned to the stairs with my palm, and took a few giant strides forward. Behind me, I felt the air shift as Stella vanished before materializing at the top of the stairs. Her slender legs went on for miles and she tapped her toes lightly on the carpet as she waited for me to make the climb. I reached the top in record time, breathless.

"You should consider yoga on the weekends," Stella suggested. "I can give you some pointers."

I grimaced. "I'm fine. Let's go."

In unison, we marched down the narrow hallway, following the sound from earlier. I paused, pointing to the door leading into my bedroom. It was partly open, and I was pretty sure I closed it before I left this morning—a habit I formed living with a personal-space-invading mother most of my teenage life. There was another shuffle behind the door, and I cocked an eyebrow at Stella, who dropped her chin. My body shook as I reached for the brass handle, readying to burst into the room to protect what's mine. I cupped the knob and sucked a breath in through my teeth. *Now or never.*

Crashing into the bedroom, I swung the tire iron over my head and yelled my best battle cry. Behind me, Stella snickered, oblivious to the badass bravery I was displaying. In her defense, my battle cry sounded a bit like a rooster with a head cold.

Paying my familiar no mind, I yelled, "I'm going to—"

My amazingly clever threat died in the air. Fingers loosening, I dropped my arm, letting the tire iron fall from my grip. It crashed on the carpet with as much bravado as my earlier yell, rolling a couple inches away from my feet. My eyes saucered.

"You must be joking," Stella huffed behind my back. Her neck craned to look over my shoulder and her features twisted in disgust as she took in our intruder.

I cocked my head to the side. "Harry Houdini?"

Sitting beside my nightstand, the raccoon raised his dark eyes and his grabby paws tightened around an object in his hands. He held it protectively close, nose sniffing the air between us. I narrowed my eyes and focused on the object. "Is that—"

"Your failed truth-seeking potion?" Stella interrupted. "Correct."

"What does he want with it? And how in the name of coffee did he get in here?"

Stella pointed to the muddied prints on the floor, and I followed their trajectory from the window to the door, then down the hallway and toward the downstairs living room. It seemed the magician climbed through my open bedroom window and snuck his chubby butt inside while I was gone. I wasn't sure what he was doing downstairs to create such a mess, and I didn't care to find out. If he made it all the way to the farmhouse, there was no telling what other mischief he'd gotten himself into while he was here. I really needed to barricade the windows. Though, knowing Harry, he probably had keys cut to the place already.

Carefully, I slid off a sneaker and aimed it at the empty spot next to Harry. As I did, I noticed my undone duvet and groaned. "Gross! I think he took a nap in my bed."

"Well, at least now you can say you've had someone else in there."

I swiped the sneaker through Stella, who dodged it like a freaking ninja. The movement startled Harry, and he bounced against the nightstand, knocking over the few items I stored atop. As they clambered to the floor, he glanced at me, then at the potion bottle in his paws. The bottle was in his little wet mouth in seconds. Before the gluttonous creature swallowed ingredients that could hurt him, I whipped the sneaker in his direction. It hit the side of the mattress, bouncing off and landing next to Harry. The raccoon hissed, got up on his hind legs, and in his panic, dropped the bottle on the floor. The contents spilled all over the carpet, staining it a permanent shade of green.

Face-palming, I shooed Harry out of the way. It took forever and a day to get the monster away from the spill and back out the window. I had no idea where he'd gone or how long he'd stay away, but my gut told me this wasn't the last of our Houdini break-ins.

Dropping to my knees, I picked up the items on the floor. My heart squeezed tightly in my chest when my fingers grazed the stack of envelopes we found in mom's suitcase. I ran my thumb over the string, eyes welling with tears.

"It's fine if you don't want to read them," Stella said.

Snapping out of my self-pity parade, I looked up at her. "I do and I don't," I told the ghost. "On the one hand, these might have answers about my magic that I desperately need. But on the other..."

"They might have other answers too," Stella finished for me.

I nodded. Then, seeing her for what felt like the first time, I finally understood. The walls Stella put up, the dodging of every question I had about her death; it all made sense now. Stella was as afraid of answers as I was. Probably even more so, considering it was her life on the line. Well, her afterlife. I slid the stack back on the nightstand and said, "Today is not the day for these."

"Oh?" Stella asked, pouting. "What is today for, then?"

I followed the tiny brown paw prints to the window and stared out at the sprawling land beyond. On the horizon, the copse of trees lining the property appeared as a thick, dark line; a border marking the beginning of the ley lines. The forest beyond reminded me of magic, and my chest tightened as my mind settled on the more important things at hand. My personal magic, whatever it was, would have to wait. I had the entire town to worry about.

"Today," I said, eyes never leaving the trees, "we talk to a man about some missing money."

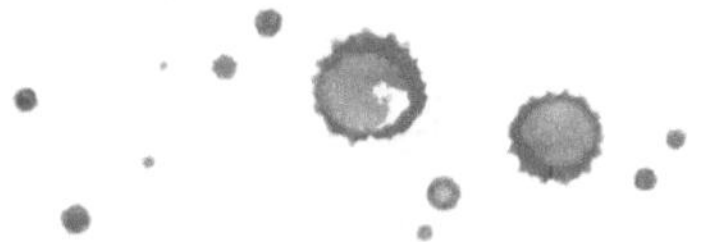

The man in question was Ray Langton, and while I was all bravado when I told Stella my plan, sitting in a booth at The Drunk Elephant now, I was shaking in my boots. Stella, on the other hand, was not bothered at all. If anything, she looked bored to tears while we waited for Ray to arrive. Drinking the worst coffee I'd ever tasted, I gagged and checked the door again.

"Enjoying your mud water?" Stella asked.

I pursed my lips and cradled the cup in my fingers, arching my head around the booth's cushiony back to look for the bartender. As predicted, I was one of the few here this early in the afternoon. When I messaged Ray to meet up, feigning interest in the book tour and lying about having information on the hauntings in the Rose Hollow, he suggested we meet here. I wondered why he'd prefer this place out of everywhere else in town. Who even went to a bar this early?

As I glanced at the sad lineup of patrons peppered through the dimly lit space, I started to understand the appeal. This was as much privacy as you could get at Orchard Hollow. Not only were we sitting far enough away from everyone, but the people that were here looked to have other things to worry about. In fact, most of them seemed like they had been here all night. I winced as Arthur Finbury stretched his arm across the table and slammed his head down. His mouth opened and a series of snores echoed through the bar. A good way away, the bartender, a young woman I didn't recognize, rolled her eyes, and continued to arrange clean glasses on one of the shelves. While she busied herself, I watched the door, waiting for it to boil.

"What's taking him so long?"

Stella yawned, inspecting the bottom of her ponytail for split ends. "Are you sure we're in the right place? This seems depressing," she said. "Even for you."

"He said the Drunk Elephant at noon. Trust me, it's not my first choice for a meeting either."

I raised the chipped coffee cup to my lips and was about to take another sip when the door of the bar swung open. A burst of sunlight pierced the dusty darkness, and I was pretty sure I heard someone hiss from the back. *Am I in a vampire hangout? Shut the blinds, people! The sun brings death!* I laughed at my own stupid joke, ignoring Stella's grossed out face on the opposite bench of the booth. Straightening out, I nudged for her to move over, and we watched Ray approach with a shuffle. His swagger was a lot less confident than I remembered, and he knocked into a couple of tables before finally reaching our booth. The stench of booze and toothpaste rushed my system. I slid the coffee cup to the side, certain that if I drank anything right now, I'd upchuck it right back.

Great. Ray Langston showed up to our meeting hung over, or possibly still drunk. I tried not to let it bother me, even when Stella said, "This is going to be a waste of time."

Then she disappeared.

Paying her no mind, I half-stood in my seat. "Hi, Ray. Thanks for coming out."

"Do they have food here? I'm starving." He wobbled and slid into the booth with a loud sigh, reaching for the menu in the center of the table. One glance at the beer selection had Ray looking ocean blue. "Ugh. No."

I tried counting to ten to stop myself from reaching across the booth and slapping the fool. Why agree to a meeting when you weren't going to show up in your right mind? Anger swirled in my chest as I realized Stella was right. This was a colossal waste of my time. Especially since—

"Sorry about my whole thing right now," Ray mumbled. "I had a little too much fun last night. Right at that table, actually." He nodded toward the spot Arthur occupied, now sprawled entirely over the table like it was a king-sized bed. "Geez. I don't know why I told you that."

Hmm. Perhaps this wasn't such a waste after all. Drunk lips were loose lips and loose lips talked. I reached for the coffee cup again. "It's fine," I said. "We can meet another time if you want. I figured with everything that happened, you might not be in town for long. But if you're not up for it..."

Ray's hands shot up. "No, no. Now works." He tried to sit up straight but proved unsuccessful. "I can't be slacking on the job, anyway. We can't afford anything else to go wrong on this tour."

"I could only imagine," I said, coating my words in molasses. Inside, I raged. A girl died, his co-worker, and Ray talked about her death like it was a minor inconvenience. I wondered if the sheriff had a chance to look into this guy. I knew the working theory was a paranormal killed Zeta, but Ray was looking more and more suspicious by the second.

"Sorry, that was really shitty of me," Ray said, proving me wrong. "I don't know how to act right now. It's horrible what happened to Zeta. It's just that Archer is, well, I'm sure you saw for yourself."

I gritted my teeth. "He's tough to deal with, huh?"

"Something like that."

"Well, you know what they say about creative people," I said, immediately regretting it.

Ray's interest peaked, and he leaned in, crossing his arms on the table. His curly hair fell into his eyes, and he let it hover there for a few moments before tucking it behind his ears. "What do they say?"

"Just that—" I scrambled around for words because, in truth, I had no clue what they said. In the end, I settled on, "That they're very particular."

In front of me, Ray nodded in agreement, and I loosened a breath. "That's right on the nose," he said. "Particular. It's a good word. I like it! Describes Archer perfectly."

"So, your boss is tough to please?"

*Take it easy. You don't want to scare him away.* I flashed some teeth, hoping to make the conversation appear as casual as possible. Lucky for me, Ray's defenses were down, and he didn't seem to notice my digging. His shoulders slumped, and he hiked one leg up, resting his dirty shoe on the torn leather seat. "He's not that bad as far as bosses go. I think he's tougher on Viv. And he definitely wasn't hard on Zeta."

My interest peaked. "How about you?"

"He's alright," Ray answered. "Actually, scratch that. He's pretty cool most of the time. Even after the crap Zeta pulled, he—"

Ray's eyes widened, and he stared at me in disbelief, as though I rang out the truth from him. I looked around, making sure no one was eavesdropping, and said, "It's okay. Vivien told me about the misunderstanding you and Zeta had."

Hoping my phrasing made it appear that I was on his side, I waited for Ray to speak. He stayed silent for a while, likely weighing the pros and cons of sharing information with me. In the end, his less than clear mindset won.

"It wasn't a misunderstanding," Ray explained. "Zeta made some bullshit up about me stealing and tried to have me fired. None of it was true. I don't even know what she was talking about. I would never jeopardize my job. But she wouldn't let it go."

"And Archer believed you over her?"

Ray scoffed. "Obviously. Because she lied. I didn't steal anything." His head shook in anger, and he fisted his hands. When he caught me staring, he uncurled his fingers and ran them through his oily hair. "Anyway, all she did was make herself look stupid. Doesn't matter now, I guess."

"Right," I whispered. "I'm very sorry for your loss. It's awful what happened."

"For sure. Can't believe someone would do that."

My eyes narrowed, and I locked them on Ray, pinning him with my glare. "Me either," I agreed. "Especially since you're all just visiting. Zeta didn't mention knowing someone in town, did she?"

"Nope," Ray said, shaking his head. "But she was completely against coming here. Kept trying to get Archer to let her stay behind. He wasn't having it, of course. This tour is a big deal for him, for us, so the entire team had to be present. I think she mostly worked since we got here. Her and Vivien are very driven. They mostly spent time together going over tour plans." A glassy stare flashed over his eyes. "Archer must feel pretty shitty now. Zeta wouldn't even be here if he didn't ride her so hard about the tour."

Memories of Zeta's phone conversation rolled through my mind. My body froze. What Ray said matched what I overheard that night—for some reason, Zeta wanted to stay away from Orchard Hollow. Could it be she knew her life was in danger? If she did, it put an entirely different perspective on her murder. It's possible this wasn't a crime of opportunity. Someone knew Zeta was going to be in town and they planned to have her killed here. The idea that a paranormal did this was looking more and more appealing.

I hated that.

"But hey, maybe she needed to get away from Declan."

My heart stopped beating for a second as I inhaled the words. "Who?"

"Dec. Her boyfriend. A piece of work, that guy," Ray said. "Real jealous type. Last I heard, Zeta threatened to leave him. Not sure what came out of it, but as far as I know, they're still a thing. Or were, I guess." His eyes darted sideways. "You didn't hear it from me, but I think the guy is on steroids. That stuff will mess with your head."

"Why do you say that?" I asked.

"Trust me, if you met Declan, you'd agree. You know he thought I had an affair with Zeta? Can you believe that? His girlfriend was trying to get me fired, and the idiot thought we were shacking up on the side." Ray shook his head and yawned. "I know I probably sound like an ass, but those two were both a little out there."

On the table, Ray's phone's screen turned on and I saw a familiar name pop up in a message bubble. I leaned over, not caring how obvious it was that I was snooping. Looking back at Ray, I asked, "Tabitha? As in Tabitha Pogue?"

Surprise flashed over Ray's features.

"You know her?" he asked. "Of course, you know her. Small town."

I didn't simply know Tabitha. She was a resident witch and a member of the coven Nancy and Cilia belonged to. Why was an Orchard Hollow witch messaging Ray? Alarm bells rang out, and I dug my nails into the wooden top of the table. "How do you know Tabitha?"

"I don't," Ray said. "I mean, not really. We met here last night."

His cheeks reddened, and he looked down at his shoe perched atop the seat. "She's kind of the reason I'm—" Ray waved his hand over his sorry form.

"You two got together?" I asked, trying to mask the shock in my voice.

"She's alright. A little weird, but cool," Ray said, refusing to answer my question. That was answer enough for me. Ray and Tabitha hooked up last night after what appeared to be way too many drinks. I wished Stella was here to hear it because this was some juicy gossip. Nancy's coven mates were as stuck up as they came; one of their own getting together with a tourist was bound to cause ripples. How I wished I was there for it.

Feeling like a hypocritical idiot, I slapped myself mentally. This was not the time to milk my petty grudge against Nancy and her coven. A girl was dead, and I was nowhere closer to finding out what happened.

"Anyway, I should call her back," Ray said. "You said you had some information on the hotel and the hauntings?"

Shoot. I completely forgot that I lured him to the bar with blatant lies. I racked my brain for a story believable enough to call him over here but didn't have time to dig myself deeper into the web of deceit I had spun. The front door swung open and a tall, muscular man poured into the bar. His bald head limned in the light of the backlit doorway and his teeth slammed together as his gaze flicked Ray.

"No freaking way," the cameraman whispered.

"I knew I'd find you here, you slimy piece of garbage!" the giant roared. "What the hell did you do to Zeta? I'm going to kill you!"

Then the brute ran toward us and leapt straight for Ray.

# CHAPTER 11

Limbs were everywhere.

I ducked out of the way as another fist flew by me; it missed my face by an inch and I slammed into the cushioned back of the booth, sliding across, and slipping away. The giant—Declan—raised another fist and rushed it toward Ray. The cameraman shielded himself with his forearms and I shielded my eyes to avoid seeing a nose break. Somehow, the hit never made contact.

Opening one eye at a time, I focused my attention on the fighting duo, realizing another man was in the mix.

"Cool it or you'll both regret it," Joe said calmly.

He held Declan's fist in one hand and used the

other to push Ray out of the way. And he wasn't even breaking a sweat. I thought vampire strength was a myth—a piece of gossip spread to make people fear the creatures—but watching Joe pull the two morons apart proved me wrong. Not only was he not even remotely struggling despite Declan's massive size, but he was also smiling. Joe gave Ray another shove, then grabbed Declan by his back collar like a mother cat herding a misbehaving kitten. His eyes met mine. "You alright?"

Nodding, I straightened out my shirt and stood up taller.

"I called the police!" the bartender yelled out.

I watched her shake her phone at us to make a point before returning to the glasses that apparently required her full attention. Judging by her lackluster behavior, I assumed she'd seen her fair share of fights in this place. Two drunks fisting it out was likely nothing out of the ordinary.

When I realized her attention would not return to the four of us, I said, "We'll take care of them. No need to bother the cops." Glancing at Joe, I whispered, "Let's take the big one outside before he does something stupid."

The vampire tipped his chin and shoved Declan toward the exit. "You heard the lady," he said sternly. "Get a move on."

While Joe escorted a struggling Declan out the door, I scribbled my phone number on a napkin and handed it to Ray, telling him to call me if he thought of someone who might have crossed paths with Zeta while they were in town. I wasn't going to hold my breath waiting for a call, knowing full well Ray would be avoiding me like the plaque considering how well this meeting went over. I was, however, holding what breath I had left watching Joe's back muscles tense while walking in front of me. My cheeks burned, and I averted my eyes. A big mistake. When Joe opened the door to toss Declan outside, his back collided with the side of my face, and I threw my hands up instinctively to brace for impact. Unfortunately, they didn't make it all that far, and I ended up cupping his butt cheeks. Hard.

"Now is probably not the time for that," Joe teased, chuckling.

I backed up, cramming my hands in my pockets before I could do any more damage. My face burned from the heat of a thousand suns and my throat was so bone dry, I couldn't make out any words. I did the next best thing. I giggled like a desperate schoolgirl.

"Smooth," a sarcastic voice sounded behind me.

I didn't need to turn around to gauge the joy my embarrassment brought Stella, who chose this exact moment to reappear. Rubbing my temples, I ran my tongue over furry teeth. "Go away. I have enough to deal with right now."

Huffing annoyingly, my familiar listened for once and I felt a slight breeze on the back of my neck as she left. Thank the coffee gods for small miracles. As soon as she was out of sight, I watched Joe walk Declan further down the street and away from the bar. A few bystanders crossed the street when they passed to avoid us, their disapproving faces making me turn beet-red. We reached a bench next to a row of potted plants and Joe lowered the struggling brute onto it, keeping his hand on Declan's shoulder to make sure he didn't make a run for it.

"Now that we're all calm and collected," Joe said, "you want to tell me why you attacked my friend?"

I would be lying if I said the word "friend" didn't sting.

Accepting his fate, Declan looked from Joe to me. "Her? I wasn't attacking her! She was in the way."

"Not winning any points here, bud," I said. "Why did you threaten Ray?"

Declan's lips tightened into a thin line, and he crossed his arms defiantly. I noticed Joe's fingers tense on his shoulder and the giant winced, trying to shake him off unsuccessfully. "Okay, fine! Ease up, bouncer man! Geez."

"Answer the question," Joe instructed. "Without the theatrics this time."

Face scrunching, Declan resembled a toddler that didn't get his way, but he wasn't about to test Joe's patience. Smart man. His nostrils flared as he said, "That piece of human trash is the reason my girlfriend is dead. He should be behind bars, not getting wasted with your friend at one in the afternoon."

"First, no one was getting wasted," I cleared up. "Second, there haven't been any arrests because the police are investigating what happened to Zeta. If you think Ray was responsible for what happened to her, you should speak to the sheriff."

It surprised me I had to suggest that. Why would Declan take it upon himself to go after Ray if he had information that could help catch the person he claimed killed his girlfriend? Either he was lying, or Ray was right about his mental state. Judging by Declan's evasive body movements, both seemed like plausible options right now.

"You don't think I already went to your useless sheriff?" he asked, scoffing. "The guy brushed me off. All but told me to get out of town. Like I'd leave when Zeta's killer is running around free! Your dumb police aren't doing anything to arrest the prick, so I'll handle him myself."

Joe cocked a dark eyebrow. "By beating him to a pulp in a bar?"

"Hey, man. The guy deserves a lot more than a beating."

"Do you have any proof to back up your allegations?" I interjected. "Proof you can take to the police to help your case before you get yourself arrested for assault?"

Frustration coated Declan's face as he worked his jaw. "I don't need proof!" he exclaimed. "Zeta found the scumbag stealing and threatened to get his ass fired. The loser threatened her, came to our apartment to tell her she needs to back off or else. I was there! What more proof do you need? She caught him red-handed, and now she's dead. I can't believe the two of them had something going on behind my back. Zeta would never let that prick touch her." Declan seethed and his eyes reddened. "Let me go! I need to finish this!"

His chest puffed out as he struggled against Joe's hold, attempting to free himself. Fists balled, he tried to pummel Joe, but his lame attacks barely made a dent. Grunting, Declan threw a couple more punches, then gave up. His back arched, and he threw himself onto the bench, the force of his body shaking the metal. Red eyes tearing, Declan raised a fist and slammed it into the bench, crushing his knuckles into hard iron. Blood welled on his skin, and he gritted his teeth together, cursing under his breath.

Slumping further down, defeat and sorrow washed over the large man that no longer seemed as threatening as before. "You don't understand," he whispered. "You can't possibly understand."

I took a step closer to the bench, avoiding Joe's warning gaze, and lowered to sit.

"Last year," I said quietly, "I lost my grandmother. It wasn't the same situation, and I know that, but it hurt like hell. Still does. She was my person, my everything, and then she was just gone. I know what it's like to lose someone you love. And I'm sorry you're going through this."

The attitude shifted in Declan. His fists relaxed and, for the first time since he arrived, his eyes landed on mine. Deep creases lined his forehead and all the blood drained from his face when he said, "I never got to say goodbye. She didn't even know I was here."

"You didn't come with Archer and his team?"

Declan's head shook. "No. I took the train in with Aria, our roommate. Zeta's best friend. It was supposed to be a surprise. I was—"

His mouth closed and silence filled the street. Declan shifted uncomfortably, his weight pressing down on the bench and making the metal groan. My eyes widened as realization hit me square in the face.

"You were going to propose, weren't you?"

I didn't know why the idea popped into my head, but it seemed to be the right one. A surprise visit to a small town? Orchard Hollow had plenty of marriage proposals yearly. The seaside views and the hidden nature of the town drew in the romantics. In fact, I was willing to bet that our slice of land had one of the highest proposal rates in the country. Only last week, a guy took a knee in front of Ray's ice cream shop. The woman said yes, of course, and the two celebrated over a double scoop of Rocky Road. On the house.

"I can't believe she's gone."

Declan's tear-filled statement burned a hole in my heart, and I was about to offer my condolences, ones I was sure would do little good, when my phone rang. Checking the Caller ID, I stood up and walked a few feet away, putting some distance between myself and the men before I answered. When I was out of earshot, I pulled the phone to my ear. "Hi, sheriff."

"Miss Addison," the sheriff's gruff voice said on the other end. "I'm calling to see how things are coming along. Any updates on our...arrangement?"

The way Romero referred to him needing my help was ridiculous. It wasn't so much an arrangement as it was Romero turning to me as a last resort out of sheer desperation. I should be billing the guy for my services, though considering how little progress I'd made in Zeta's case, it wasn't an option. That, and I was sure Romero would laugh in my face if I so much as suggested some form of payment. What would he even pay me for? Being a witch? That would be the day.

I swallowed the lump in my throat and snapped myself back to reality. "Nothing yet," I admitted. "I'm following some possible leads, but so far, I don't think anyone from the paranormal community had contact with Zeta. Were you able to track the call I told you about?"

"We were. It went to a burner phone. We're working on trying to get more information on the person Miss Huxley spoke with," Romero answered. "You're certain no one with your abilities talked to her while she was here?"

*Abilities. Rich.* "Not from what I gathered." I thought back to the day Zeta died. Goosebumps crawled up my arms and legs and I shivered like a pigeon over a grate. "And no one at the cafe was a paranormal except me and Rory. How could someone with my 'abilities' poison her if they weren't even there?"

On the other line, the sheriff mumbled, and I pressed the phone tighter to my ear. "What was that?"

"I said it wasn't in the coffee."

*Color me pink and slap a bow on my head!* What

did Romero say? My body rigid, I asked, "Are you telling me she was poisoned some other way? But she died after she drank the latte. You said it was what killed her!"

"I know what I said, Miss Addison," the sheriff grumbled. "The coroner confirmed this morning that the poison was in Miss Huxley's system for a full three hours prior to her death. Which would imply the latte was not what killed her."

My head hurt. "That means literally anybody could have done it!"

"Correct," the sheriff said, adding, "anyone of paranormal nature. I remain firm on the motive being the information Miss Huxley had on your kind. She was a threat to your entire community. It's enough to kill for."

Boy, this guy sure had it out for paranormals. It was as though the sheriff had already made up his mind about what happened, and he needed me to confirm his suspicions. Suspicions that didn't appear to be rooted in any real fact. This was too close to how things played out the last time someone died in our town, and I didn't like where we were going. Mostly because the last time I almost got myself shot.

I took a deep breath to calm down and asked, "What exactly did you find on Zeta's laptop, sheriff?"

Romero grunted. "Nothing I can speak to at the

moment," he said. I assumed that meant he wasn't alone and likely didn't want to arouse suspicion. "If you'd like to come by the station later this week, I'd be happy to share more information."

Hint received. I made a mental note to pay the sheriff a visit sooner rather than later. "I'm going to keep looking. If anything comes up, I'll let you know," I promised.

"I certainly hope so," the sheriff said, and hung up.

Tossing the sheriff's rudeness aside, I hissed out "you're welcome" and pocketed my phone, walking back to Joe and Declan. The sheriff may have been a blowhard with a paper-thin theory, but he did reveal new information which could help *me* help *him*. Kneeling next to Declan, I caught his deadpan gaze. "Were you in town the morning Zeta died?" I asked.

"Uh-huh," Declan answered. "I was at the old lighthouse with Aria. We were setting up for—"

"Got it," I said, sparing the pain of reliving the proposal that never happened. "Why did you need Aria to help? Were you two close?"

Declan shrugged. "I guess. She was constantly hanging around, so I didn't have much of a choice. And she really wanted to be here for the whole thing. Said she wanted to see how happy Zeta was, but—"

He stopped short, almost as though he felt he said too much. "But, what?"

"Look, this is going to come off conceited," Declan said. No shock there. "Aria kind of had a thing for me. I know it bothered Zeta sometimes, but they'd been friends since high school, so she let it go."

"And you all lived together?"

What type of weird setup was this? Never, in a million years, would you catch me living in the same house as a girl who had a thing for my boyfriend. Granted, I'd have to get a boyfriend first. The thought made me glance at Joe and my neck burned immediately. I looked at my feet, suddenly finding my shoelaces to be the most interesting contraption invented.

I was so embarrassed, I almost missed Declan say, "Zeta was planning to ask Aria to move out. She said she had enough of her flirting with me and friend or not, we needed to be on our own."

*Huh.* I thought Ray said Declan was the jealous one in the relationship? Maybe Zeta had a hot temper like her boyfriend. Could she have crossed someone she shouldn't have? The vague outline of a theory started to form in my mind but got cut off when I replayed Declan's statement.

"Do you think Aria found out?"

"I don't think so," Declan said. "Aria isn't exactly super sharp. She's sweet and all but not the brightest. She's over there right now, you know? At the lighthouse. Kept going there every day since we found out about Zeta. She said it made her feel closer to her. Aria is always doing weird stuff like that, so trust me, I was kind of relieved when Zeta suggested we ask her to move out. But I also felt sorry for her. It's kind of sad."

*And yet you didn't stop her from flirting with you?* What a slimeball.

A door slammed open, and I caught movement from the corner of my eye. My blood pressure spiked when I saw Ray exit The Drunk Elephant, checking the street. Jumping to stand, I tugged on Joe's sleeve and motioned in the direction of the bar. When he noticed Ray, he tilted his body to block Declan's view. Softly, he patted the boy's shoulder and said, "How about we go get something to eat? You look like you could use a meal."

Relief flooded my body when Declan nodded, stood, and allowed Joe to lead him away.

Crisis averted.

"You two go ahead!" I yelled after them. "I'll call you later."

As I watched them disappear, my thoughts jumbled in my head. Ray was in the cafe when Zeta was poisoned, but I now knew the latte wasn't how she died. He may have seen her earlier that morning, but I felt confident he wasn't our guy. Despite what Declan thought, Ray never got fired, so whatever dirt Zeta had on him couldn't have been true. Case in point, he continued to work for Archer Lee. I doubted the author would keep someone around if they stole from him.

Then we had Declan. Self-absorbed, quick-with-a-fist Declan. His alibi was plausible, though that was only if I took his word for it. And he did genuinely seem to care for Zeta. I wasn't falling for someone's words again, not after last time. I had to make sure Declan's alibi was solid, which left me with no other option than to talk to the other person in Zeta's life, someone who happened to be in town when she died.

The third wheel roommate.

Who was Aria and why did she follow Declan to Orchard Hollow to watch him propose? Either she had a self-deprecating streak or there was more to the story. I was leaning toward the latter.

Could she have killed Zeta to have Declan all to herself?

I couldn't imagine anyone killing for that man, but I had no right to judge. My longest relationship was with my coffee maker and even that was starting to fall apart. Looking past the rolling road of Cliff Row, I focused my eyes on the lighthouse in the distance. The decrepit old thing should have been torn down by now, but it refused to crumble. Year after year, it stood stoic and tall. And year after year, it dragged in tourists. People like Declan, who had beautiful notions of the place.

My heart pinged, thinking of the proposal.

There were too many uncertainties around Zeta's death, and unlike what the sheriff thought, most of them had nothing to do with paranormals. Unless Aria was one? The girl's name made my brain hurt. She was one more person Zeta dragged into town and one more messy complication which could have gotten her killed. I looked at the lighthouse, my eyes narrowing to slits.

I needed to speak to Aria. And thanks to Declan, I knew exactly where to find her.

# CHAPTER 12

Wind slapped my face until it was a deep shade of red as I walked against its current to the entrance. Despite the lack of cars in the parking lot due to the lighthouse being out of order for the last forty years, I parked further away. At the time, it seemed like a good idea, so I didn't spook Aria when I arrived. I quickly realized the error of my ways a minute into the excruciating walk. Gravel crunched under my sneakers with each step, and I climbed the long hill, losing momentum by the second. In the near distance, the lighthouse grew larger, and I noted the years of decay on its once pristine facade. Ivy crawled up the first two levels of the structure and pushed its way past the stones, causing parts of the tower to crumble. Above the decrepit wooden door, a sign read "Lighthouse not in use. Enter at your own risk."

An Orchard Hollow inside joke.

From what I remembered; kids used to party in the broken-down place long before I was even born. These days, the lighthouse was a makeshift tourist attraction for a small number of visitors each year. Most came for the views; for the sprawling sea and the waves that crashed against the rocky cliff the structure sat on. Though there were plenty people like Declan who considered the lighthouse to be a cherished piece of the town's history and good enough to form lasting connections in.

I rolled my eyes up the tower to the shattered glass that once held a beam of hope.

History looked sad from where I was standing.

With one final glance at the beetle, which was nothing but a dot in the field, I pulled the door handle and slipped inside. Dust circled me and I coughed into the turtleneck of my sweater, my eyes watering from the stench of mold in the air. Before me, a less than solid spiral staircase unfolded, leading all the way to the roof of the tower. I checked my phone, making sure I had reception, and started to climb. The steps were wide and further apart than a normal staircase, and each forward movement made my sides pinch.

Stella was on to something; I really needed to exercise more often.

By the time I reached the lantern room, I was out of breath and covered in a thin layer of sweat that chilled me to the bone. I wiped my brow, walking along the pathway circling the cupola. Not far from me, there was a shuffle of feet, followed by the unmistakable sound of someone blowing their nose. I stopped in my tracks. Maybe it was a mistake to follow Aria here. I didn't want to scare the girl by showing up unannounced. What if she thought I was here to hurt her?

One foot behind the other, I started to back away. My hip nudged the wooden railing surrounding the glass encasement where the main light fixture was once held, and I heard a loud snap before half the stupid thing tumbled to the floor. I winced, kicking the busted railing piece to the side.

"Hello?" a soft voice called out from around the bend. "Is someone here?"

Great. I did the one thing I tried not to do: scare the living daylights out of Aria. At least, I hoped it was Aria. Hands up in surrender, I dragged myself toward the voice, emerging on the side facing the sea. "Sorry if I scared you," I said. "I come in peace."

I started to raise my fingers in a salute and stopped. The girl was already looking like she might bolt, and any sudden moves could send her over the edge. My eyes glanced out the large windows of the dome and I took a couple of steps back to put her at ease.

"Oh," the girl said. "I didn't realize anyone else comes here."

Her eyes scanned the round walkway of the lighthouse, searching for an escape route should she need it.

Smiling, I leaned against what was left of the railing to appear nonthreatening. "They usually don't," I said. "Your friend Declan told me you might be here."

"Declan sent you? Why?" A glimpse of fear appeared on Aria's thin face, but she didn't move. Her slender arms crossed, and I watched her pull a phone out of her bag. An insurance policy. Smart kid. Not that I planned to hurt her, but she was right to be weary. There was no one at the lighthouse except the two of us, and I wasn't exactly doing a stellar job at explaining why I came here.

I widened my smile, examining the frail girl in front of me. There was a peaceful demeanor about her, as though the world couldn't reach her, no matter how hard it tried. She wore a light pink rain jacket and the tiniest hint of a lace collar peeked out from beneath it. Even her clothes resembled someone who stepped right out of a portal to another world. The air around Aria drew my attention. I couldn't quite put my finger on it, and it made me wonder if she often had this effect on people. It also made me wonder if I was wrong about my earlier assumption. This girl was far too sweet to be a killer, wasn't she?

Ugh. I was taking forever and a day to answer. Worry lines formed around Aria's eyes and I quickly recovered, saying, "He didn't send me. I ran into him in town. He seemed upset and told me you're here, so I thought I would check in."

Aria frowned. "I was there when your friend passed away," I explained. "It happened in my cafe."

"I'm sorry, I don't understand," Aria said.

"I'm not making any sense," I agreed. "Let me try again. My name is Piper and I'm helping the police find out who might have wanted to hurt your friend."

Barely relaxing, Aria's pink lips twitched, and she lowered her phone. "Oh. Okay. You're a police officer?"

"Not at all," I said. "More like an assistant. But your friend died in my place, and I wanted to help in any way I can." The lies felt awkward falling from my lips, but they seemed to be working, so I kept going. "Declan was understandably upset when I spoke with him. When he mentioned you were up here by your-self, I thought I should make sure you were alright."

For a moment, it looked as though I had done a profound job of scaring the bejesus out of the young girl. Her eyes widened so much she resembled a cartoon character. Aria rolled her shoulders and wisps of mouse-brown hair fell over her coat. She blew a strand away from her face, pinning me with a serious look. "Is he okay?"

"Declan?" I asked. "He's fine. The other guy probably wouldn't have been if we hadn't interfered."

A string pulled at her lips.

"Is Declan always so—"

"Harsh?" Aria asked. "Pretty much. He's a very passionate person. I think that's why Zeta and he got along so well."

Uncertainty filled the air between us at the mention of her best friend's name and Aria tore her gaze from me to look out the window. Her long fingers played with a charm dangling off a silver bracelet, and my eyes caught on it glimmering in the light shining through. I tried to make out its shape, giving up when Aria curled a fist around it. "Have you had any luck?"

I stared at her, open-mouthed, trying to decipher what she meant.

"Finding out what happened to Zeta," Aria whispered.

Right. The reason I told her I was here. I really needed to keep my act going if I was to gain this girl's trust. I dared to venture toward her, closing some of the distance between us. "Not yet. But the police are doing everything they can. As am I."

"That's good," Aria said, continuing to watch the waves crash to shore beneath us. "Declan said we should stay until we have some answers. And until they can release her body."

Nodding, I took one more step in. "That's a smart move. What do you think?"

She side-eyed me. "I think it won't make a differ-ence. She's gone, and he's broken-hearted. Finding out what happened won't change that."

"Can I ask you a personal question?" When Aria nodded, I said, "Declan mentioned you three lived together. How was that going?"

This got her attention. Aria spun around, stopping me in place. Regret filled my gut, and I realized I said too much, gave too much away. Aria's cheeks sucked in, and she bit her bottom lip. "I guess there's no point hiding it now," she said.

"You had feelings for him, didn't you?"

She nodded, her chin dipping low. "I was in love with him," she admitted. "Still am, I guess. You know I met him first? I was the one that introduced him to Zeta. I thought we had something too, Declan and me. So stupid. The second he met her; it was all over. Zeta was like that, you know. When she was in the room, all eyes were on her."

I recalled the girl I met the first day Archer's team came to Bean Me Up. The way she carried herself, the way she spoke. It was exactly as Aria described it. Zeta was a force; one you couldn't help but watch. My heart ached for the poor, broken girl in front of me. She never stood a chance.

"I didn't mind it most of the time," Aria said, making my chest squeeze tight. "I loved them both, and they were so happy together. I couldn't get in the way of that."

"So, you kept your feelings to yourself?"

She nodded again. "Yep. You probably think I'm a loser."

"Not at all," I told her. "You're stronger than I am, that's for sure."

Smiling, she rolled up her sleeve and the charm she played with fell from her fingers, dangling in the air. My eyes snapped to it, unease settling in the bottom of my stomach. Electricity sparked within me, and I wet my lips, realization smacking me in the forehead.

The charm: it was a talisman. A magical talisman.

Aria was a paranormal.

Catching me staring, Aria tried to tuck the bracelet back into her sleeve, but it was too late. The truth was out, and we both knew it. She spread her feet wide and shoved her hands in her coat pockets, her full attention landing on me. "Which one are you?" she asked.

I sucked in a breath between clenched teeth. "Witch. You?"

"My dad was a warlock," she answered. "But I'm not anything."

"Your gene never activated?"

Aria shook her head, her eyes lowering. "I'm his biggest disappointment. My parents never had other children, so unless I have kids and the gene passes to them, the family magic dies with me."

It all made sense now. The ethereal way about her, the pull I felt when I first stepped foot in the lighthouse. Paranormals were drawn to their own kind, and I could sense Aria's magical background despite her not having any abilities. "I can relate," I told her.

"Your gene didn't activate too?"

I scoffed. "Oh, it did. But I'm useless with magic." As though to mock me, my magic chose that moment to manifest, and I felt sparks fly from my fingers. I looped my hands behind my back to keep them out of sight. The electricity build-up released, and I zapped myself in the back. Jumping, I rubbed a painful burn and coughed to cover my yelps. "I'm also a bit of a disappointment," I said. A thought occurred to me, and I added, "Your best friend worked for a man who hunts our kind. How did you manage to hide your background from her?"

*Or did you not manage it at all?* Did Zeta find out about Aria's magic, and she killed her for it? I had trouble picturing the frail girl before me going to such extremes, but that didn't mean it couldn't happen.

Aria laughed, a high-pitched sound that dragged me away from my thoughts. "It's not hard to hide magic you never had. Besides, Zeta never bought into the whole magic thing. She thought it was a ruse to sell books."

"But she worked for Archer Lee," I said.

"Uh-huh. She said it paid the bills and her plan was to get enough experience to bulk up her resume. There was some program she was dying to get into, and Archer Lee is a big deal. His name looked good on an application. At least that's what Zeta said."

I wondered if Archer knew his prized employee thought he was a joke. Maybe it was why Zeta didn't want to come on the book tour. I thought back to the conversation I heard that night and frowned. It didn't add up. Zeta was adamant that she didn't want to be in Orchard Hollow. Not on the book tour, but in our town specifically. Why? What did she have against coming here?

Thoughts jumbled; I focused on Aria. "Did Zeta

mention someone in town she was talking to? Someone who could have been helping her with a project?"

"Oh, you must mean Tabitha," Aria said.

*Come again? Did she say Tabitha?* Deep creases formed on my forehead and heat rose up my back. "Do you mean Tabitha Pogue?"

"I don't know her last name. But Zeta said she was working on a big story, one that was going to get her into the program for sure. I think I heard her mention a Tabitha once or twice," Aria explained.

Knots twisted my gut, and my body shook. Why was Zeta in contact with Tabitha Pogue? My stomach turned as I thought about the only reason Archer's assistant might have for speaking to an Orchard Hollow witch. To get proof that magic existed. Was Tabitha giving up paranormal secrets on the sly? And if she was, why did Zeta keep them from her boss? It was clear Archer knew nothing of the proof the sheriff found on Zeta's laptop; if he did, he would have already blown the whistle for his fifteen minutes of fame.

I steadied a shaky breath and ran a finger along the window on my right. Beads of water formed over the line in the foggy glass, dripping down like blood from an open wound. I caught Aria's gaze in mine. "Do you think your friend planned to go behind

Archer's back and write her own story about para-normals?"

"No way," Aria said without a second thought. "I'm telling you; Zeta didn't believe in that stuff. If anything, she'd be working to disprove that pompous man and his allegations."

And yet she was talking to a witch in secret.

The girl checked her watch, then her phone, then her watch again. It was enough to let me know she was done speaking. Either that or I managed to creep her the heck out. Both were viable options. Choosing not to keep her any longer, I thanked Aria for her time and let her know that if she needed to speak to someone, to reach out.

"Thanks," Aria said, giving me a wide berth on her way to the staircase. "And thanks for trying to help Zeta. She didn't have anyone except Declan and me. Nice to know someone else is looking out for her."

I reached out and squeezed her shoulder, surprised when she didn't slap my hand away. "We'll get to the bottom of this. And I mean it, you can talk to me anytime. Even if it's not about Zeta."

Lips curling lightly, Aria nodded, catching my drift. I felt for the girl. If anyone understood what it was like to be a failure at magic, it was me. That and her love life was even more complicated than mine, which I didn't think was possible. Offering an ear was the least I could do. As gran told me, when you have the chance to help someone, take it.

I waved goodbye and watched Aria disappear into the belly of the lighthouse, her steps fading as she left. My eyes rolled over the encasement I stood in, noting the lack of life around me. I wondered what it was like to stand in this same spot when the lighthouse was operational. When the center of the tower wasn't an empty hole but held a beacon to guide travelers home. Turning to the window, I looked at the horizon and the turbulent sea stretching long before me. Rays of sun cut through the clouds and reflected off the water, turning it into a gargantuan mirror that reflected all my current doubts.

Despite what Aria said, a gnawing feeling crept through me. There had to be a reason Tabitha and Zeta were in contact, a reason I was sure was bad news for paranormals. I didn't know why Tabitha, a witch herself, would want to out our kind, but it was the only theory that made sense. And if I was correct, the sheriff's motive for Zeta's murder was much more plausible than I originally imagined.

It seemed whether she believed it or not, Zeta was knee deep in magic.

Deep enough to get her killed.

My attention caught on the line in the glass I drew earlier and the water dripping down the window. It flowed down to the stone wall beneath, creating dark streaks in the concrete. My jaw clenched shut. There was a rough carving on the wall, right under the railing my behind tore off earlier. I bent over, pushing my face closer to it.

Knees buckling, I traced my finger over the crude sketch that looked as though it had been cut out with a knife. A line cutting across an open triangle. I knew what I was looking at instantly.

Someone carved a spear into the wall of the lighthouse.

Words floated in my head, and I pressed my palm to the wall to keep myself from falling. "Meet me at the spear tonight."

My mom's letters from the mysterious M. Was this the spear they referred to? It was all too coincidental not to be related. I shut my eyes, a headache careening from temple to temple. In my back pocket, my phone vibrated, and I swallowed the saliva pooling in my mouth before picking it up. "Hello?"

"Piper, where are you?" Joe's voice sounded urgent on the line.

I cleared my throat, regaining some of my composure. "At the lighthouse," I answered. "I stopped by to talk to Aria, see if I can get some information from her while I knew where she'd be."

"Good. That's good."

"Is everything alright?" I asked.

"Yes, nothing to worry about. I went looking for you after I dropped Declan back at the hotel but couldn't find you. Wanted to make sure you were safe."

Was Joe worried about me? *Take that, Stella!* I smiled, but it fell away when I saw the spear again. "Hey, Joe?" I asked. "Do you have any plans tonight?"

"Not at all," he answered eagerly.

"Think you can swing by my place? I have something I want to run by you, something strange I found at the house. I don't know how to make sense of it yet, but I think it might be a clue about my... um...situation."

There was silence on the other line and my cheeks reddened, embarrassment setting in. Did I just ask Joe to come by my house so I could show him things? It sounded like the worst pick up line ever. What was actually wrong with me? Fanning my face, I bit my tongue and slurred out, "Joe?"

"Sorry, yes. We're on for tonight. I can be there at eight."

Relief washed over me, and I nearly fainted right there in the lighthouse. "It's a date," I said.

*What? No! Stop talking!*

"Sure is," Joe said. I could feel his grin widen through the phone and my body vibrated in return.

"And you can tell me what you got from Aria while I'm there; two birds, one stone."

After we hung up, I stayed at the lighthouse for a while longer, my eyes never leaving the spear. Jumbled thoughts crowded my mind, and I tried to keep them straight, though they refused to be controlled. Between the strange circumstances around Zeta's death and the even stranger clues my mom left behind, I didn't know where to start. My life had become a tangled mess, and that wasn't even counting the fact that I had a business to run—when the sheriff would finally let me open the cafe—and apparently a date tonight to think about.

What was it Joe said before he hung up? Two birds and one stone?

Shrugging, I forced myself to stand on weak legs. I had way too many birds flying and not a stone in sight.

# CHAPTER 13

"Did you remember to shave your big toe?" Stella asked, her face poking in through the crack in the bathroom door.

I turned around to tell her off, forgetting the eyeliner I was applying. The pencil slid over my skin, drawing a perfect line from my eye to my ear. "Ugh!" I howled. "Get out of here! I'm trying to get ready. Joe will be here any minute and look at me now."

Rubbing at the black line on my face, I reached for a cotton ball, hoping I didn't have to start over. Makeup and I were not on the best terms, and it was hard enough to figure out the tools and contraptions laid out on the counter without Stella's annoying interruptions. Why did I let her talk me into this? Joe had seen me looking a hot mess plenty of times; one more night would not make a difference.

I doused the cotton ball in makeup remover and smeared it on my face, smudging the thick line into a blob.

"Happy now?" I said with a huff.

Stella's body pushed its way into the room, and she shoved her perfect, cost-more-than-my-house nose closer to the mirror. "Maybe some glitter will help?"

"No. Absolutely not. I'm washing all this nonsense off and I don't want to hear you whine about it." Stella pouted, but I ignored her. "And my big toe is perfectly fine, thank you very much."

"Sure," Stella said, smirking. "If you're protecting it from cold weather."

Blood boiling, I grabbed the hot curling iron from the counter and pushed it through her bratty head. Stella shrieked, her body shimmering as she disappeared. I waited, counting the seconds for her return. She was going to be so pissed I did that.

On cue, Stella materialized behind me, her hands cocked on her hips and a disapproving look plastered on her face. "That was entirely uncalled for. I'm trying to help you. No need to get defensive."

"You're only making me more nervous," I said. "Tonight is not a big deal, and you're blowing things out of proportion."

No surprise there. Blowing things out of propor-tion was Stella's specialty. That and avoiding any conversation with substance. If I didn't know better, I'd have thought my familiar was a teenager and not a grown woman. Behind me, Stella stuck her tongue out, thinking I couldn't see her.

Definitely not grown.

"Can you please get out of here so I can finish?" I asked.

Before Stella had a chance to reply, a knock sounded on the downstairs door and we both stopped breathing. Well, I stopped breathing and Stella stopped talking. I wished I had time to appreciate the silence, but Joe was waiting and there was no time to waste. As quickly as humanly possible, I rubbed off the clown makeup I applied earlier, tied my hair into a messy top bun, and rushed to the front door. Behind me, Stella shouted unsolicited advice, and I hummed as I skipped down the stairs, pretending not to hear her.

Breathless, I opened the door to greet Joe right before he knocked again.

"Hi," I said. "Come on in."

He looked back at the porch and rubbed the rear of his neck, stepping inside. I watched him shift his weight from one foot to the other and he white-knuckled a bottle of wine, his eyes dancing around the room. From his vantage point, Joe could see the entire downstairs of the farmhouse and I wondered what he thought of the place. I kept it tidy enough, but it had an unmistakable cottage feel and Joe struck me as someone who was used to finer things in life.

Standing at the entrance, Joe seemed completely out of place. Even though he ditched his usual slacks and suit jacket attire and opted for dark jeans and a casual sweater, he didn't quite fit in. If anything, he looked uncomfortable, maybe even a little nervous. Was Joe as out of sorts about tonight as I was? It couldn't be. He didn't have a Stella to stir up doubts before our so-called date.

To break the unbearable awkwardness between us, I pointed to the bottle, asking, "That for me?"

"Yes, sorry," Joe said sheepishly. "I wasn't sure what you enjoyed, so I settled on a French cab. Hope that's alright."

I couldn't bring myself to tell him that I wouldn't know the difference one way or another, so instead, I nodded, taking the bottle from him and setting it on the kitchen counter. "Make yourself comfortable," I yelled out from the kitchen. "I have a pizza in the oven that's almost done."

Checking on the food, I poured two glasses of wine and carried them into the living room where Joe was perusing the collection of photographs lining my fireplace mantle. His eyes inspected every image, and I blushed, remembering some of the unfortunate ones gran kept around.

"I really need to replace some of those," I said.

Joe chuckled, the sound making me melt into the floor. "Don't. It's sweet you kept them."

"After gran passed, I couldn't bring myself to redecorate," I admitted. "This place still feels like hers sometimes. It's strange, but it's almost as though she's here, watching over me."

Gaze jumping around the room, Joe sat the frame he picked up back on the shelf.

"She isn't, right?" he asked. "Here, I mean."

I laughed. "Nope. No grandmother ghosts in the farmhouse. It's only Stella that I can see and trust me, she's plenty to handle."

I half-expected the ghost to pop up and argue and when she didn't, my chest rose and fell with relieved breaths. At least Stella had the decency not to ruin tonight any more than she already had.

"It's interesting that you can't see anyone else, considering your family's background."

Right. My great-great-aunt who was possibly crazy. I didn't know why I let that part slip out when I told Joe about my ability to see Stella, but he believed it was the reason I had a ghost familiar in the first place. That the witches in my family had some sort of connection to the realm of the dead. According to Joe, with enough practice, I could actually see dead people. He was under the wrongful impression that my "gift" was a good thing.

No, thanks. One ghost was plenty. I wasn't about to add ghost wrangler to my list of weird magical abilities.

Speaking of....

I walked back to the kitchen and snatched the stack of envelopes from the bar counter, bringing them to Joe. "This is what I wanted to show you," I said and handed them over.

With care, Joe inspected the envelopes, looking at me briefly before opening the letter I already read. I waited while he got through it, his eyes widening. Joe flipped the letter over and checked the back, asking, "Where did you find these?"

"In my mom's things in the attic. They were stitched into the lining of a suitcase," I said. "It was Stella's suggestion to check there because it turns out she's got some good ideas at times. What do you think it means?"

"I'm not sure. Any idea who M is?"

I shook my head no. "There's no one in the family with that initial."

"Could it be someone she met in the city?"

"You think it's someone from the coven she

joined?" I asked. My stomach twisted at the implication. If M was part of the dark magic coven mom ran off with, that would mean she was in contact with them long before I was even born. The dates I could make out on the envelopes went as far back as mom's teenage years, which would explain why I found them hidden in her childhood suitcase. How would she have even met them? The thought of it made me uncomfortable. How long had mom been planning to leave?

While I spun out of control, Joe opened several more letters and read their contents. His brow furrowed as he skimmed them, settling on one. "There's no name in any of these. Just the initial. But this one is interesting."

He handed me the letter, and I bit the inside of my cheek, reading it aloud.

"My dearest Sylvie.

I'm sorry to hear the latest news. Are you certain it is what we feared?

If your hunch is correct, we must find a way to protect her. No one can ever find out the truth. For her safety, and for yours. For all of ours.

I will do my best to find a temporary solution. Please continue to monitor her magic and I will write as soon as I have more information.

Yours always,

M."

Panic shot through me and I dropped the letter, looking up at Joe. "What does this mean? Who is M talking about?"

The vampire didn't answer and only handed me another piece of paper.

"My dearest Sylvie,

Enclosed, you will find the spell required to bind her magic. You must perform it immediately. I must warn you, the spell requires immense energy, so I'm afraid you will need help. Find someone you trust but do not disclose more than you need.

I will meet you at the spear this weekend as agreed.

Good luck.

Yours always,

M."

Head spinning, I grabbed the envelopes from Joe and rummaged through them. This was the last one of the bunch. It couldn't be. I checked again, defeat swallowing me whole. Tears pricked at the back of my eyelids, and I shut them tightly, refusing to cry. When I was sure I wasn't going to break down in front of Joe—because worst date ever—I looked at the date on the final envelope. "This isn't right. If these dates are correct," I said, "I would have been five when they were sent. How did I not know mom was talking to someone in the coven this whole time? And gran? She would have noticed. She noticed everything."

"Unless she did," Joe suggested.

I let my eyes wonder over the letter again. "Unless gran was the person mom trusted for the binding spell," I whispered.

Joe nodded slowly.

"But what were they binding? I've never heard of a spell to bind someone's magic. And why?"

There was a moment of silence as Joe worked his jaw, considering his next words very carefully. His eyes burnt into me, and he reached out, his large hands obscuring mine from view. "Do you remember what I saw when I was a kid?"

"You mean me bringing a squirrel back to life?" I scoffed. "I'm pretty sure you imagined it."

"What if I didn't?"

My heart raced inside my ribcage and my vision spotted. I blinked to clear the black dots swimming at the edges of my sightline and my breath hitched as I said, "It can't be. Why would mom and gran bind my magic? And how would I even have the magic you described? Our family is pure witch blood. What you think you saw is dark. It's unheard of."

"It does line up with these letters," Joe said.

"If they're not a hoax. For all we know, this is some stupid game mom made up to mess with gran after she left. She was constantly doing things to get under her skin."

Joe's chin tucked into his chest and his lips thinned. "I know you don't want to believe this, and it opens up a new can of worms, but I think these letters are the real deal."

"You seriously think I have some sort of dark magic inside me that needed to be kept hidden?" I asked.

"Maybe," Joe said. He took the letters from me and placed them on the coffee table, guiding me to the couch. When I sat, he handed me the glass of wine I was yet to try, tipping his chin toward it. "How about this? We forget about the letters for tonight. I will see what I can find in the bookstore tomorrow and let you know if anything comes up. And in the meantime, we focus on things that are less confusing."

I sniffled, taking a giant, super classy gulp from the wineglass. "Like what?"

"Why don't you tell me where you're at on the Zeta Huxley case? Take your mind off this for now."

A chuckle escaped me. Only someone who really understood me would know that discussing a murder might be less dark than talking about my magic. Ears pounding, I tried my best to fill Joe in on what I learned from Aria. When I got to the part where she mentioned Tabitha, Joe's head spun, and he had the same look of interest I did when I first heard it. We spent the rest of the evening doing the least romantic thing I could think of: bouncing theories on why Tabitha Pogue would want to out the paranormal community and what that meant for Zeta.

Stella was going to be so pissed when she found out my date wasn't a date, after all.

By the time Joe left, I was an empty shell. My body was drained and tired, and I could barely keep my eyes open. I wasn't sure if it was the emotional turmoil from mom's letters, or the wine, but whatever it was, I knew I needed rest.

Casting a side glance at the stack of envelopes left on the coffee table, I carried my sorry butt upstairs. Falling asleep as soon as my head hit the pillow.

# CHAPTER 14

The beetle's engine huffed and puffed as I maneuvered it down Cliff Row, heading for the cafe. This morning, I received a call from the sheriff's office letting me know it should only be a few more days until I could reopen and the first thing I did was call Rory in. I was dead set on making sure the place was ready to go when we got the go ahead.

I also desperately needed a distraction from last night's events and from the fact that it seemed Zeta's case was on a fast track to become an unsolved crime. Romero was yet to find the person who killed her and considering how little luck I had on my end, it was looking like both of us were at a dead end.

Though you'd never hear the sheriff admit it.

Jumpy from too many morning coffees, I put the car in park and slammed the door, rushing to reach Bean Me Up. I wanted to get there a little earlier since Rory didn't have keys to the place, but when I arrived at the door, she was already leaning against it.

"Morning!" she announced in a chipper voice.

I looked her up and down, gauging the reason for her excitement, and unlocked the front door. "You're here early."

"Aunt Cilia dropped me off on her way to work." She pointed to the hotel behind us. "It was getting here early or taking the bus. An easy choice. Obviously."

I thought of the dingy, old bus going through town and our only form of public transportation. "Obviously," I agreed. Dropping my purse off in the office, I took an inventory of what had to be done. Chills spread through me when my eyes landed on the spot Zeta died at. There might as well have been a giant chalk outline on the floor because I was sure I could never get the image of her lying there out of my mind.

"Want me to sweep and mop the front?" Rory offered.

Her lack of disgust with being back here surprised me and I cocked one eyebrow, asking, "You don't mind?"

"No way," she said. "I know it's like super grim, but this place kind of made me popular. Everyone wants to know what happened. And trust me, being here beats hanging out at home with the monsters, so you're doing me a favor."

The monsters, as Rory called them, were her three older brothers, all of whom were the bane of Rory's existence, as far as I could tell. In the short time I've known her, she had never said one nice word about the boys. It made her spending most of her time with Cilia that much clearer. If I grew up in a house full of testosterone, I'd be itching for female company too. A part of me wondered if Rory took the job to get out of the house and meet people that weren't her brothers.

I watched her sweep piles of dust into the corners of the cafe and leave them there, my eyes rolling. "You sure you're fine doing that?"

"One hundred percent!" she yelled.

While proceeded to work at her version of a hundred percent, I put in an order for milk and baked goods. Luckily, the bakery down the street agreed to partner with me when I first opened, and I didn't need to think too far ahead with orders. Mrs. Cevil, the sweet old lady who ran the bakery, told me to call her any time, even if I needed an order mid-day when it was especially busy. I used to think I'd never have to rely on her generosity, but that was before I met Harry

Houdini. With his grabby paws, you never knew what might go missing and require replenishment.

My eyes instinctively shifted to the back door, which remained closed.

Where was Harry spending his time these days? I hadn't seen him since the break-in at the farmhouse and with the cafe on lockdown, he had nowhere to go to cause his mischief. As much as I hated to admit it, I worried about the little guy.

Thinking of the raccoon made me remember the night I spied on Zeta, and my knees knocked together. Who was she talking to? And what did she mean when she told the person on the other end to handle things?

An uneasy feeling rushed through me, and I pushed back from the desk, walking to the front.

"Will you be okay here if I stepped out for a bit?" I asked Rory.

The girl saluted me, hiding the phone she was on behind her back. "Sure thing, boss."

Pretending I didn't see her slacking—because Rory was doing me a favor by being here, paid or not—I pushed the front door wide open and made my way across the street to the Rose Hollow Hotel. The familiar feel of the plush carpet under my feet made me want to turn around and run back to the cafe. The last time I was here, things didn't exactly go as planned and I ended up getting involved in solving an old murder, a complication that was fast becoming a regular occurrence in my life. At least Cilia and I were on better terms now than we were then. We weren't best friends by any means, but I didn't want to punch her in the nose as much these days. And I was pretty sure I had her to thank for the lack of appearances Nancy Steeles had been making in my life lately.

Although the witch's attitude toward me might go back to hatred once she heard what I came here to ask.

I tiptoed to the reception desk, avoiding making eye contact with the few guests mingling in the lobby. They paid me no mind, instead focusing on a large map of Orchard Hollow spread out on a coffee table in front of them. I noticed a few familiar haunts marked off with red circles and knots formed in my throat when I realized the lighthouse was one of them. Now that I knew it was a meeting spot for my mom and whoever this M character was, I was never going to see it the same way.

When I reached the front desk, my palm hovered over the large brass bell on the counter. Did I really want to drag Cilia into this mess? It was bad enough her niece witnessed a murder in my cafe; now I was going to grill her about a member of her coven?

It seemed fate decided for me.

Before I had a chance to back out, Cilia's blonde

bob rounded the corner, her eyes twinkling when she saw me. "Hi, Piper," she said, with shocking enthusiasm. "Everything alright with Rory?"

"Oh, hi, Cilia. All good. She's being very helpful today," I lied.

"What is she *really* doing?"

I chuckled under my breath. "I left her glued to her phone," I admitted. "Or sweeping, as she calls it."

"Teenagers, huh? So, how can I help you?"

*Here goes nothing.* I tapped my index fingers together, fidgeting in my spot. "I'm not sure exactly how to say this without sounding like I'm crossing boundaries," I said. "But I need your help."

I expected her to tell me to march my butt out of the hotel, similar to how she behaved the last time I questioned her. Except Cilia did no such thing. She smiled warmly, and leaned over the counter, her teeth sparkling from the light of the overhead chandelier. "Anything you need," she said.

*I'm sorry, what?* Who was this person and what did she do with Cilia Craven? I knew we were on better terms now that her niece worked for me, but I didn't know we were on anything-you-need terms. This was a turn of events I didn't expect. I kind of liked the new and improved Cilia.

"Earth to Piper."

Blinking rapidly to clear my mind, I scolded

myself for zoning out again, and looked at the witch. "Whoops," I said, laughing uncomfortably. "I tend to lose myself in thought. Sorry. I know this is probably going to sound like I'm pushing it, but do you think I can ask you about Tabitha?"

"Pogue? My coven mate?" Cilia's face scrunched. "What about her?"

Deciding not to beat around the bush, I laid it all out for her. "I'm sure you're busy here, so I'll cut right to the chase," I said. "I'm trying to find out what happened to the girl that died in the cafe and Tabitha's name came up. It's probably nothing, but I wanted to know if you noticed her acting odd in the last few weeks."

I waited for Cilia to tell me to bite it.

She didn't. At all.

"You'll have to be more specific," she answered with a laugh. "Tabitha is always acting odd. It's her signature personality trait. How come you're getting involved?"

Shoot. How do I phrase what I'm doing without telling Cilia about my deal with the sheriff? I felt guilty enough that I ran my big mouth to Aria, but she wasn't from town and when she left, my secret, unpaid side gig would remain under wraps. Cilia lived here. She knew the sheriff. If she found out he tasked me with spying on paranormals, it wouldn't go over well.

I chewed on my tongue, thinking. "Bodies keep piling up around me," I finally said. "I don't want to get the reputation of someone who's bad luck. Not sure if you noticed, but we don't exactly have the fastest moving police force in town. I figured I could help speed up the process. Especially since one of our own might be involved."

"You think Tabitha had something to do with that poor girl dying?" Cilia asked.

"I don't know what I think," I said, adding, "yet. It's why I wanted to check with you when her name was mentioned, since you probably know her well."

Darkness settled over Cilia's face. "It's true then," she whispered. "A paranormal killed the girl?"

"What? I never said that."

"You don't have to, Piper," she said. "Rory told me all about what those four were here for. A book tour exposing our town's magic and the author's research assistant drops dead. You don't have to be a genius to figure out one of us did it."

*Hmm.* Cilia and the sheriff both came to the same conclusion, but I wasn't convinced. It was the obvious choice, which was exactly why I didn't buy it. "Do you think Tabitha is capable of murder?" I asked.

"No way! She's strange and very opinionated, but I can't picture her killing someone. Tabitha is too preoccupied with moving up in the coven to care about anything else. Honestly, I don't even know how the bank hasn't fired her yet since she's late for every shift. She's been training with Gemini, our lead seer, to strengthen her magic. From what I can tell, it was working too. What I mean is, Tabitha is all about herself. Going so far as to kill someone to protect others is not on her radar."

I rolled Cilia's words over in my head, trying to make sense of them. If what she said was true, Tabitha would have to be a fool to expose our secrets to Zeta, as I originally thought. Why bother working your butt off to rise to higher ranks in the coven if you're going to throw it all away by snitching? And if Tabitha was somewhat selfish, as Cilia implied, our secret getting out would do her no favors. Then why was she talking to Zeta? What could they possibly have to discuss?

Could it have been her on the phone that night?

"I'm going to tell you a secret, but it stays between us," I said. "I found out Tabitha was talking to Zeta, the girl who died, but not what about. And she hooked up with Archer's videographer. That's a lot of connections to a man who wants to expose our kind. More than I'd think a witch would want to have."

Standing perfectly still, Cilia's features gave nothing away. She leaned further over the desk, her face inches from mine. "Look," she said, her voice nearly a whisper. "I really don't think she did it. And I have no idea why she'd get herself so wrapped up in this whole book tour. But I will say that Tabitha has been distracted lately."

"Distracted how?"

"Just out of it. Usually, she is all about the coven and her position as a seer after Gemini steps down."

My breath came out short. "Your lead seer is leaving?"

"Uh-huh," Cilia said, nodding. "But not a word to anyone. I'm not supposed to advertise coven business to outsiders."

My insides twisted. Being called an outsider by a fellow witch was worse than getting boiling water thrown in my face. I knew being a solitary witch was my decision, but still. Ouch. I shook off my hurt feelings and said, "Maybe she was distracted because she was up to no good and her actions could hurt every paranormal in town."

"Why, though?" Cilia asked. "Why would she want to expose magic when she's a witch?"

I shrugged. "That's what I'm trying to find out. Right now, she's the only paranormal I can connect to Zeta, and it doesn't look good."

Looking past me at the guests crowding the lobby, Cilia blew a wavy blonde hair off her face, her eyes darkening. "I'll be honest with you. I wasn't close with her. She was a little stuck up for my tastes." *And yet you're friends with Nancy Steeles*. As though she could hear my thoughts, Cilia's lips curled up. "Even more so than Nancy, if you can believe it."

"Oh, I wasn't—"

Cilia held her hand up. "It's fine," she said. "I know you two don't get along. Nancy isn't so bad when you get to know her, but Tabitha.... Well, let's say she was a tough one to get close to. I don't think anyone in the coven spent time with her outside our meetings except her sister, Vera."

"That's not much to go on," I mused.

"Sorry I couldn't help more. If you do want to get into Tabitha's twisted head, your best bet is to talk to her directly."

I scowled. "I doubt she'll talk to me. I've never spoken to her before and I'm sure she doesn't have the best impression of me. I don't think anyone in your coven does."

Memories of Nancy turning half the witches in this town against me flashed through my system and I brushed them off, refusing to let the nasty little witch get to me. After gran died, things with Nancy got even worse. She'd never try half the stunts she pulled when gran was around. No one messed with my grandmother and for most of my life, I lived under the protection of her reputation. I didn't realize how much I depended on it until she passed. Without gran, and even mom, I was nothing more than a failed witch in a town full of powerful paranormals.

I glanced at my idle fingers. Now, with this bizarre magic I held, I was worse than a failure. I was an anomaly. Nobody liked those.

"She'll meet you at her and Vera's place tomorrow at noon," Cilia said. My head did a double take as she slid a piece of paper across the counter, nudging it towards me. "I wrote the address down for you. Don't be late. She's a stickler for timing."

My jaw hit the ground, and I rubbed my chin, trying to think of what to say.

"Don't look so shocked," Cilia teased. "Not all of us are like Nancy."

Thanking her more times than I should have, I turned to leave when I heard Cilia call out my name. I spun on my heels, the paper she gave me melting in my clammy hands.

"We should grab a drink sometime," Cilia said. "I never got to properly thank you for hiring Rory."

"S-Sure," I stuttered. "That sounds great." I looked down at the wrinkled paper. "And thanks for this."

Cilia laughed. "You already said that. Five times."

Rushing out of the hotel before I could embarrass myself further, I crossed the street, my legs rubbery from excitement. Finally, I was getting somewhere. It could have been nothing, but something inside me said otherwise. Somehow, Tabitha Pogue was connected to Zeta's murder. I was so close to figuring it out, I could taste it. *Take that, Romero! Looks like late night detective show binges are paying off.*

I had to admit, I wasn't half bad at this. If things kept coming up Piper, I might have to ask the sheriff to put me on his payroll, after all. It appeared I had an unexpected knack for digging up information, and if that was the case, I could use that to help people in this town.

Maybe I wasn't the best witch, or whatever I was, but this way I could give back to the community. My head swiveled to the hotel. And who knew? I might even make a friend in the process.

# CHAPTER 15

Waiting to meet Tabitha was the equivalent of waiting for a pot to boil. Which was exactly what I was doing in my kitchen while Stella paced the length of the living room and back again. The ghost had been in a tizzy ever since I told her things with Joe didn't go according to plan. She swung her fit body around, her tennis skirt swaying angrily.

"I can't believe you spent the entire night talking about murder!"

I looked at the pot again, adding more coffee to the French press. Today was a triple coffee type of day. "Yes, well, the letters were a mood kill," I said.

"And why did you think it was a good idea to break out the depression stack on your date?"

Sucking in a shaky breath, I willed myself not to snap at her.

"I already told you," I repeated. "It wasn't really a date. I asked Joe over to help me figure out my magic."

Stella slanted a shapely brow. "Did he?"

"Not exactly. But he did say he'll investigate the spell M told mom about."

The pacing continued, and I watched Stella like a pendulum, my eyes following her fluid movements. She rubbed her chin, periodically pausing to look out the bay window. After an excruciating five minutes of silence, she finally stopped walking and twirled to face me. "Can you zippity zap something for me?"

I sighed in agony.

"Why do you—"

"Just do it, Piper," Stella pressed.

Realizing there was no arguing with a dead woman, as per usual, I let out a second dramatic sigh and pushed away from the kitchen counter. Scanning the room, I landed on a dirty dish rag that was on its final days and pointed a finger in its direction. Reaching for my magic, I felt my body tense as it crept to the surface. My finger twitched, blue electric sparks jumping over the skin. I pressed my tongue to the roof of my mouth and let the magic go. It shot across the kitchen, zapping the rag with a loud hiss. Sparks blew out from where my magic hit the rag and the nasty thing buzzed with electricity before dropping into the sink.

Stella grinned. "Not bad. You're getting the hang of it."

"Care to tell me why I had to perform for you?"

"Not yet," Stella said, her teeth still showing. "I have a theory I'm working on."

And we were back to vagueness and zero information. *Climb aboard the mystery train, folks! Next stop, Stella Rutherford's brain, a place no one has seen the deep crevices of. Enter at your own risk!* Behind me, the kettle screeched, and I turned it off, settling on having a coffee and forgetting about my interaction with the bratty ghost. When the coffee finished brewing, I poured a giant cup (a ridiculous Christmas tree-shaped one gran loved), slipped into a thick sweater, and carried my agitated self to the porch. My body slumped onto the small bench, and I watched the trees in the distance, trying to relax. A few more hours and I'd be talking to Tabitha.

I wasn't sure why I was so nervous, but it felt as though today may give me the answers I needed. At least ones about Zeta's murder. I had nothing on my own magic, so I was celebrating the small things in life.

A light wind nipped at my skin, and I breathed in the cool air, my lungs paper thin.

That was when I heard Stella scream.

Leaping for the door I accidentally left open, I rushed inside. My feet slammed on the floorboards, making the wood snap and creak under my weight. Coffee cup in hand, I slid to a stop in the living room where Stella stood, her face contorted. I followed her thunderous gaze to the couch, a laugh bubbling inside me.

"You have got to be kidding me," I said.

"Get. It. Out!" Stella shrieked, pointing to the ball of fur snuggled on the couch cushions.

I bent over, slapped my thighs, and exploded with laughter. My eyes watered as I watched Stella's panic rise while continuing to point at Harry Houdini, who not only managed to get inside the farmhouse, but was firmly nuzzled under the embroidered blanket on the couch. His paws tugged at a loose thread, and he pulled it out, shoving it into his mouth and smacking his wet lips together. Harry's eyes closed, and he wiggled his chubby body around, finding a more comfortable position.

"Piper! Do something!"

I wiped my wet eyelashes. "I don't think I can," I said. "It's his couch now."

"How can you joke at a time like this?! There is a

trash gremlin in our living room! Do we live with vermin now? Is this how far you've sunk?"

The ghost's reaction to the raccoon made the entire situation that much more enjoyable. Between her face, which appeared paler than normal, and the stomping of her feet, I couldn't help but laugh again. I really needed to thank Harry for getting such a rise out of her. It was as though he knew Stella was on my last nerve and decided to intervene.

I downed half the coffee in my cup and smiled mischievously. "We should get him a bowl of food. Maybe I can get his name engraved on it." Fumes rose off Stella Rutherford. "Oh! How about a little pillow near the fireplace so he can stay cozy when he's here?"

At this, Harry's left ear stood up higher and his beady, black eyes landed on me.

"I think he's into it," I said.

"Piper, I am only going to say this once and I need you to pay attention," Stella warned. "There is a lot I expected from my afterlife, none of which involved a disease-ridden rat. It is bad enough I am stuck here—" she waved around the room "—but quite another to share it with that!"

Stella pointed to the raccoon again, her last words hitting hard. A hiss sounded from the couch, and she gasped. "Did you hear that? He's asking for it now!"

"Fine," I said. "I'll get rid of him. Hold on."

In truth, Stella had a point. Letting Harry stick around was probably not the best idea. I knew some people who owned raccoons as pets, but I was fairly certain they didn't adopt them from the street. I was even more certain their raccoons didn't slink off to eat garbage, an act Harry was very accustomed to. As cute as the little bugger was, he was too wild to keep at home.

"I'm going to find something to lure him outside with," I said.

"For heaven's sake, Piper! Use your magic!"

I shook my head. "I don't want to hurt him. Give me a minute to think."

My minute was cut short by the sound of my cellphone ringing upstairs. I held up a finger, ignoring Stella's moans of dispute and rushed up the stairs. Leaping on my bed, I dug around the comforter until I located the phone and looked at the screen. My toes turned to ice. Pressing the call button, I brought the phone to my ear, swallowing the overflowing saliva filling my mouth. "Sheriff?"

"Hello, Miss Addison," Romero said, his voice more grim than usual. "Have I caught you at a bad time?"

"Sort of. I have a raccoon situation."

Romero let out a low whistle. "I'm not even going to attempt to understand what that means," he said.

"Don't worry about it," I said. "How can I help you?"

Muffled voices sounded near Romero, and I tried to make out what they said. I couldn't hear a word properly and there was a scuffle on the line, almost like the sheriff wrapped his hand over the phone. He spoke to someone who wasn't me and I heard a rumble, followed by the scraping of boots.

"Hello?" I asked.

"Miss Addison, there's no way to say this gently," Romero said. "So, I'll cut to the chase. There's been another murder."

My soul might have left my body. I rolled onto my back, focusing on the ceiling. "Did you say another murder?"

"Correct," Romero replied.

"Why did you call me?"

More voices rose on Romero's end, followed by the slamming of a door. I heard a sigh, Romero's, right before he said, "It's one of yours."

His words slammed into me, and my bones turned to dust, making me sink into the mattress. "A paranormal?"

"A witch," the sheriff answered.

Panic gnawed its way through my chest and my heart rate spiked. The room spun, the light streaming through the window suddenly painful. My thigh muscles tightened, and I squeezed my eyes shut, praying it wasn't anyone I knew. Praying it wasn't Cilia.

Rubbing my chest, I tried to push away the anchor holding me down. "Who is it?" I asked, my voice trembling.

"Tabitha," the sheriff said matter-of-factly. "Tabitha Pogue."

Then my entire world exploded.

# CHAPTER 16

After my body stopped shaking and I regained some of the heat that escaped it, I managed to convince the sheriff to let me stop by the crime scene. He wasn't pleased, but my insistence wore him down, and mentioning that I had a meeting with Tabitha to discuss her connection to Zeta's death helped topple him over the edge. I arrived at Tabitha and Vera's home a short twenty minutes later, the beat of my heart thundering in my ears.

The sisters lived in a tiny bungalow located on the eastern side of town, close enough to the interstate but tucked away on a residential off-road. It made the home look like it was one foot out of town, and I wondered briefly if the sisters were much the same way. I parked the beetle three houses down, the furthest from the police cars I could manage without having to walk forever to get to the front door. There were a few nosy neighbors standing on their front lawns and I ducked my chin into my chest, keeping a low profile as I made my way to the bungalow.

On first approach, a lump the size of a boulder lodged itself in my chest.

Tabitha and Vera's home was the most adorable abode I had seen in Orchard Hollow. Despite its small size, it had the curb appeal of a million-dollar residence. A cobble stone walkway led from the sidewalk to the porch, which wrapped around the entire house. There were two egg chairs to the right of the door and a small, modern table between them. Hanging flowerbeds overflowing with greenery lined the porch, and I passed an enormous oak tree on my way in. From it, string lights hung at different heights, making me wish to see the Pogue residence in the night. It must have looked miraculous.

Everything about the home screamed comfort.

Everything except the police tape criss-crossing the front door.

I spotted the sheriff at the base of the porch steps, his large-brimmed hat obscuring his eyes from the sun and hiding his solemn expression. In his hands he held the notebook I was sure the man slept with, and he tapped on its edge with a ballpoint pen, waiting for me to approach.

"Thank you for letting me stop by," I said, carefully maneuvering around the yellow tape to follow him inside.

The sheriff led me in, grumbling, through the door and down a hallway cutting through the house and leading to the backyard yard. The home was empty, save for the two of us, and I realized Romero must have sent his officers away before allowing me to come in. It was a good call. Fewer questions about why a random citizen was trampling all over their crime scene. As I walked, I spotted a small kitchen to my right and a sitting room full of books. In the corner of the room, right next to the couch, stood a decent sized cauldron. I gasped. The Pogue sisters didn't even bother covering up their witchery. What if someone popped by unannounced? Even gran had the sense to lock all our magical items in a separate room.

Seeing the cauldron made me think my theory of Tabitha running her mouth about paranormals wasn't all that far off.

While my brain grasped at random thoughts, the sheriff opened the back door, saying, "The coroner removed the body. But I must warn you, it's not a pretty sight."

I nodded.

"What happened?" I asked, still lingering in the space between the home and the yard. In the distance, I could see more police tape blocking off a small portion of the backyard and dark stains soaking into the grass. I gagged, the idea of Tabitha's body lying in a pool of blood churning my stomach.

"A break-in," the sheriff said. "There's a safe in the sister's room that's wide open and empty. My officers are trying to get a hold of her so we can see if anything important is missing, but for now, we're thinking the victim came home and interrupted a burglary. Things went south after that."

I blanched, my lungs refusing to expand. "How did they...how did she die?"

"Gunshot to the chest," the sheriff said calmly. "It was quick."

Romero was trying to make me feel better, but it had the opposite effect. A gunshot sounded so impersonal, so cowardly. I hated that Tabitha was wiped off the earth without even a chance to fight. She deserved at least that. I turned my back to the yard and the blotches of yellow in my peripheral.

"You mentioned you were coming to see her today?"

I nodded slowly. "About Zeta. In my searching, I found out the two had contact, so I wanted to follow up on a theory." I bit off a loose cuticle. "That maybe Tabitha was saying things she shouldn't be."

Romero leaned sideways on the wall, his shoulder grazing a crooked picture frame. It was a photograph of Tabitha and Vera, two sisters who couldn't be more different. Both had the same platinum white hair, but that was about all the family resemblance I could spot. They posed in front of the oak tree in the front yard; Tabitha with dark, goth-like makeup and long, flowing skirts billowing from under her black corset—a true depiction of a witch. Vera, on the other hand, sported none of the frills. Her hair was tied back into a tight bun, a complete opposite of Tabitha's unruly mane. She wore no makeup and her outfit resembled that of a soccer mom. They stood together, but the distance between them could be noticed easily. Tabitha demanded the camera's attention, staring it down defiantly. Vera was harder to read. It was as though she had one eye on Tabitha the entire time, a look of distrust crossing her gaze.

Did Vera know her sister was betraying paranormals? Did she at least suspect it?

"If you're hoping to find evidence Tabitha was the one who leaked information to Zeta, you won't get anywhere," the sheriff said.

I frowned. "Why not?"

"The incriminating video we found on Miss

Huxley's laptop does not suggest it came from Orchard Hollow."

My eyebrows hit the ceiling. "Oh?"

"It was a recording of a—" the sheriff paused "—a feeding."

"You don't mean..."

He shook his head as if to wipe the memory of whatever he saw from his mind. "A vampire, yes. In a club in King City. We traced the video's filming date. Tabitha Pogue is alibied for the days before and after, so you can rule her out."

It couldn't be. If Tabitha wasn't the one who was spilling our secrets to Archer's assistant, I had nothing to go on. But if she wasn't involved, then why would someone kill her? Unless Romero's hunch was correct, and it was a break-in gone wrong. It didn't add up.

Something stirred inside me. There was a connection between the two women; I knew it.

I simply didn't know how or why.

My eyes crawled down the long hallway and I turned to the sheriff. "Mind if I check the place out, anyway? For my own peace of mind."

"Knock yourself out," Romero said. "My guys went through everything already."

Leaving the sheriff to whatever business he had, probably making sure I don't do anything unsavory; I walked the length of the hallway. A few shut doors lined my right side, and I peered inside. Two bedrooms, one for each sister, and both as opposite as their owners. Vera's room, the closest to the kitchen, was a vacant thing. The only items inside were a queen-sized bed, a nightstand, and a small table in the corner. I crept in, careful not to move anything as I inspected the few belongings on the table. There was a stack of books on gardening and a laptop, open to a crafting blog. I quickly scanned the other tabs, finding them of little interest. Vera had a knack for DIY projects, and most were related to some sort of craft or another. There was also one article for a pie recipe and another outlining the best nightlife in the city. All in all, nothing caught my attention. Beside the table, a sliding door opened to a tiny closet where the safe Romero mentioned sat open on the floor.

I ran my finger along the door of the safe and moved on to Tabitha's room.

The small, square space was full to the brim. Where there weren't clothes strewn about haphazardly, there were potion bottles and bushels of dried herbs. Unlike Vera's room, Tabitha's had no table, but instead, a large bookcase took up most of the wall opposite her unmade bed. I noticed a few Archer Lee books on one shelf and grimaced. Was the witch a fan, or was it more?

Moving away from the bookcase, I knelt, sitting on

the floor beside a makeshift altar. A black silk cloth covered a low coffee table and atop it, candles in all stages of burnt crowded together. There was a freshly laid out tarot card spread and behind it, a beautiful crystal ball sat on a tall brass stand. My fingers itched to touch it. I reached out, hovering my thumb an inch from the ball. Without notice, sparks flew off my skin and into the crystal. I jumped back, my butt landing hard on the floor. "What the?"

"Where is she? I want to see her!" a loud voice screamed from outside and I crab-crawled through the room, peering out the door.

My eyes glued to the figure barreling through the hallway, and I instantly recognized the woman to be Vera Pogue. Her steps shook the floor as she rushed toward the backyard where the sheriff stood, his body obscuring the door. When Vera neared him, he held his hands up to stop her. "Miss Pogue, I can't let you out there," he said. "Trust me, there is nothing there you want to see."

"What happened to my sister?" Vera wailed. "Where is she?"

Romero took a step toward her, attempting to move her away from the yard. "Why don't we discuss this at the station? I can explain everything there. Follow me, Miss Pogue."

"I don't want to go to the station. I want to know

what happened to my sister," Vera stated. She spun around, and I threw myself from the door to avoid being seen.

"Who's that, and what is she doing in my sister's room?"

Oh, no. I pressed my back to the wall and tried to steady my heavy breathing. Why did I pick this exact moment to sound like someone chased me down the street for ten miles? Pulse thundering, I slowly rose to stand. Vera's footsteps neared the bedroom, and I heard Romero yell out, "Miss Pogue, I need you to follow me to the station and leave my assistant to finish what she's here for."

Vera's head rounded the doorframe and her blue eyes dug into me. "Piper Addison? That's your assistant?!" she squealed. "Someone better tell me what's going on right this instant!"

Romero slid into the room to get between us, but I stopped him short. "It's alright," I said. "She deserves to know what happened."

I tried not to watch while the sheriff informed Vera of her sister's passing, the break-in, and the possibility of valuables missing from the safe. As he spoke, Vera stayed silent, inhaling every word leaving the sheriff's lips. I waited for her to cry, but the witch was holding herself together, whether for my sake or Romero's, I wasn't sure. It struck me as odd how unemotional she was in finding out her sister was horribly killed when she was belligerent only a few moments ago. When I finally dared to sneak a peek at her face, I saw her eyes were closed and she trembled in her spot, lips shaking as she held back tears.

I had to hand it to Vera Pogue—she had more strength than me.

When gran passed, I cried for two weeks straight and even after I accepted that she was gone, I couldn't hear her name mentioned without breaking down. Vera was the opposite. I could tell she wanted to cry but refused to do so. Romero placed a hand on her shoulder, the first show of emotion I'd seen from the man, and said something I couldn't hear.

Giving them some space, I backed away, my shoulder blades colliding with Tabitha's bookcase. The edge of a hard spine jutted into my back, and I turned around, grimacing. Of course, it was one of Archer's books attacking me. I pulled it off the shelf, pretending to busy myself with the text so I didn't interrupt Vera in her moment of grief. As I flipped through the pages, a piece of paper fell from inside the book and floated down, landing at my feet. I knelt, picking up a faded photograph. In it, Tabitha had her arms wrapped around the neck of a man I didn't recognize, and their foreheads were pressed together, a look of completeness on both their faces.

I brought the photograph closer, an unsettled feeling rising in my chest.

Before I had the chance to inspect it, the photograph was snatched from my hands.

"Leave her stuff alone!" Vera snapped. "I don't know why you're here, but I want you gone."

I looked at her, bewildered. "I'm only trying to help."

"This is none of your business, Piper."

Wow. I didn't even realize Vera Pogue knew I existed. *How much of that is Nancy's doing?* I wondered. I wouldn't have been surprised to know she poisoned her entire coven against me. It would explain why Vera was so adamant I leave her sister's things alone.

Even though everything in my body pressed me to walk away, I refused to back down. Tabitha was dead, and I didn't buy the robbery story. The two deaths were tied together, and I had to find out how. Behind Vera's back, Romero gestured to the door, but I pretended not to see him. Training a serious glare on the witch, I said, "I know you're upset right now, but I need you to hear me out. Whatever you might think of me, I am trying to help find the person who hurt your sister." I leaned in closer, my words barely a whisper. "We need to stick together. You know as well as I do that this feels off. We can't leave it to the police and we both know why."

"Watch yourself, Miss Addison," Romero warned.

Maybe I wasn't as quiet as I thought I was. I didn't care. All I needed was for Vera to drop her guard long enough to understand what I meant. One of ours was dead. It wasn't only a matter of her personal grief, this was paranormal business and no matter what Romero knew of our kind, only another paranormal truly understood her loss.

I placed my palm over her wrist and squeezed. "Please, help me find the person who did this."

To my utter surprise, Vera nodded.

Looking at the photograph in her shaking hand, I asked, "Who is the man in the picture?"

"Bellamy," she answered. "Bellamy Ellison. Tabitha was seeing him for a while, but they broke up."

"Recently?"

"Two weeks ago."

I scanned the bedroom, my mind reeling. "And was he...you know?"

"A paranormal?" Vera mouthed. "Uh-huh. Vampire."

Vision blurring at the edges, my thoughts swam inside my head. A witch and a vampire dating. A video of a vampire feeding on a human leaked to an author who was itching expose our kind. And now, that same witch was dead. There were too many coincidences for Tabitha's death to be a case of wrong place, wrong time. I inspected the room. "Can I take a couple of Tabitha's things home? See if they spark anything?" Vera's face contorted. "Or I can stay here and search."

"Take whatever," she said quickly. Behind her, Romero quirked a knowing smile.

As fast as manageable, I collected the few items that drew my attention. I gathered several books into a neat pile on the messy bed—some of which were Archer's. Gross. Next, I walked around Tabitha's bed, picking up a thick, leather-bound journal.

"Not that," Vera instructed. "It's her grimoire. You're not taking it."

Deflated, I placed the journal back down and continued searching. My attention caught on the altar, and I walked toward it, glancing at Vera for approval. She didn't move, so I bent down, picking up the one thing I felt connected to before. The crystal ball. "Can I take this? I promise I'll return it as soon as possible."

"Sure," Vera said reluctantly. "I have no use for it. Tabitha was the one with the sight."

Grabbing the ball and the stack of books, I snaked by Vera, thanking her on my way out of the bedroom. As I left, I felt the sheriff's eyes on my back, and I was certain I would get a call later asking me questions I had no answers to. The thing was, I had no clue why I wanted to keep anything of Tabitha's. All I knew was I couldn't stay here, in Vera's home, and go through her dead sister's things. Not only was it widely inappropriate, but it made my skin itch to be somewhere I was clearly not wanted.

Leaving the two in the bedroom, I walked down the hallway when a thought nipped the rear of my mind. I backtracked, taking a quick peek into Vera's room and the laptop on her table.

If this was a robbery gone wrong, why would they leave the laptop? It was worth more than my car. If I was a thief, it would be one of the first things I'd take.

There was so much lingering in the air, so many unknowns, but there was one thing I was one hundred percent clear on. Tabitha Pogue did not walk in on a robber. Someone killed her and covered their tracks well enough to throw the police off. I cast a solemn glance over my shoulder.

*Who killed Tabitha?* I asked myself. *And why?*

# CHAPTER 17

"It was the vampire in the yard with a gun."

I deadpanned on Stella and placed my hands on my hips, annoyed beyond reason. Sitting cross-legged on the floor of my bedroom, I folded a piece of paper towel several times, attempting my best at origami. Then I remembered I didn't know how to origami. I gave the paper another lame fold and shoved it aside. "This isn't a game," I told Stella. "A woman is dead. Another one."

"Who's playing?" the ghost asked.

Stella had been guessing at Tabitha's killer for the better half of an hour, her insane theories bouncing off the walls like a tennis ball. Every hunch was more ridiculous than the other, but this time, she may have hit the nail on the head. My fingers itched to pick up the paper towel again.

"Why would Tabitha's ex kill her?"

"I think the real question is why was she dating a blood sucker?"

I flinched.

"Sorry," Stella said, fake wincing. "I'm sure your fella is different."

"He is. And we're not dating, so it doesn't matter."

The ghost rolled her eyes skyward and tapped a long finger on her temple. "You don't have to remind me." Under her breath, she said "booooring" blandly. "Anyhoo. It has to be the ex, right?"

I remembered the photograph I found in Tabitha's books and creases formed at the corners of my eyes, an unwelcome addition to the bags under them. Why did the witch keep the picture? Was she hung up on Bellamy, or was there more to it? The tips of my fingers danced on my hardened thighs. If Tabitha was in love with the vampire, why did she spend the night with Ray?

To get close to Archer somehow? The books suggested she was a fan, but sleeping with the author's employee was weird, even by paranormal standards. It was stalker weird, and I couldn't quite picture Tabitha being that creepy.

"Don't you think that's too on the nose?" I asked.

"They break up and he kills her. Why? What's the point?"

Stella strained and lifted her hand toward a picture frame hanging on the wall. It was of gran and I standing outside the greenhouse. She looked so happy there. I held back tears as I watched Stella straighten the frame by a fraction of an inch, then step back, smiling in satisfaction. Was it wrong to yeet your familiar across the room?

"Could be a crime of passion," she said, staring at the photo.

"Maybe," I whispered and reached across the bed to grab my phone.

The ghost glanced at me questioningly, and I held up a finger, motioning for her to shut it while I dialed Joe's number. As much as I didn't buy Stella's theory, we didn't exactly have anything more to go on. I knew the police would want to question Bellamy sooner or later, so I had little time to test the assumptions my familiar was stuck on. That said, I did not want to bombard a vampire without backup. And who better to bring as personal armor than another vampire?

I waited for the phone to ring, holding my breath.

"Hello?"

"Hey, Joe. It's Piper."

"I know," the bookstore owner answered. I slapped my forehead hard enough to leave a red palm mark across it. *Caller ID, idiot. Welcome to the modern world.*

Flushing, I asked, "Any chance you'd be up for another field trip?"

On the other line, Joe mumbled words I couldn't make out but assumed were detailing his frustration with my incessant need to go on dangerous excursions. With all the dead bodies in my orbit, it was becoming standard procedure for me to drag him along or ask him to research one death after another. No wonder our "dates" always ended before they began. I was a walking mortuary.

I was about to tell Joe to forget it when he said, "Sorry about that. Had to tell a customer we're closing for the day. What did you have in mind?"

"He's a keeper," Stella sing-songed.

I stuck my tongue out at her and turned around, my back firmly blocking out the ghost's stuck-up face. "So, long story short, someone else died. And before you say anything, I know. It's dangerous to get involved. But I have a hunch. Well, Stella has a hunch, and I want to check it out."

And now I was rambling.

When Joe didn't say anything, I continued. "I'll fill you in on the way," I said. "But you should know, we have a possible suspect. And it's a vampire."

"Piper!" Joe hollered.

"I know, I know. Stay away from vampires. Except you. I get it." I let go of a breath slowly. "But are you in?"

If frustration had a face, I was willing to bet it was Joe's. I could all but feel his want to argue over the phone and was relieved when he didn't. Instead of telling me off, as he likely should have, Joe said, "Meet me at the bookstore. I'll drive." Then he asked, "Where are we going?"

"Yeah, about that..." I said sheepishly. "Do you happen to know a Bellamy Ellison?"

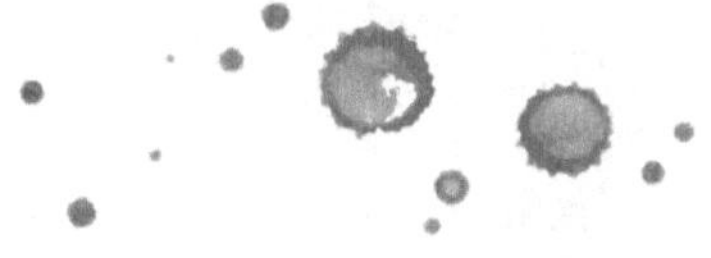

As it turned out, Joe didn't need to drive after all. By the time I made it down to Cliff Row and the bookstore, he informed me Bellamy was on his way to meet us. I didn't ask how he got a hold of the man so quickly, and I had a hunch Joe wouldn't share. His distaste for vampires was apparent, and I felt terrible about dragging him into this meeting. Then I reminded myself I'd feel even worse if Bellamy was the killer, and I ended up being his next victim. Especially if there was a chance I'd be stuck as a ghost with Stella for the rest of eternity.

With that image securely in the forefront of my mind, I thanked Joe for doing all the heavy lifting and settled into one of the dusty couches in the shop to wait for Bellamy.

Less than a half hour after I arrived, a knock sounded on the front door and Joe cast a solemn glance my way before opening it. His back rigid, I watched as he stepped aside, giving Bellamy a wide berth to enter. When the man walked in, my jaw dropped.

I could certainly see why Tabitha might have been hung up on the vampire.

Bellamy was super model hot.

His broad shoulders barely fit through the door as he made his way inside and he had the most surreal gray eyes that sparkled as diamonds against his dark complexion. There was an air of easiness about him, and he carried himself as someone who was completely unaware of his good looks. Which only made him that much more attractive. When Bellamy reached the center of the shop where I perched, he grinned, a row of pearly whites lighting up the bookshop.

Neck flushing, I stood up and stretched out a hand, feigning a lack of interest. From the corner of my eye, I could see Joe work his jaw, his body straight as an arrow as he watched me.

"Hi, Bellamy," I said, shaking his hand. "Thank you for stopping by. I hope it's not too much of a nuisance."

The vampire's grin widened. "Not at all," he said smoothly. "Happy to help a beautiful woman."

*Holy mother of.... Tabitha should have dug her talons into this one.*

Near to us, Joe cleared his throat and possibly growled. I wasn't sure. Gesturing for Bellamy to join me on a chair opposite the couch, I waited until Joe got over his evident discomfort and sat beside me. Together, we stared at Bellamy like he was a trapped in a glass jar, his wings fluttering.

"I'm not sure if you heard about Tabitha," I said, interrupting the silence.

Dark clouds settled over Bellamy's eyes, and I gulped at the storms gathering in those gray orbs. He looked down at his shoes, shiny designer loafers, then back to me and Joe. "Vera called me this morning," he said. "I'm still processing."

*Processing or plotting an escape?* I thought.

"I told her to lock the front door," Bellamy stated. "Tabitha was stubborn, even when it came to something so small as a lock. Every time I mentioned it, she laughed. 'Nothing happens in Orchard Hollow,' she told me." His wide shoulders drooped, and his chest rose up and down slowly. "You know, you live here your entire life, and you get complacent. You think because everyone knows everyone that you're safe. But that's not the case. Even a town as peaceful as ours has its monsters."

His words shook my core, and I leaned into Joe to keep from slipping off the couch. I couldn't think of a better way to describe Orchard Hollow. On the surface, it was a magical place; quite literally. But underneath, people were people. Some were good and some weren't. Some were killers.

I stole a glance at Joe, then settled my narrowed eyes on Bellamy.

In any other situation, one might consider the monsters the vampire spoke of to be the ones sitting in this bookstore.

Noticing my questioning stare, Bellamy said, "Whatever you're thinking, you're wrong."

"I'm sorry?"

"The police called me right after Vera," he explained.

Hmm. The sheriff was one step ahead of me, it seemed. I put on my best poker face, but as Stella often said, it was garbage. Bellamy saw right through me even before I opened my mouth.

"I'll tell you what I told the sheriff," he said. "I was out of town until late last night."

"I wasn't suggesting—"

The vampire cut me off, his face unreadable. "Don't bother. I know how this looks. Tabitha and I broke it off and I'm the first person fingers would point to. But I didn't do it. I had no reason to want her dead."

"Not even after she dumped you?" Joe asked.

Bellamy shook his head and scoffed. "Not sure where you're getting your information, but no one dumped anyone."

*Yeah, Joe. What gives?* I didn't remember saying anything about Tabitha breaking it off with Bellamy. I had the distinct feeling that Joe's disgust with his own kind was clouding his judgment and it was going to make the conversation with Bellamy go south super fast. I had to get control of the situation quick before my botched-up interview turned into a blood sucker fist fight.

"What happened to you two?" I asked. "If you don't mind me asking."

A low growl sounded from Joe's puffed out chest and I nudged him with my elbow. *Tone it down,* I thought into the space between us. *You two can measure whose fangs are bigger when I'm done here.*

Joe shifted his weight away from me but stayed quiet.

"Nothing happened," Bellamy said calmly. "Tabitha and I, we had an understanding. We had fun, but that was all we had. I'm sure you understand why."

I so didn't.

Bellamy's lips quirked as he looked from me to Joe. "A vampire and a witch are not a pair that can last. It was unfortunate; Tabitha was great. When we realized we were getting in too deep, we decided to part ways. Amicably and without any hard feelings, in case that was your next question."

If I was smart, I would have pressed him further to explain, but my brain latched onto one thing and one thing only. A vampire and a witch are not a pair that can last. *Why not?* I wanted to ask him. Rationally, I knew what he meant. Paranormals did not mix. Our gene specific magic did not play well with others. To continue their bloodlines, each paranormal species stuck to reproducing with humans. It was the way it had been for centuries, and I did not know of a couple that proved it otherwise.

My stomach lurched and I tried not to look at Joe. I wondered if he was thinking the same thing I was.

"Do you buy into the break-in story?" Joe asked. Clearly, he was not on the same page.

The vampire's eyes widened, the storm returning. "Who else would want Tabitha dead?" he asked.

"That's what we were hoping you could help us with," I said.

Sitting up straighter, Bellamy chuckled, and I cocked my head to the side, trying to see what was so funny. He shook his head, looking me up and down. "The sheriff said I should expect to hear from you," he explained. "Now I see why."

*Romero, I'm going to kill you.*

I leaned back into the couch cushion. A book someone left behind lodged itself into my back and I squirmed, my pretense at playing bad cop flying out the window. Keeping my eyes locked on Bellamy, I removed said book as smoothly as possible and placed it on the coffee table. "I'm helping him out," I said. "Paranormal death and all that."

Bellamy nodded.

Joe huffed out an exasperated sigh.

I shifted my weight uncomfortably.

"Honestly, as much as I cared about Tabitha, she was a handful," Bellamy finally said. "I think you're reaching to think there's more to the story than what the cops think, though. I mean, sure, she got on people's nerves and was pushy when she wanted her way, but I can't picture anyone wanting her dead."

For someone who cared about Tabitha, he was much too nonchalant. Was it a vampire thing? I knew his kind were not well regarded by other paranormals, mostly because of their hunger for human blood, but Bellamy was acting too detached. Too much like someone who didn't give a rats behind that his ex-girl-friend was shot down in her own backyard.

My lips pressed tightly together. "Is there a particular time you can think of where Tabitha may have been too pushy?"

This earned me another laugh, and I felt Joe start to move beside me. I placed a hand on his knee, urging him not to punch Bellamy's pretty face in no matter how much I wanted to see it happen. It was official. Joe was the only vampire I could stomach. I was starting to question why Tabitha kept this fool's photograph around. Cute but absolutely revolting was a good way to describe Bellamy. Reading the room, the vampire reeled himself in and said, "There were too many times to keep track of. As I said, Tabitha was a handful." He looked away, scanning the shop, deep in thought. "If I had to point you to anyone, I'd say talk to Gemini."

"Her coven mate?"

He nodded. "And mentor. A few weeks before we broke up, Tabitha showed up to a date, fuming. I guess her and Gemini got into it. She wouldn't tell me why, and it was the first time I heard of the two disagreeing. But it made Tabitha very angry. We had to cut our date short because she couldn't stop complaining."

"No one else?" I asked.

"Not at all," Bellamy replied. He looked at his

watch, also designer, and rose to stand. "I wish I could help you out here, but I'm with the police on this. Tabitha should have been more careful."

A bad taste coated the inside of my mouth as I watched Bellamy head for the door, Joe on his heels. The two stood in the doorway for a few moments before Bellamy walked out and Joe slammed the door behind him. He clicked the lock, stomping back to the center of the shop to join me. "What a piece of work," he said. "Completely useless."

I had to disagree with him. Sure, most of what Bellamy said didn't raise red flags, but he did clue me in to my next direction. The argument Tabitha had with her mentor required looking in to. Nothing was more volatile than two witches going at it and I had the feeling that Tabitha and Gemini both had tempers that could set the world on fire. I needed to find out what they fought over and if it was worth killing for. Goosebumps covered my skin. There was something the vampire said that I couldn't get out of my mind.

Tabitha *should* have been more careful.

I looked out the window of the bookstore and down the street, picturing whoever broke into her house walking around out there, free.

Maybe we all should be.

# CHAPTER 18

With a few helpful hints from Cilia, I was able to track down Gemini Hollis to the local occult shop on the far edge of town. I hadn't stepped foot in The Witch's Safe in over a decade and when I walked in, I quickly realized why. While the shop boasted an endless supply of magical related items, it was impossible to find anything in the place. Random bobbles crowded the many shelves tightly crammed into the small space and there was no form of organization that I could discern. To make matters worse, the shop was located on the second floor above a burger joint and smelled like a solid combination of grease and old bacon; a scent I was hoping would wash out of my hair later.

I squeezed between a large chest filled with old books and an armoire missing its front doors. My shoelace caught on the base of the armoire, and I yanked it out, glancing down. A rusty nail stuck out of the filthy leg of the furniture; a piece of my shoelace clutched in its tetanus-filled grip. I groaned and kept walking, turning myself liquid to get by the things in my way.

By the time I reached the belly of the shop, I felt like I had survived an obstacle course from hell.

No wonder gran ordered all her magic supplies from the city. This place was atrocious.

My battle with The Witch's Safe, an ironic name in my opinion, was well worth it when I clawed out of the mess in the front. Standing a few paces from me, leaning on the front counter, and chatting to who I assumed was the shop's owner, was Gemini. She wore a dark hooded coat, but I could see her signature blue braids popping out from the collar. I rolled my shoulders, taking a leisurely stroll inward.

"Welcome to The Witch's Safe," the owner announced.

It was a man in his late sixties who appeared to be at least twice that age. His long, white beard reached past his belly button, and he resembled a wizard from an old movie. Thin, silver-rimmed glasses perched on his prominent nose, and he had more wrinkles than my un-ironed bedsheets back home.

"Can I help you find anything in particular?" the wizard asked.

I glanced behind me. *Good luck with that.* Smiling, I crept closer. "Nothing specific," I said. "I came here a few times with my grandmother when I was younger. I was in the area and decided to pop in."

The wizard gave me a once over.

"Piper? Piper Addison?" he asked. "My, my. You have grown up, young lady. Sorry to hear about your gran. She was a stand-up woman."

The way he spoke about gran made me wonder if the two were friendlier than I knew. *Ew. Gross, gran.* At the mention of my name, I felt Gemini turn toward me. A look of recognition crossed her face, followed by a questioning quirk of the eyebrows. I had the feeling she was wondering what I'd be looking for in this place, considering my all-around lack of magic.

Pretending to be oblivious to her staring, I glanced between her and the wizard, plastering on my best clueless grin. "I don't mean to interrupt," I said.

"It's fine," Gemini said politely. "I was wrapping up here, anyway. Thanks for the help, Bob."

Bob? Really? Talk about the name not matching the face.

She turned to leave, patting the dusty counter

twice. Before she could crawl into the labyrinth of the shop, I twisted my body toward her. "You're Gemini, right?" I asked. "Gemini Hollis?"

Behind the counter, the wizard stopped rearranging the decks of tarot cards on display and leaned in, not bothering to hide his eavesdropping. I assumed this must have been the highlight of his day, as no doubt he rarely got frequent customers. Paying him no mind, I took a step to the right, putting myself directly in Gemini's path.

"That's me," she said warily.

"I thought I recognized you." I wracked my brain for the next thing to say that would keep her from leaving. The edges of a lie started to form, and I grasped them with sticky fingers like Harry Houdini grasped chocolate. "Tabitha mentioned you were a mentor of hers. I'm sorry to hear about what happened."

At this, Gemini's ears perked. With her blue hair and large hood, she looked almost elvish from this angle. She licked her bottom lip, surprisingly not eating away at the burgundy lipstick covering it. "You were a friend of Tabitha's?" she asked.

"She knew my grandmother," I said. The lie burnt my tongue, and I bit it hard to keep from showing my bluff.

"Ah, right," Gemini replied, seemingly satisfied with my answer.

The way I figured, someone as magic-less as me would never cross paths with a coven witch. Gran, on the other hand, knew everyone, so it was likely my lie wasn't a lie at all. There was a very good chance Tabitha and my grandmother really did speak, or at least were on familiar terms.

Gemini's brow furrowed, and she reached up to lower her hood. Under her hat of hair, I noticed the gleam of a locket and feverish energy rushed through my body. As though pulled by an invisible magnet, I battled the urge to reach for the necklace, cramming my hands in my pockets. The locket must have been Gemini's talisman; there was no other explanation for why I craved it so.

Since when was I a talisman magpie?

I didn't want to think about why I wished to touch Gemini's locket so badly or why it reminded me so much of the effect Rosemary's pendant had on me. It was the same feeling I got when I was around Nancy's and Aria's talismans, and it worried me beyond belief.

Tucking the development away for later dissection, I trained my eyes on Gemini. Behind her, the wizard was blatantly staring now, and I tried not to let his nosiness break me.

"I hope they find out who did this," I said.

"Me too," Gemini agreed. "I didn't realize you two

were close. If I'm honest, I didn't realize anyone in the coven knew you personally."

Ouch.

Gemini shook her head. "Sorry. What I mean is we don't usually socialize with unattached witches."

Double ouch.

"Um, right," I said. "Well, we weren't close. I only wanted to offer my condolences."

Whatever I said must have made her guilt kick in, because Gemini's facial expression changed instantly. No longer did she look at me like I was covered in mildew or was some magical leper to be avoided. She unfolded her crossed arms and said, "I didn't mean to offend. Thank you for the well wishes."

I half-turned to the counter and pretended to look at the tarot cards, turning each one over. In truth, I had no idea how to use them. Gran relied on green magic, and I followed suit. The work of a seer was not in our wheelhouse; I was amazed by people such as Gemini and Tabitha, who could glimpse the future using their magic. It was a sought-after skill, one that was not taken lightly in the witch community.

Gemini's presence was suddenly all encompassing.

Was there a chance she wasn't as good of a mentor to Tabitha as I was led to believe? Bellamy mentioned a heated argument between the two, one that left

Tabitha shaken. Could the relationship between the seers have been darker and more sinister than that of a mentor and mentee? I looked at Gemini from the corner of my eye. What if Gemini had no intention of stepping down from the role of the coven's lead seer? What if she killed Tabitha to keep her spot?

In my inner musings, I completely missed what Gemini said. Her words sounded underwater, and by the time I snapped back to reality, she was glaring at me through hooded eyes. "Can you repeat that?" I asked.

"I said, are you looking into the practice?" Gemini repeated, pointing to the deck of cards I clutched close to my chest.

I pulled away from the cards. "I'm thinking about it. Any tips?"

"Are you asking me to mentor you?"

I thought about the fate of her last mentee and shook my head. "No, nothing quite so serious. And I'm sure Tabitha would be hard to replace. I don't know you well, but I assume you two were close."

A quiet sadness surrounded the seer, and she ran her hand over the stack of decks beside me. Her golden bracelets clashed together, the sound of metal on metal ringing through the shop. For the first time since I walked in, the wizard got a clue and mentioned needing to check the back before rushing off. I followed him, intrigued to know the maze had another hidden space. The wizard parted a row of beaded curtains and vanished, leaving behind only a trace of patchouli in his wake. So theatrical.

"We weren't all that similar," Gemini said, hands still on the cards. "Tabitha and I, we fought a lot."

"Oh?" I asked. "Nothing serious I hope."

Gemini's eyes twitched. "Usually, no."

The way she spoke made it appear there was more to the story. It was almost as though the seer had a weight on her, a secret she needed to unload before it buried her. I picked up a random deck, looking it over. "You know, my gran and I, we had the most explosive arguments. We're talking call-the-cops explosive," I said. "It didn't mean we didn't love each other. Or that I don't miss fighting with her now that she's gone."

Gemini's eyes shot up, but she didn't look at me. "You get it," she said. "I didn't speak to Tabitha for weeks. We had a fight, a big one, and I stopped talking to her. I wanted her to come to me. So foolish."

"And you never got a chance to sort it out," I said.

Gemini's shoulders shook, and she clutched one card out of the deck, harrumphing. She flipped it over to show me. I doubled back, the Death card prominently displayed in the seer's palm. "I kept getting it in all my readings," she said, the card hovering between us. "After the fight, every time I pulled a spread, there it was, staring at me from the table. I thought it was mixed messaging, that I was meant to learn a lesson. If I knew.... You must think I'm the worst seer ever."

"Of course not," I assured her. "I might not be the greatest witch out there, but I know that's not how the sight works. You couldn't have predicted this. Don't blame yourself."

"But I could have gotten off my high horse and reached out to her after she told me about Vera."

*Come again?* I stopped breathing to look at her. "Her sister? What about her?"

There was a scuffle behind the beaded curtains and Gemini closed the distance between us. She lowered her voice; suddenly aware we weren't alone. "It's nothing I want repeated," she said in hushed tones. "Unlike some witches in my coven, I am not keen on gossip."

I swallowed excess saliva and nodded in agreement.

"The fight, the one Tabitha and I had, was about her sister. Tabitha found out Vera had been sneaking off into the city to follow some author around. I can't recall the name, but it had Tabitha in knots. I couldn't understand why at first, then she told me about this man's books. He writes about—"

"Exposing paranormals," I interrupted.

"That's right. You know him?"

I coughed into my hand. "Sort of. You're telling me Vera was a fan of Archer Lee?"

"More than a fan, from what Tabitha told me," Gemini explained. "According to Tabitha, her sister went as far as reaching out to one of his employees. A research assistant, I believe. Anyhow, it made Tabitha furious. She told me she can't sit by and watch her sister fangirl over a man who's set on destroying our kind. That she hated being related to her."

If this was a cartoon, stars would appear before me, and I would drop right on the spot. Funny how Vera didn't mention being obsessed with Archer Lee when I was asking about her sister. Was that why Tabitha had his books in her room? To find out why her sister was so intrigued by the man? Bile rose up my throat. Both sisters knew Zeta.

What was Vera hiding?

"Is that why you fought with Tabitha?" I asked. "Because she was upset with her sister?"

"Goddess no! I have no business getting between two siblings, especially ones as strong-willed as the Pogue girls. We fought because Tabitha wanted to cast Vera out of the coven, and she wanted my vote to do it." Gemini rubbed her forehead and groaned. "I wasn't going to, of course. Vera's life is her own, no one else's. I tried telling Tabitha that, but she wouldn't hear of it. Stormed out on me after saying a few choice words I'd rather not repeat. It was quite a scene."

I wanted to ask her to expand, to tell me every detail of the argument, but the beaded curtains shimmied, and the wizard appeared out of thin air. His white beard pushed its way between Gemini and me, ruining whatever moment we were having. "I really must clean all this up," he said, motioning to the decks on the counter.

*Yeah, right, buddy. You haven't cleaned anything in here for ages.* I wanted to tell him I needed more time, but it seemed his presence stirred an urgency in Gemini. She pulled up her hood, a part of it covering her eyes. Her blue hair hung in pieces over her chest, and I could barely make out the glimmer of her talisman behind the thick, dark fabric.

"I need to get going," she said. "Thanks for everything, Bob. And nice talking to you, Piper. You're not so bad."

I assumed she meant not as bad as what Nancy Steeles made me out to be. Deflated, I also thanked Bob—though I wasn't sure for what—and slid myself through the mess of the shop until I got to the exit. The tornado of thoughts within me raged, and I tried to steady my speedy breaths, attempting my best to make sense of what I discovered. I sat out to find a connection between Tabitha and Zeta and now, I had a different connection in place. I knew Vera didn't lie, not exactly, but she left out pertinent information and, in my mind, that was as good as a lie.

Jumping down the last two steps, I pushed my way outside, my face freezing as I ran into a cold and gray mass. I blinked, the taste of death on my tongue. "Stella?"

The ghost's disturbed face told me she was not pleased my clumsy butt barreled through her.

"What are you doing here?"

"I think I figured it out," Stella said.

In my back pocket, my cellphone rang, and I shushed her, saying, "Hold that thought." Pressing enter, I lifted the phone to my ear. "Hey, Joe. What's up?"

"I think I know what your magic is," Joe said at the same time as Stella yelled, "I know why you can zippity zap!"

My forehead tilted up, and I stared at the gray sky above me. Body aching and head full of questions, all I wanted was to crawl into a bath and stay in it until my skin pruned. Unfortunately, life had other plans in mind and judging by Stella's sucked in cheek bones and Joe's rushed voice, it would be a while until I got to relax.

# CHAPTER 19

**M**eet me at the lighthouse. Those were Joe's instructions before he hung up the phone. I wanted to ask why there specifically, but the vampiric bookshop owner ghosted me before I had a chance to speak. When I attempted to ask Stella about her announcement, she was no use.

"See you there," she said right before disappearing.

I really needed to surround myself with less cryptic people.

The lighthouse was a good half hour drive from the occult shop, and I spent the majority of it trying to guess at what Joe figured out. It seemed he and Stella had some ideas about my magic, but with neither of them willing to talk, I was left to my own devices. Those were, regretfully, few and far in between.

"Maybe mom thought my magic was so unpredictable she had to bind it?" I asked the empty beetle. The engine growled in response. "No, you're right. That can't be it. There are plenty of paranormals with hard to control magic; she could have simply trained me to work with it. Especially if gran was involved."

Then why? Why did M believe it was unsafe for me to have any magic at all?

This was all assuming I was the one the letters referred to, which, despite Joe's insistence, I didn't quite buy. It was hard to imagine a world where my magic was so powerful it required to be hidden. My fingers curled around the steering wheel, the cracked leather chafing my skin. I considered the lightning I controlled, or sort of controlled, and the energy of it bubbled to the surface. My skin burst with blue lights and sparks flew off in all directions. I gasped, swerving to the right. The beetle's wheels slid off the road and into the shoulder. Ripping my foot off the gas, I brought the vehicle to a stop, catching my breath. Luckily, it was only me on the road.

"Think non-magic thoughts. Think non-magic thoughts. Think non-magic thoughts," I urged myself. My eyes landed on the dashboard clock, and I collected myself before starting up the car.

I spent the remainder of the drive solving math equations and singing show tunes.

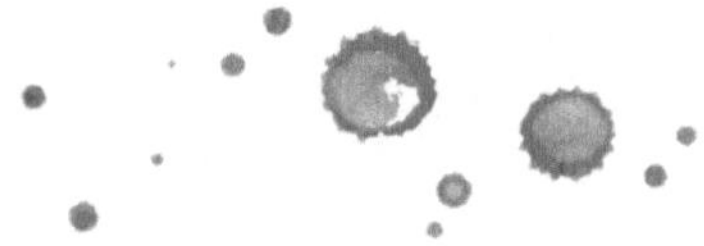

"Up here!" Joe called from the top of the lighthouse.

Closing the rackety old door behind me, I filled my lungs with air and climbed up the stairs, this time avoiding touching the railing. As I reached the lantern room, I was surprised to see Joe standing by a window-pane, Stella directly behind him. He turned, the ghost taking a step back to avoid colliding with his wide back.

"You got here fast," he said.

I looked at the vintage watch gran left me. "No traffic."

"Is there ever?" Stella asked. The sarcasm in her voice did not go unnoticed.

Glancing between the two of them, I stifled a laugh. "We have company."

At my words, Joe jerked his head around the cupola, searching for the woman he would never get to see. He waved aimlessly at the empty air next to the ghost. "Hi, Stella."

She rolled her eyes, pretending to smack his palm away.

"She says hello," I told Joe. "Looks like you both had epiphanies today."

Under her breath, Stella hissed out, "I thought of it first."

Walking around her, I took a few steps to cross toward Joe, settling in beside him at the windows. Beyond the lighthouse, the sea was angry. Waves crashed into the cliffs, and I could see the milky white of sea foam exploding in the air. Ripples covered the water, and I looked past the horizon at the trees lining one cliff. Their bodies swayed from side to side, a frosty wind tearing them from slumber.

I pressed a hand to the glass, sighing. "Why did you want to meet here?"

Joe wasted no time getting down to business. He reached into his coat pocket and produced a thin book. The binding was made of old, worn-out leather and I could see aging on the spine and pages. "This," Joe said, lifting the book in the air, "is why."

I craned my neck to read the title at the same time as Stella.

"To Hell and Back," I read aloud. One eyebrow cocked; I tilted my head to the side.

Next to Joe, Stella's grin widened, a note of approval on her face.

"You know something about this, don't you?" I asked her.

"Talk to the man," Stella instructed. "And for heaven's sake, straighten your head. You look like a Cocker Spaniel."

I made a face at her and turned back to Joe, head only slightly lifting. Touching the spine of the book, I asked, "What's in here?"

"What isn't?" Joe replied. "It's a short read, but packed with information. Some interesting stuff if you ever want to check it out. But—" he flipped the first half of the book open, landing on a page marked with tape "—this is what caught my eye."

Joe turned the book around so I could read. Saucer-eyed, I took in each word. Heart beating faster and faster, I let my lips part so I could breathe in the dusty air of the lighthouse. The hand I pressed to the glass slid down, and I hugged my sides, looking up at Joe. "This can't be real, can it?" I asked, baffled. "It says here the only time a binding spell has been used successfully on a paranormal was three hundred years ago."

"Keep reading."

Unquestioningly, I did. This time, my mouth flopped wide open, and I was pretty sure a little bit of drool escaped. I wiped it with the back of my hand, my body frozen. "Did I read this correctly? The binding spell was to block ancient magic passed through—" I flipped the page over. "The lineage of the old gods."

"Strange, isn't it?" Joe asked.

"Not strange," I said. "It's unimaginable. It must be fake. What old gods?"

I knew little of the original creation of magic. Gran tried to teach it to me when I was young, but it all sounded jumbled. Bloodlines and family trees weren't as fun as spells and the magic I grew up with. It was clinical and calculated when my favorite part of magic, the absolute reason why I was so entranced by it as a child, was the unexplainable factor of its existence. I didn't want to know how magic came to be; I only wanted to wield it.

Joke's on me. I didn't have it to wield in the first place. My eyes narrowed on the book. Or did I?

"That part I haven't figured out yet," Joe said. "But it's a start. This was the only mention of a binding spell I could find. If it's the one your mother used, we're looking at something a lot bigger than witch magic."

I scowled. "You don't truly believe there is ancient god magic out there? Or that I have it."

"Maybe."

"Okay, but if that's true, how come no one talks about them?" I asked. "Have you ever heard of the old gods before? Because I sure haven't, and I think I'd remember that."

While Joe and I stared at each other, a throat cleared around the bend from us. I looked down the length of the lantern room, realizing Stella was no longer near Joe. My head swerved right and left, trying to find the ghost.

"Yoo-hoo!" her voice sounded not too far away. "Over here!"

Pulling Joe after me, I walked the circular path to the opposite side of the cupola. There, crouching down with her index finger extended, was Stella. There was a knowing smirk on her face, and she waited until we approached to say, "I believe this is the answer you're looking for."

I followed her polished nail to the familiar carving on the wall.

"The spear," I mumbled.

"The one from the letters?" Joe asked. "How does it tie in?"

Stella cleared her throat again, this time in annoyance. "If Loverboy would let me speak, I can tell you what I know."

Head dropping back, I sighed loudly.

"Stella would like to speak. She wants us to shut it." As Joe nodded, I turned to my familiar. "Alright, the stage is yours. Dazzle me with your profound intellect."

Slow as molasses, she lifted her skinny butt off the floor, dusted off her skirt and waved her hand over the carving. From here, Stella looked like a circus presenter welcoming the next act; I half expected a microphone to drop down from the ceiling and fire-works to go off behind her. She pulled at her long ponytail, twirling the ends before letting it drop down her back.

"When you first got your zippity zap magic," she started. I bit my tongue to keep from arguing over her description of my powers. "You said it wasn't witch magic because you didn't need your talisman to control it, remember?"

I nodded, recalling that exact conversation.

"Well, it got me thinking. It had to come from somewhere, right? And if not from your paranormal gene, then somewhere else," she explained. "I couldn't quite put my finger on it. The lightning, the energy you felt inside you when you used it, the mention of a spear. It all sounded so familiar. Then I remembered the mythology class I took in college."

*Stella Rutherford went to college? For what?*

I shook the questions off, urging for her to continue.

"Anyhoo, while you were off playing detective, I

came by here," Stella said. "I had to see this spear for myself and when I did—" she made an explosion motion with her hand "—lightbulb!"

I waited for her to reveal the big event. And waited. And waited. Finally, when I couldn't take it anymore, I asked, "And?"

"It's not a spear," Stella replied. "It's a bident."

At that same moment, Joe nudged my side, clearly interested in what the ghost was saying. I opened my mouth to speak, then closed it again, formulating the sentence before I spewed it out. "She says it's a bident," I told him.

"Hold on, a bident? As in *the* bident?"

Stella shrugged, saying, "So he's not all looks and muscle. Excellent."

While my familiar stared at Joe hungrily, a look I'd rather die than see again, I tried to recall my high school mythology classes. The weapon tugged at my brain, and I was so close to the answer, I could taste it. The memory returned to me, slamming into me like the cliffs were pummeled by the sea below us. It crashed into my mind, knocking the breath out of my lungs. "You're not implying that my mom got it on with—"

"Hades himself?" Stella asked. "Of course not."

I breathed out, relieved the insane notion was vetoed, and I didn't have to worry about a nonsensical story as the explanation for the absurdity of my magic. My relief was short-lived because Stella's cheeky grin returned.

"But she most definitely knocked bits with one of his descendants."

Beside me, Joe's muffled voice asked a question, probably to relate what the ghost said. I couldn't even hear him. All I could think about was the lightning and energy I felt inside my blood whenever I used it. There was no sense denying it; I knew deep down that my magic was not that of a paranormal. At least, not entirely. Which meant that Stella had a point. I knew nothing of my father or his background. In fact, I always assumed he was a human my mom used and left behind. Now, I wasn't so sure.

Gazing past Stella to the carving, I thought of mom. *Sylvie Addison, you have some explaining to do.*

# CHAPTER 20

"**A**re you sure you don't want to sit down?" Joe asked. "This is a lot to take in."

I wasn't sure of anything, but the last thing I wanted to do was waste time sitting around in the lighthouse. What Stella suggested was preposterous. No way would mom be so dumb as to fall for a paranormal. Were descendants of Hades even paranormal? What would one call a family member of a freaking ancient god?

My legs wobbled.

No. Absolutely not. I was not getting dragged into whatever drama Sylvie got herself into and I certainly wasn't opening the can of worms that came with assuming what Stella said was true. *I am not*, I repeated, *related to the devil. No way.*

"You're pasty," Stella sniped.

Cold air slapped my cheeks as she waved her hand in my face like a fan. I trained her with a nasty look. "Cut it out. I'm fine."

"Cut what out?" Joe asked.

"Not you," I told him. "And I don't need to sit. None of this is real. It's too crazy, even for Sylvie."

Behind me, Stella whispered, "Methinks the lady dost protest too much."

A ticking bomb of anger and annoyance built within me, and I strained to keep my cool. I was so over my life being guided by forces beyond my control. My reputation as a witch was ruined because Nancy Steeles decided she didn't like me in high school. My cafe shut down, twice, because people died on its premises. Even my magic wasn't really my own. What was it about me that screamed "easy target"? I didn't know how to handle the Hades discovery. Not because I wasn't strong enough to deal with it, but because if I admitted that it might be true, I would also have to admit that gran and mom lied to me. My own family didn't keep me in the loop and if I couldn't trust family, who could I trust?

I looked at Joe, then Stella.

Maybe not even them.

Refusing to succumb to self-pity, I straightened my collapsed spine and brushed my hair back. Handing the book to Joe, I said, "You can keep this. I don't want to think about it right now." Then I turned to Stella. "And you," I hissed out. "If you don't stop with the attitude, I'm going to move Harry into the spare bedroom. I mean it."

The ghost quirked her lips. "Geez, Piper. I'm only teasing. You need to relax, maybe ask Hot Pants Book Nerd over here if he wants to go out tonight. Go dancing. Live a little."

She spun around, giving me a perfect view of her even more perfect behind. Not bothering to say goodbye or tell me she'll see me later, the ghost disappeared, leaving the lighthouse that much emptier. I instantly felt like a traitor. Stella, in her own twisted misguided way, was only trying to help, and I bit her head off because I couldn't handle my own garbage life. I really needed to make it up to her tonight. Maybe I should go dancing with Joe. It would probably get her off my back for a while.

Facing Joe, I thought about the closest nightclub a few towns over and—

"Sweet mother of coffee and biscuits," I whispered under my breath.

"Excuse me?" Joe asked.

I hopped in one spot, giddy with the thought that

cleared my clouded mind. "I think I figured it out!" I screeched, a little too excitedly. "I have to go. I'll call you later to explain!"

With that, I ran down the stairs and out of the lighthouse, fading from view faster than Stella.

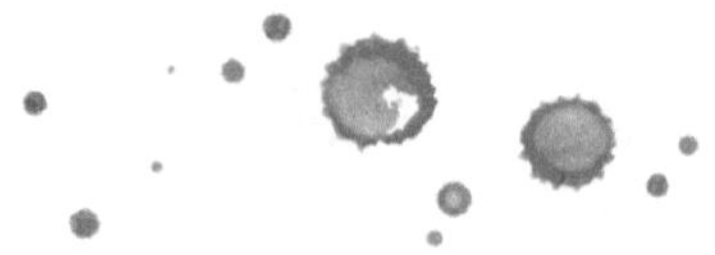

I arrived at the Pogue house quickly, mostly because I sped like a maniac. The sun had started to set, and the front porch of the house was lit in a faint shade of pink, adding to the magical setting it already had. I noticed the string of lights on the oak in the front yard were on, indicating someone was home.

My knuckles rapped on the door, and I spread my legs wide for balance.

There was the sound of a lock clicking open before the door swung out, Vera's face poking out to greet me. Confusion laced her features, and she shut the door slightly. I tried not to take offense at the gesture.

"Piper," she said. "What are you doing here? Did you bring Tabitha's things back?"

She looked at my empty hands, lips thinning.

"Not yet. I wanted to talk to you if that's alright," I told her.

Vera looked about as impressed with me as Stella was with Harry Houdini moving in. Her eyes beaded, and she gave me a once over, the opening narrowing another inch. I knew I had only a few seconds before she slammed the door in my face; I had to move fast. Not wasting time to think of the best approach, I blurted out the first thing that came to my mind, which was the reason for my unannounced visit. "I know you talked to Zeta Huxley," I said, the words mashing together. "And I know why."

The door opened slowly, but only wide enough for Vera to slip outside. I guessed the thought of having me over worried her, considering what I said. I didn't care. As long as the witch talked, it didn't matter where it happened. And it wasn't as though I had plans to befriend the woman. With all the things I found out today, I wanted to have less contact with the paranormal community, not more of it.

*Maybe I should stay away from Cilia as well.*

A pang jolted my heart, and I rubbed at my chest; I didn't realize it before, but the idea of becoming friends with another witch excited me. As I was so often reminded by my familiar, my social life was pretty dry, and it would be nice to have a witch to talk magic with. Or someone else to interact with other than a dead woman and a raccoon. Because yes, I counted Harry as a confidant.

Pathetic.

A foot tapped on the porch boards, and I jostled myself back to reality.

"How did you find out?" she asked.

It was interesting she wasn't denying it or pretending I had my facts wrong. Up until I got here, I was operating on a hunch, but now, I was certain my theory on why Vera reached out to Archer's assistant was correct. I buttoned up my tweed coat, then unbuttoned it again. "It's not important how," I said, refusing to drop Gemini's name. "The 'why' I figured out when I was here last. You left a tab open on your laptop. I didn't take you for the clubbing type."

There was a chance I was dead wrong about this, but my gut pushed me forward. "You're the one who leaked the video of the vampire to Zeta, aren't you?"

Vera's face stayed straight, but I could see her neck turn red. Angry splotches climbed up her skin and peaked out from under her turtleneck—her guilt showing. She rubbed her brow and smacked her lips together like she was parched for water.

"It's not what you think," she finally said.

I scoffed. "You're *not* trying to tell the entire world about paranormals? What did Archer Lee offer you? Cash? Fame? What could possibly be worth betraying your own kind?"

"I did it for Tabitha!" she howled. Her palms

slapped her thighs, and she stomped a foot down, her emotions swirling around us.

Taken aback, I leaned away and asked, "How would people finding out about magic help your sister?"

For a moment, Vera didn't speak, and I thought I lost her. *Here it comes. She's going to push me off her porch and tell me not to return.* I was ready to argue until she answered my questions, but Vera didn't move a muscle. Her body curled in on itself and she took a few careful steps toward one of the egg chairs, lowering herself into its cocoon. Somehow, in the span of seconds, Vera Huxley shrank two sizes. I walked to stand in front of her, staying silent until she was ready.

"The vampire in the video, the one feeding on a human in the nightclub," she explained, "it's Bellamy. I knew he was no good. I caught him feeding on a tourist in the Drunk Elephant last summer."

*Huh? No way.*

I nodded slowly, keeping my mouth shut.

"Tabitha and him, they had this unhealthy relationship; on and off again. When she started dating him this time around, I couldn't let it go on. The guy is bad news, and not only because he's a vampire. So, I followed him to the city on one of his business trips—" she made quote signals with her fingers "—and as expected, the creep was all over some floozy in a dance club. Feeding on her in front of everyone. No concern at all if anyone could see him." Vera looked at her furry slippers. "I didn't know what to do, but I knew I had to show Tabitha, so I filmed him on my phone. I figured if I had proof, she'd break it off with him."

"And she did," I said.

"Ha! Not at all," Vera yelped. "She told me I was jealous and to leave her boyfriend alone. Can you believe that? I'm showing her a video of the scum with another woman and she's making it seem like I'm the problem? Typical Tabitha."

My head spun as I tried to keep up with her story. "But they did break up and when I spoke to Bellamy, he mentioned it was an amicable break."

"They *always* broke up! That's the point. It was only a matter of time until he slimed his way back into my sister's life and I couldn't let it happen. We had our differences, but I loved Tabitha. I couldn't let her waste her life with a vampire."

*Do not think of Joe.* I cringed, asking, "But why send the video to Zeta? You must have known once Archer Lee got a hold of it, our entire community would be in trouble. I mean, the guy is here on a tour to expose us based on the video you sent."

"I figured," Vera ground out, "that if she heard it from someone who wasn't me, she might actually pay attention."

"I'm sorry. Are you saying you were willing to let humans know paranormals exist to break your sister up with her boyfriend?"

I seriously could not believe what I was hearing. Either Vera was the most selfish person in the world, or she was deranged. The more she told me, the more I started to understand Tabitha's point of view. It sounded as if Vera was jealous. Enough to ruin life for everyone to prove her point.

Swaying the chair back and forth, the tiny psycho scrunched her nose at me. "Don't be silly, Piper," she said. "No one was going to be exposed. You're over-reacting."

"You sent a video of a vampire to an author who writes about paranormals!" I bit out every word, hoping my emphasis came through.

"No," Vera corrected. "I sent the video to his research assistant."

*What in the coffee bean is this woman on about?*

"Zeta was never going to show the video to her boss."

My brain hurt. Scratch that, my entire body hurt trying to understand her reasoning. I flashed Vera a steely look and sucked in a breath to calm down. "It was her entire job to show him things like that video," I said.

"Trust me, she wouldn't. Zeta didn't believe in

magic. I told her it was a costume party and Bellamy was very good at playing a part. As far as she knew, the video was of two people getting it on in a club."

Okay. I supposed that made some sort of sense. But it didn't explain one thing, and it was this one detail which stuck in my mind while Vera swung in the chair. "If you thought the video would never make it into Archer's books or his tour videos, how did sending it to Zeta help you expose Bellamy? The video would never be made public."

"I didn't need it to be public, Piper. I only needed Zeta to have it."

She said this in a frustrated tone, implying Vera believed me to be the biggest idiot of all time. Maybe I was because no matter how hard I tried; I wasn't following her logic. I was about to ask her to explain, but she beat me to it.

"You know Tabitha and Zeta knew each other, right?" she asked.

*I sure do.* I nodded in agreement. "It came up," I said. "But I don't know how they would have crossed paths."

Vera pushed off the floor and swung higher, her legs flopping all over the place and almost hitting me in the shins. "Tabitha was Archer Lee's financial advisor," the witch said. "Her and Zeta met regularly to go over his business accounts. They've known each other for years. And anyway, it didn't matter at all. Zeta told Tabitha her guy was cheating, and my sister still couldn't care less about the garbage person she dated."

"Did your sister figure out it was you who got Zeta involved?" I asked.

Vera shook her head in disgust. "Yes. We had a big fight over it and everything. I interrupted her during one of her sessions with the crystal ball, figured it was a good time to catch her off guard," she explained. "And you know what she told me? That she didn't care what Bellamy did with his free time or who knew about it."

That couldn't be right. Was Tabitha truly so self-absorbed she wasn't the least bit bothered to know her boyfriend got it on with humans and used them to feed? What kind of witch would behave this way? What kind of person?

I didn't wish to speak ill of the dead, but Tabitha Pogue was one horrible individual.

"I don't even know why I bothered with the whole charade," Vera said, her voice small and defeated. "The last few months, all Tabitha cared about was that stupid crystal ball. I swear, when she wasn't at work, she was locked up in her room. I know you probably think I'm a terrible person for what I tried to do, but the truth is, I lost my sister long before she died."

"I'm really sorry," I said.

"It is what it is. I should get back inside," Vera said quietly. "If you can bring her things back soon, please. Tabitha loved that crystal ball, and I want to make sure we have it for the service on Sunday." She looked at me questioningly. "I'd invite you to come, but the entire coven will be there."

With that, Vera stood up and went back inside, leaving me alone on the freezing porch.

# CHAPTER 21

The walk back to the beetle was slow and cold and I dragged my feet across the asphalt, the Pogue house growing smaller behind me. In the dark crevices of my mind, an idea took shape. Though I could barely call it a full-fledged thought. If I had to describe what I was feeling, I would equate it to a forgotten word. A few letters, a vowel, all of them mingling together and perching on the tip of my tongue but never forming a concrete shape.

Amid a sea of guessing, one thing stood out clearly: Tabitha and Zeta went further back than I, or the sheriff, I wagered, knew.

I doubted Romero bothered to check the two cases

against each other. As far as I could tell, he wrote Tabitha's death off as an unfortunate run in with a robber. But I knew otherwise; I could feel it in my bones.

When I reached the car and climbed in, I didn't start the engine. Instead, I picked up my phone and dialed the sheriff's number, the one he gave me in case I needed to discuss things out of the police's earshot. The line rang and rang and for a moment; I thought I'd have to ramble my incoherent theories over Romero's answering machine. When the sheriff finally picked up, I had a speech ready to go.

"Miss Addison," Romero said, sounding unhappy to hear from me as per usual.

"Hi, sheriff. How are things?"

*Really? How are things?*

On the line, Romero wasn't buying my transparent small talk. "Cut to the chase, Miss Addison," he said. "I'm a little tied up here."

For a second, I pictured the sheriff physically tied up in his police station office.

"Quick question," I started. "If I wanted to get information on someone's bank account, how would I go about doing that?"

A good ten seconds passed; I had to look at the phone screen to make sure we were still connected. We were. Romero was simply refusing to talk. I gave him another moment and cleared my throat, hoping he got the clue. For someone who was "tied up" he sure was taking his sweet time answering my question. When he did answer, I wished he hadn't. Actually, answering was not a good way to describe it because what Romero did was the verbal equivalent of a slap in the face.

The man laughed at me.

His chuckle started low, a rasp in the base of his throat, and grew exponentially. By the time I realized I wasn't going to get anything out of him, the sheriff was full-blown giggling. Annoyed, I considered hanging up on him but held off, saying, "A simple answer would suffice."

"I'm sorry," Romero croaked out between chuckles. "You took me by surprise. Why is it you need to see someone's banking information?"

"I have a lead," I answered. *And a possible theory.* I kept the last part to myself since it wasn't so much a theory as it was me trying to organize my wild thoughts. "So, how do I do it? Go to the bank and ask them? Do I tell the bank manager it's for an investigation or is there papers you need to sign off on?"

Again, a loud, bellowing laugh pierced my ears. When Romero finally got a grip, he said, "Miss Addison, you can't get access to a person's accounts based on a—what did you call it? A lead?"

"Tabitha was Archer Lee's financial advisor," I stated. "Her and Zeta knew each other for a long time. I think it's worth looking at Archer's business banking to see if it points us in the right direction."

"Which direction would that be?"

"I don't know!" I said, exasperated. "The right one. I know you don't believe this and have your own theories you're following up on." *All of which are wrong.* "These aren't unrelated murders. Look, it might be nothing and if it is, I'm sorry. But what if it's not? If I can get my hands on his account book and Tabitha's logs, I can link the two girls together. See where and when their paths intersected and go from there."

The sheriff made a gurgling sound with his throat. "So now you also need access to the bank's secure employee information?"

"Yes, that would be great."

"How about a unicorn? Can I get you one of those while I'm at it?" the sheriff asked, his tone demeaning.

I banged my head against the steering wheel, the rough, torn leather leaving a red mark across my forehead. My knees knocked together, and I clenched my teeth to keep from screaming. Was I asking for too much? I didn't know a lot about police procedure, but this didn't strike me as an unreasonable request. In all the shows I watched while downing copious amounts of popcorn, the police had access to all the victim's financial files, usually instantaneously. I knew Archer Lee wasn't a victim, and he had rights and such, but Tabitha was dead. Shouldn't that at least get me a foot in the door with the bank she worked in?

Removing myself from the clutches of the wheel, I rubbed at the sore spot it left behind.

"I don't mean to be insensitive," Romero said. *Could have fooled me.* "But even if I did think there was sound reason to drag a man's business through the mud, which I don't, there are procedures in places for this sort of thing."

Hope fluttered in my chest. "What type of procedures?"

"Well, for starters, you'll need a court order."

"How do I get that?"

Romero sighed heavily, letting me know he was not enjoying our conversation. I wasn't having the time of my life either, so I completely ignored his melodramatic reactions. "You'll need to show probable cause and a police report that signifies the bank records have a direct link to the case."

"Oh."

I didn't have any of that. This was not looking great for Team Piper.

To deflate my ego even more, Romero added, "And once submitted, it could take a judge up to two weeks to approve the request. Plus, the time it would take the bank to gather all the information."

"In other words, it's not happening."

"I'm afraid not," Romero said. "Now if there's nothing else?"

"One more thing. Did you find anything relating to the Orchard Hollow Royal Bank on Zeta's laptop? Any files or notes she kept?"

The sheriff sighed again, this time lighter and more defeated. "Nothing of the sort," he answered. "Anything else I can help with?"

*Because you were so much help so far.* I rolled my eyes and ended the conversation, hanging up quickly. Tossing my phone on the passenger side seat, I gripped the steering wheel with all my might and let a groan escape my tight jaw. My brain buzzed and my eyes swung to the phone as I reached to pick it up again. Pulling up a GPS app, I typed Orchard Hollow Royal Bank into the search bar and clicked "enter".

Seventeen minutes to get there from where I was. If I stepped on it, I could make it in time before the bank closed.

I looked at the map and the zigzagging line leading me to Tabitha's place of employment. If Romero couldn't help, I had to take matters into my own hands. With the phone secured in its holder on the dash, I started the car and drove forward, heading straight for a misdemeanor.

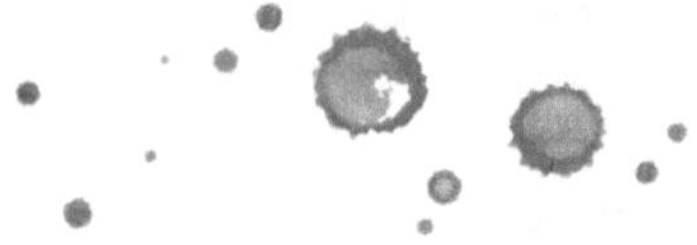

Orchard Hollow Royal Bank was a beautiful two-story traditional building. Two wide columns framed a set of doors that were updated to glass about thirty years ago; the name of the bank etched above them in classic, bold letters. Inside, the bank opened to a large, open-concept area with the sprawling teller desk set against the back wall. Behind it, a door leading to the rear of the building and the safe room was left open. No one worried about bank robberies in our town.

I walked inside, the smell of money and citrus cleaner wafting up my nostrils. There was a small line of patrons waiting to be served, and I counted two tellers on duty. I couldn't remember the name of the girl, but the man was Peter Widenstance—an old high school acquaintance of moms. When Peter spotted me, he curtly nodded, and I waved hello, waiting. I was hoping it would be him to serve me, so I didn't feel so guilty about asking too many questions.

The girl, Theresa, judging by the gold nameplate on her chest, finished first and the next customer in line walked up. It seemed Peter was dealing with a particularly difficult customer, and I chewed my nails as I bounced from foot to foot nervously. *Come on, come on, come on.* My stomach muscles tightened.

By the time the man grabbed his paperwork off the counter, I had developed an ulcer.

I started for Peter when my eyes caught a glimpse of the man, and I paused. Passing by him, I edged myself closer, appearing in his direct sightline. "Hi, Ray," I said.

Archer Lee's cameraman stopped to look up from his phone.

"Hi again," he said.

Looking down at his stack of papers, I asked, "Getting some banking done while you're here?"

"Uh-huh." Ray nodded and shoved the papers into a letter-sized plastic envelope, secured the top, and held it tightly between his fingers. "Hey, I never got to thank you and your friend for saving my ass in the bar."

I waved him off. "No worries. I'm glad it didn't get too far."

"Tell that to my left eye."

For the first time, I noticed the dark bruise adorning his face. The eye in question looked rough for wear and it was so red it appeared infected. Zeta's boyfriend sure did a number on this guy. I grinned toothily. "It doesn't look so bad."

"Right." Ray shrugged. "Lucky it's Archer on camera and not me."

This was my chance. I had a clear opening to bring up Archer Lee and I couldn't stop smiling. Ray pretty much fell into my lap, saving me from the suspicious questioning I was going to put poor Peter through. I lifted my chin, checking the teller counter over Ray's shoulder, and loosened a breath. It seemed that Peter had no plans to wait until I finished chatting and had moved on to the next customer in line. Phew!

"Speaking of your boss," I said, pausing for effect. "Do you know if he banks here, too?"

Wow. *Way to make it obvious you're prying for information.* Thankfully, Ray didn't appear to have noticed the desperation in my voice. He wiggled the envelope between us, saying, "As a matter of fact, I'm here for him."

"I thought you were in charge of videos?"

"I am. But after Zeta...you know...Archer asked me to take over his business accounts. He's so busy with the tour and the upcoming releases, and it's the least I can do after our previous misunderstanding."

*When Zeta accused you of stealing money from the business,* I thought. Keeping the conversation friendly and non-confrontational, I flashed my teeth and gave

Ray some breathing room. "He's got you busy, I see. It sounds like a lot of extra work."

"Not really," Ray admitted. A loose curl dropped into his eyes, and he pushed it away only for it to fall down again. "It's simple stuff. Some expenses for the trip, balancing the check book. Nothing major. He has someone else taking care of the important things."

Someone like Tabitha? I wanted to ask so badly; it left an imprint on my tongue. Before I could, Ray started to shift his weight around and look at the clock on his phone. I was running out of time, and I really didn't wish to be stuck making Peter hate his job later. Guessing I only had a few minutes before Ray excused himself and left me in the dust, I went for the jugular. "Did Zeta take care of the important things for him?"

Ray paused, scratched his chin, paused again.

"You know, I have no idea," he said. "Probably. She was constantly doing more than she should for the guy. If you ask me, she had a crush on Archer. But don't repeat that; I don't want to get fired over gossip."

"Of course not," I agreed. It was hard not to laugh. If Ray didn't want to lose his job because of gossip, he probably shouldn't have been gossiping. I truly could not picture anyone having a crush on Archer Lee. "This is a little far for business banking, no?" I asked. "I'm sure they have great banks in the city."

I was praying Ray didn't pick this particular time

to get a clue because my questions were starting to get too intense, and I didn't even know where I was going with any of it. But it did strike me as odd that Archer Lee would pick Tabitha, of all people, to be his financial advisor. Why her and not someone closer to his main base of operations? It wasn't as though Orchard Hollow was known for its stellar stocks.

Oblivious to my overstepping, Ray said, "It's not so weird if you know Archer. He always says, 'Never put all your eggs in one basket.' The guy has an account with branches all over the place. It makes it easier when we travel."

Ray checked his phone a second time and skirted around me. "I have to run. We're setting up for the big signing event on the weekend, and I still need to get the lights in place at the hotel. Can't film a ghost hunt without the proper atmosphere."

So that was Archer's big reveal? I should have known he would milk the haunted hotel story. Now that I knew that's the case, I wondered if the author had any real proof of the paranormal or if the entire tour was staged for publicity. What was it that Rory called Vivien? Archer's marketing guru. Maybe I was wrong to worry about him and his books.

Archer Lee may have been nothing more than a story chaser; one with zero knowledge of the truth.

Getting out of Ray's way so he could leave, I

waited until both tellers were occupied before slinking out the front doors and heading back to my car. The drive home was longer than usual since I decided to take the scenic route along the sea to clear my head. While I was lucky to run into Ray at the bank, I didn't get any concrete answers, though that was more because I didn't know the right questions to ask. So, what if Archer Lee had multiple bank accounts? It wasn't illegal, and it's not like I understood much about running a business. Everything I knew was tied to the cafe and by no means was Bean Me Up making the same amount of money Ray's boss brought in. For all I knew, having multiple accounts was standard procedure.

I made a mental note to ask Joe about it since he had more experience with these things on account of being a lawyer in a previous life.

When I reached the farmhouse and pulled into the driveway, it was pitch black outside. I dragged my tired legs up the porch steps and pushed the key in the lock. As I turned it, the hint of a breeze cooled my neck. I spun around, hand on the door lock. "Hey, Stella," I told the ghost, who was staring daggers into me. "I know I'm later than usual, but—"

"Get your witch behind into that house now!" Stella yelped.

"What's going on?" I asked.

My hand fumbled with the key, twisting it around so I could pull it out while simultaneously turning the handle. Behind me, my ghost familiar took several quick breaths and rapped her foot on the porch's wooden planks. "Something's wrong with the beast. He's not moving."

# CHAPTER 22

***Harry Houdini***

There was a stink in the air tonight. The delicious scent stuck to my nose and pulled me out from under the bench. Shaking off my fur and leaving a trail of crumbs from last night's breakfast, I stood up on my hind legs and sniffed. The witch left something behind before she walked out for the day. Something tasty.

I dropped to all fours and stretched, back feet sliding on the floor of my hiding spot.

A few nights ago, I heard the witch call this place The Greenhouse, but I'm sure she meant it ironically.

I looked around, nose up. Whatever plants she had in here were not faring better than the dead fly in the spiderweb on the window. Green or not, this was a great place to spend the day when the sun was up, and my belly was full.

Scraping my fur against the dirt covered floor, I tiptoed for the door. Stopped. Looked behind me. I pushed my paw in my mouth to wet it and pressed it to the ground; the crumbs gluing to my skin. Darting my eyes around the House of Not Green, I slid my tongue over the crumbs and swallowed.

No one gets left behind.

My nails scratched the floor as I crept forward and I hunched my back, lightening my steps. I was pretty sure I heard the witch's chariot roar in the afternoon, but not of it returning, though there was a chance I slept through the noise. I doubted it. The metal box carrying the witch in and out of my life made too much noise to miss.

Nudging the door frame with my nose, I stepped over a rusty nail and hung half my body out of my hiding space. An owl hooted overhead, and I ducked low to the ground, crawling along the stone pathway toward the house. I started for the metal pipe attached to the side of the building and began the climb to the upstairs window. Stopped.

Rolling away from the pipe, I shook myself off and stuck my head around the corner to check the front. I was right—no chariot in sight. It relieved me to see the front of the house clear of any visitors, specifically the furless human who delivered packages for the witch every morning. The man wore a strange costume with an image of a box on his back and he never seemed to take it off. Odd behavior for a human, considering even I shed my fur and replaced it with a fresh set occasionally.

I had to admit I was a bit upset over his absence tonight, mostly because I had him to thank for bringing me here. If it wasn't for the thoughtful gift of dried apricots I found in a package stored in his large, wheeled contraption, I wouldn't have ended up at the witch's house. The furless human never even saw me behind the stack of boxes in the back and, when the noises stopped and we quit bouncing up and down, I watched him get out to walk to the front of the house, leaving a brown box near the door. The place smelled the same as the cafe I frequented, so I made it a point to climb out and slink around the back while the furless human started up his metal canister.

This was five days ago.

Despite the loud shrieks of the gray woman the witch kept around, I had no intention of leaving. The cafe was great and there were plenty of snacks when I could get my hands on them, but it was hard work. Here, in the middle of nowhere, with the witch gone for most of the days, I was in my element.

I twisted around and hobbled back to the pipe, my hump hitting the side of the house a few times on the way. Then I started to climb.

A couple days ago, when the witch finally caught on I was here, I heard her mention boarding up the windows, but I was able to nudge one open without any issues. I should have known it wasn't anything to worry about; she had too much on her plate to worry about little ol' me invading her home. *Hmm...plate....* I rolled over the windowsill and landed on my behind, tumbling to the side before righting myself. *What will we have for dinner?*

After a few days, I was well acquainted with the house and knew which spots to avoid if I wanted to stay away from the loud gray woman. Sticking to the shadows, I slinked down the stairs with the aptitude of a viper. My nails made tiny rapping sounds against the wood and I flattened my paws, landing on the soft bits when I walked. I was in the kitchen in no time.

From here, it was easy to get a good lay of the land. I lifted up and sniffed. My nose caught the yummy scent, and I followed it to the counter. Using all my strength and the handles on the cabinet doors, I hoisted myself up.

Victory was mine.

It seemed the witch left in a hurry and the sink was full of unwashed dishes. Dishes covered in food.

My paw dunked into the metal basin and I pulled out a wooden stick covered in a sticky green residue. Without pausing, I shoved half of it in my mouth and chewed.

*Sweet, marvelous treat.*

My eyes rolled to the back of my head with excitement and I continued to lick the goodness the witch had left behind. It stuck to the roof of my mouth, making me smack my gums loudly. I looked around, checking for the gray woman, but the house was abandoned.

Suddenly, my stomach growled, and I hissed at it.

Not a good time.

I pressed my tongue to the stick and tried to lick again, my stomach once more interrupting. This was unprecedented. Never have I found myself in a position where I couldn't eat. I smacked my aching belly and—

Vision flickering, I rolled onto my back. The house floated around me and I was pretty sure I lost my sense of smell. Garbled noises sounded from somewhere in the room and I heard the gray woman yell something in my direction. I pried my lips open to hiss at her, but I was so sleepy. So very, very sleepy.

*I'll take a little nap, then back to the goodies, I* thought.

Hugging the stick to my chest for safety, I rolled on my side and closed my eyes, dreaming of cookies.

# CHAPTER 23

"The beast is not moving."

Stella's words rang in my ears and I all but karate kicked the front door open to get inside. My stomach pitched violently as I rushed through the farmhouse, following Stella's directions leading me to the kitchen. When I saw Harry lying on the counter, I almost threw up. His body was curled on the side and even from halfway across the room, I could see he wasn't moving. "Harry!" I yelled and leapt toward him.

Not caring about whatever germs the wild animal might have had, I dug my fingers into his shabby fur and turned him over. His eyes were closed, a wet, sticky substance dripping from his half-open muzzle. I placed my palm on his chest and waited for movement. His breathing was so faint I almost missed it, but it was there.

Tears stung the rear of my lids. "He's breathing!" I screamed at Stella.

"I can hear you fine," she said. "And good."

"What did he get into?" I looked around the kitchen, my eyes landing on the wooden spatula clutched in his paws. "No, no, no!"

I tugged at the stick several times before I was able to free it from his grip, then tossed it behind me, as far away from the raccoon as possible. "He ate one of my potions!"

"The ones from last night?" Stella asked.

When I couldn't sleep the night before, I did what I often did on such occasions. I played with magic. I loosely remembered grinding up some of gran's crystals and herbs and boiling them into a thick paste. The plan was to brew a potion that could help with the random spasms of my unknown magic, but as many times before, the plan backfired. Testing it on my fingers, not only did I not succeed in what I set out to do, but I ended up burning my skin in the process. If Harry ate the foul mixture I concocted, I didn't know what would happen to him.

I peered at the raccoon's limp body. "We need to get him to a vet."

"You can't bring a raccoon to a vet, Piper," Stella said. "It's not a pet." She peered over me at Harry Houdini. "And I don't think you'll make it in time."

I followed her gaze, my heart sinking as Harry's breathing slowed down further. His chest barely moved now and his closed lids began to flutter, like he was having a bad dream. "This can't be happening. What do I do? I need to help him!"

My familiar stood stone still, and I knew she was thinking the same thing I was; we were too late. Whatever effect the potion had on Harry, it moved fast. He was in worse shape than when I found him only minutes ago and I was certain if I didn't act that instant, Harry would not make it. A fat tear rolled down my cheek, and I pressed both my palms to the raccoon's chest, my fingers sinking into his fur. I wanted to scream.

Prying my lips apart, I sucked in air, the tears continuing to stream down my face.

A memory flashed before me and I saw Joe's face in my mind as he explained the magic he saw me perform as a child. The dark magic I had no business knowing.

I paused my sniveling and turned up my chin at Stella. "I have an idea," I said. "It's crazy."

Without waiting for her to ask what I was going to do, I scooped up Harry's chubby body and cradled him to my chest, carefully laying him down on the tile floor. He looked so peaceful, a direct opposite to the savage creature he usually was. If it wasn't an emergency and I wasn't going out of my mind with worry, I would have envied his deep sleep. Harry's eyes fluttered rapidly, then stopped. I was running out of time.

My body moved on instinct and I gave into its flow before I had the chance to spiral out of control. In any other given moment, what I was about to do would have given me pause. Not today, though. Harry was in trouble and I may have been his only shot at making it out alive.

I hovered my hands an inch above his motionless body and closed my eyes. Inside me, the magic I didn't know how to maneuver rustled and I did my best to calm my restless mind. I tried to connect to whatever energy the little girl Joe remembered may have used, but since I had no recollection of the event, all I could do was settle for what I knew and trusted. Well, sort of trusted.

Imagining the lightning magic I carried, I waited until I felt it on the tips of my fingers and opened my eyes. The lightning danced on my skin, ready. I breathed in slow and steady, continuing to keep my palms close to Harry's body but not touching it. "Whatever this is," I told the energy I harnessed, "help me fix him. Please."

With my lame incantation out in the world, I pressed the flats of my palms to Harry's chest.

The lightning didn't hesitate, and it jumped from my body to the raccoon in the blink of an eye. Harry convulsed, and I fought the need to pull away. Continuing to feed the energy into his body, I kept my eyes wide open and watched for any signs of life from the little rascal. In my head, I pictured Harry coming to, alive and well. Hungry.

The raccoon's body jumped again and then it stopped moving entirely.

I sucked in a shuddering breath.

"Did it work?" Stella asked.

I didn't answer. All I could do was watch Harry lie on my kitchen floor and fight the never ending tears flowing down my face. They dripped down my neck and into the cowl of my sweater, cooling my skin. My breath hitched and my chest tightened. Harry still didn't move. I started for his chest again, my palms connecting with his rough fur.

Suddenly, the raccoon's eyes popped open, and he looked right at me. His lips drew back to reveal sharp canines and he let out a feral hiss as he flipped from his back to his stomach, then curved his spine to the sky. The green, sticky potion I brewed lingered on his breath as he continued to tell me off in raccoon language. I held up my hands in surrender. "Whoa there! I'm not going to hurt you."

I couldn't be completely sure, but I thought I heard him scoff.

Harry teetered backward to put some space between us, and the overwhelming joy I felt at seeing him alive brought me down to all fours. My body heaved with heavy sighs and my hair hung clumsily over my face. Above me, Stella said something about me turning into a raccoon, and I chose not to entertain her with a rebuttal. I did it. I saved the troublemaking fur ball. My magic actually worked for a change.

Looking up from between loose locks, I spotted Harry beeline for the poison spatula lying on the floor. I jumped up, hopping over his clumsy, round body to pick up the stupid stick before the clown could hurt himself again. Waving the spatula at Harry's nose, I growled. "You never learn, do you?"

The ungrateful bugger hissed at me again and waddled out of the kitchen. I watched him climb the stairs and disappear somewhere I knew I would regret allowing him to go later.

"You're really letting him have a run of the place now?" Stella asked.

I looked at the spatula in my hand. "He almost died. Let him have his moment. I'm afraid to think what would happen if I didn't show up when I did. I wish the little guy would learn to keep things out of his mouth. It's as if he's—"

I stopped talking.

"As if he's what?" Stella asked.

"Oh. My. Latte," I whispered. "I think I know how the poison got into Zeta's system."

Tossing the spatula into the sink and dousing it with water to rinse off the potion, I skidded by Stella and ran to the front door where I dropped my purse. My arm dug at the bottom and I pulled out my cellphone, dialing Romero's number. "Come on," I begged. "Answer."

The sheriff picked up the phone on the fourth ring. "Miss Addison. Good evening."

"I'm sorry to call so late, but I just saved a raccoon, and it made me realize an important piece of Zeta's death. See, Harry Houdini needs to chew on stuff. Cookies, paper bags, potion spatulas, you name it. Anyway, I know how the killer poisoned Zeta." I was rambling, and it was beyond embarrassing. "What I mean to say is you need to test her pens. Zeta was constantly chewing on one. If there was poison in her body, I'm willing to bet big it came from one of her pens. Which means the killer had access to them. If you can figure out who was close enough to get into her pen stash, you'll find your killer."

"Hmm," the sheriff mused. I pictured him twirl his mustache while he thought and tried not to laugh.

"You believe me, right?"

"I do. And what you're saying might help us quite a bit tonight," the sheriff said.

I straightened out, pressing my shoulder blades into the wall behind me. "Why tonight?"

"I was going to call you tomorrow morning, but since you don't seem to have office hours, now's a good a time as any." Romero's voice was chipper and it worried me. Romero was never happy. Something was wrong. "We arrested someone for the murder of Zeta Huxley tonight and if what you're saying turns out to be true, it would make the case easier to close. The person we have in custody had plenty of chances to take one of the victim's pens. I'll have my guys test the pens in Miss Huxley's belongings and I'll keep you updated."

There was a rustle on the phone and I panicked. No way was this man about to hang up on me without spilling the beans. "That's great," I said, a little too urgently, so the words came out jumbled together. "Who is it?"

Romero didn't answer.

"Sheriff, come on," I begged. "After everything I've done trying to help you with this, I deserve to know who the killer is."

"Of course," Romero said. "Of course you do. We have Ray Langston in custody as of seven this evening."

"Wait, what? Ray? He didn't do it."

"I'm afraid you're wrong," the sheriff said. "Mr. Langston was reported by his boss earlier today after an altercation regarding some business accounts. It turns out you were correct in your hunch to speak to the bank. Mr. Langston moved quite a large sum of money from his boss's account. Our victim must have figured out what he was planning, and he killed her for it."

*Huh? No. That's not right.* I bristled in my spot. "That doesn't make any sense," I said. "Ray said it wasn't true and that Zeta tried to have him fired for no reason. He said Archer Lee believed he was innocent."

"I'm not sure what to tell you," Romero said. "Whatever Mr. Langston told you, he lied."

My back slid down the wall and I crumbled into a ball on the floor.

"I really need to get going, Miss Addison," the sheriff said. "You have my gratitude for the help you provided. I will have someone at the station write a check for informant services. You can pick it up later in the week."

"A check?" I asked.

"It's the least I could do for running you around

town. Hopefully, it helps offset the temporary closing of the cafe."

I thanked the sheriff and put the phone down next to my sneakers. My body felt hollow. After what happened with Harry Houdini and now the news the sheriff delivered, I wasn't sure what was up and what was down. Ray killed Zeta. If what Romero said was backed by evidence, I had no reason to question him. And yet I did. I definitely questioned it all.

Even if I did believe Ray was capable of poisoning his coworker, which was a big "if", it didn't explain Tabitha's death. No matter what the sheriff concluded, this case wasn't closed. I shuddered.

The killer was still out there.

# CHAPTER 24

The night was a complete blur, and I tossed and turned for hours on end, unable to rest. Between Harry's incident and speaking to the sheriff, I was going out of my mind with worry. The sun's first rays streamed through my curtains and I rubbed the sleep, or lack thereof, from my eyes and got dressed. I reached the kitchen in record time, considering how exhausted I was. What I needed was a stiff coffee and a few minutes of silence to get my thoughts in order.

While the kettle heated, I wracked my brain for clues.

It was incredibly difficult to work past the idea that Ray was the main suspect. He had access to Zeta's pens, held a grudge against her for their previous altercation, and if anyone could catch him stealing from Archer Lee, it was the girl who handled the author's business banking. I hated to admit it, but Ray fit the bill. If this was the case, perhaps he also killed Tabitha to cover his tracks.

He already knew where she lived after their rendevouz, and the connection between them was hard to ignore. Did Ray target Tabitha in the bar? It seemed impossible that their meeting was an accident.

Behind me, the kettle screamed, and I shut it off, pouring the water into a carafe fit for six. "How much money are we talking about here?" I asked the empty kitchen.

I pulled out my phone and typed "Archer Lee net worth" into the search bar. There were several websites offering the answer if I signed up for their mailing list and I scrolled past them, continuing to dig. As I scrolled, I came across multiple articles on the author, all of which made my stomach turn. Archer was no more pleasant in his interviews than he was in real life. "Geez," I whispered. "The head on this guy." I skimmed a few articles and gagged in my mouth, then one site caught my eye.

"Holy coffee bean..."

My mouth gaped, and my throat felt tight and full.

Archer Lee had sold an estimated of six million book copies to date. The article listed all of Archer's books and I was surprised by how prolific he was. I remembered some of what I read with Joe. I supposed it was easier to publish faster when everything he wrote was made up. The worst part was that six million people believed the author was the real deal. The article stated that Archer Lee's latest book tour—the one he was currently on in our small town—pulled in some massive backers, something to the tune of half a million dollars.

I thought back to when the author filmed at Bean Me Up. You'd think with all that money being pumped into this tour, he'd have a more elaborate setup. When the author showed up at my closed cafe after the death of his employee, I got the sense he enjoyed luxury. Most people didn't have an avert reaction to drip coffee. Not this guy, though. Archer was all about acting and being treated like a star. Then why did Ray film his tour? Why ask Zeta to handle his accounting? I would have imagined that someone with such success would have a crew of people shutting down every street in town.

Cradling my coffee mug, I dragged my tired self to the living room and plopped down on the couch. The cushions swallowed me whole, and I pulled the fluffy blanket over myself until I was a witch-sized cocoon. A foul smell permeated the air, and I pushed the blanket off, dry heaving.

"Ugh!"

I had completely forgotten to wash it after Harry Houdini rolled around in it.

Trying not to think about the possible rabies I had inherited from the raccoon, I kicked the blanket to the floor. A heavy object clambered at my feet and the sound of rolling woke me from my daze. Beneath me, Tabitha's crystal ball made its escape, heading for the fireplace wall. I slid the mug onto the coffee table and gave chase, catching it before it cracked open on the bottom tile.

I could only imagine the lecture I'd get from Vera if I shattered her dead sister's prized possession a few days before the viewing.

Carefully, I carried the ball back to the couch and set it up on its base in the middle of the coffee table, next to the few books I grabbed from Tabitha's bedroom. My fingers itched to touch the ball again, but this time there was no magical pull as it was curiosity driving my body. Since I was a little girl, I was amazed by the magic seers possessed. What a gift —my young mind thought—it was to tell the future. As I grew older, I understood that wasn't quite how the magic worked. Seers didn't have glimpses of what was to come any more than a witch could create something out of nothing. They received messages, or paths, as gran called them. The way she explained it when I was old enough to understand was a seer could see all the outcomes of a situation and every scenario that might unfold. When I looked at it this way, it made the entire system feel flawed. And way too complicated. I couldn't imagine walking around with multiple possibilities in the way of making decisions.

When I asked gran about it, she only shrugged. She said it was incredibly rare for a seer to have a concrete answer to any of the questions they posed during their readings, because their magic could not interfere with personal choice. Unless someone's choices were set in stone, a seer would always see multiple paths. And gran said people were too flighty to be that decisive.

*The last few months, all Tabitha cared about was her crystal ball....* Vera's words came back to me and I stared at the ball blankly, wondering why her sister was so entranced with it lately. For the life of me, I couldn't see the appeal. Then again, all I saw was a shiny orb.

I picked it up and brought it to my face to study it. My eye enlarged through the convex surface and I laughed at the skinny view of the fireplace on the other side. Pulling away, I stretched to put the ball back on its base; something caught my eye in the metal. On the rounded platform that held it in place was a small dot, almost in the shape of a tiny button. It was black when the rest of the stand was golden and it stood out like a sore thumb now that I saw it. Of course, with the ball on top, I wouldn't have noticed it at all.

Settling the crystal orb on the couch, I nestled it between two cushions and picked up the stand. My index finger hovered above the dot for a moment before I pushed it down. I expected nothing to happen. Boy, was I wrong! The dot dropped into the metal and a loud clicking sound rang in my ears.

A lock unlocking.

I twisted the stand around and looked for a change. That was when I spotted it. The bottom part of the stand was no longer smooth; a piece of it jotted out about a half an inch. I pulled on it, the piece coming out of the stand easily. "What the..." I whispered, bringing it closer to my eyes.

In my fingers was a USB stick. The back of it was glued to a sewed off portion of the crystal ball stand to make it blend in without notice. It was a simple stick, one of the slimmer ones that one could easily carry in a pocket or attached to a keychain. I twirled it around in awe. Cupping the stick in my clammy fist, I jogged up the stairs and ran into my bedroom. Half-lying on the bed, I grabbed my laptop from the nightstand and typed in my password—a security measure against Stella's nosy butt. When the laptop powered up, I inserted the USB stick, clicked on the only unnamed file there, and started to go through the contents.

There were a few documents with numbered labels I didn't understand and several photos. I clicked on the first one, then the next, and the one after. My lungs expanded, and I let go of a shuddering breath.

With the documents open, I dialed Joe.

"I got it!" I said when he picked up.

"Hello to you too," Joe said.

I collected myself, glancing at the computer screen, then freaked out internally. "Sorry, hello. I got it!" I seriously had no chill. "Look, I don't have time to explain, but I know what happened to Zeta and Tabitha, and I need your help."

"Piper, is this going to be dangerous? Because I don't want you doing anything foolish."

"It won't be," I said, meaning it.

Joe sighed heavily, and I pictured him shaking his head at me on the other side of the phone. "What do you need?"

My lips peeled back into a smile. "I want to use Brooks Books for an event," I said. "A celebration of a well-known author to congratulate him on his tour."

# CHAPTER 25

Getting an event organized last minute was not as easy as I thought it would be, especially considering it was one big fake. After a little convincing and a lot of promising to make it up to him later, I got Joe to agree to contact Archer Lee while I rounded up a few other people. The guest list was minimal: Myself and Joe, Archer, Vivien, Vera, Declan and Aria. I also invited Cilia, but that was more for moral support than the plan I had. I figured it would be nice to have another witch present in case my theory was correct and things went south.

We awaited the group at the bookshop while I rearranged the snacks and drinks Rory helped prepare earlier. If I was wrong, at least we could all enjoy oat matcha lattes together.

The last member of the group, one that wasn't going to show his face, was Sheriff Romero.

When I called him to tell him what I planned, he immediately told me to drop it. Then he told me to sit tight while he attempted to get Ray's confession. Ray was very lucky sitting tight was not part of my DNA and I called the sheriff seven times in a row until he picked up and agreed to meet me at Brooks Books. As soon as he arrived, I explained everything I discovered and promised that if he gave me an hour to go through with the charade I was putting on, I would have the real killer ready for him to cuff and drag to the station.

It all looked great on paper.

I looked at the crescent-shaped arrangement of chairs Joe set up and frowned. My history with things going according to plan were not great, and I started to get quite nervous about the outcome of this meeting. The more I thought about it, the more I realized how insane my ruse was. What if everything I thought I found out was true? I was so wrapped up in organizing the perfect false event; I hadn't stopped to think what that would mean.

Soon, if people actually showed up, I would be in the same room as Zeta and Tabitha's killer. Not only that, but I'd be tricking them into a confession.

*Then what?*

I shook my head and shifted the row of lattes one inch to the left. I had not thought it through that far ahead.

"Are you sure this is the best play?" Joe asked, checking his watch.

*I'm so not.* Nodding, I moved the lattes again and turned to the tray of scones. I cut a few in half, placing the knife back on the table without wiping it off. "I think so. After last time, I really don't want to confront anyone alone and Romero is not going to believe me unless I bring him proof." I looked out the window and across the street toward Ray's ice cream shop, where the sheriff would be waiting. "And what's the worst that could happen around so many witnesses? Safety in numbers, right?"

I didn't want to tell him that the only reason I felt even remotely safe was because he was here. Joe's badass vampire skills would come in handy if the maybe-killer tried to escape. It wasn't my physical safety that I was so concerned over as I continued to mess around with the drinks table. What had me tied up in knots was the possibility that I was wrong. My theory, while solid in my head, was a lot more far-fetched than what the police believed happened. No matter how hard I tried to stay positive, I had to face reality.

There was a very good chance Ray was the killer, and I was wasting the sheriff's time with my half-brained schemes.

Spiraling, I held onto the table for dear life.

"For what it's worth, I agree with you." Stella's voice was a welcome reprieve, and I loosened a breath, turning my head to face her. She stood at the cash register of the shop with her elbows on the counter and her chin resting in her palms. The ghost glanced at the refreshments table. "But I don't agree with your choice of hors d'oeuvres. If you want people to think this is a real celebration and not a complete farce, you should scale it up a notch."

I side-eyed the table. "What's wrong with scones and lattes?"

"Nothing at all," Stella said. "If you're celebrating the fall of humanity."

"You're impossible. How can you be worried about class right now?"

The ghost shrugged. "All I'm saying is caviar goes a long way."

"A long way through my savings," I muttered under my breath and shoved a scone in my mouth to annoy her. At my back, the bell on the front door rang out, and I bit off a giant piece, swallowing it and breathing in at the same time. The stupid scone shot into my throat and I felt it lodge itself in my esophagus. I covered my mouth, coughing up an entire lung next to the snack table.

A flat object slammed into my back and I toppled forward, fingers gripping the table's side for support. Another hit between my shoulder blades sent me into a coughing fit, and tears streamed down my face as the giant piece of scone jumped up from my throat and hit the back of my teeth. I straightened, heaving long breaths and wiping my wet face. Turning around, I hiked up two thumbs to let Joe know I was okay and to thank him for the makeshift Heimlich.

He rubbed my shoulder, half facing me and half the door. "Ready?" he asked and handed me a latte.

I took a big sip to wash down the remnants of scone from my mouth, nodding.

"You know what goes down real smooth?"

"If you say 'caviar', I will end you," I warned Stella. Eyes glued to the door, where a few people, Cilia and Vera, gathered. "Now hush up and let's get this over with."

After greeting the two witches, I led them to the chairs where Joe waited to entertain people until we had a full house. It didn't take long for most to arrive and we had everyone present within a half hour, save for Archer Lee. I briefly looked at Vivien, who made a face that told me the author moved to the beat of his own drum. Butterflies danced in my stomach while we waited. Scratch that, full on pterodactyls flew around in there. I was so nervous, I thought I might throw up.

I downed the last drop of my latte at the same time as the door of the bookstore swung open and Archer Lee made his appearance. The man moved slowly, gazing around the room, almost as if he was expecting a standing ovation. His tweed suit made shuffling sounds as he strolled toward us and he wore an arrogant smile on his even more arrogant face. The fake glasses he usually wore were gone, the contacts making his eyes appear more golden. I tried to keep my nausea at bay as I watched him get nearer.

The author walked by Joe, tipping his newspaper boy hat in a pretentious salute. He whisked by Cilia, who rolled her eyes at his back, and came to stand beside me in front of the other guests. As he took in the few people in the chairs, the pretense dropped and he took on a confused, fast-blinking stare.

If I didn't act fast to keep up pretenses, I was going to lose him.

I gestured to the table behind me, one I had set up in a hurry, holding copies of Archer's books as well as a standing banner I borrowed from Vivien with the author's photo and name. I bit my tongue reading the tagline: Magic Unlocked. The only magic this fake unlocked was the ability to sell books full of lies to an obscene amount of clueless humans.

"Welcome everyone," I said while Archer settled in. He grabbed a pen from the pile I tossed on the table and got ready to sign copies I was pretty sure no one wanted. "As some of you know, we have somewhat of a celebrity here in town. I wanted to throw a small celebration to congratulate Archer Lee on his upcoming book release and to welcome him the Orchard Hollow way. I'm sure you're all as excited as I am to find out what kind of magic Mr. Lee discovered in our small town."

From her chair, I noticed Cilia arch one eyebrow in my direction.

"I thought it a good idea to keep the group small and intimate. That way we can all have a chance to welcome Mr. Lee and wish him luck on his tour." I turned to Archer. "Welcome to Orchard Hollow! I, for one, am very excited to hear all about your new book."

Archer shifted his weight, and I wondered if he was seeing through my performance. He cleared his throat and said, "Thank you. It's great to be appreciated."

Ugh. This man was the absolute worst.

"No problem at all," I said. "I'm sure that the recent events had an effect on the tour, so anything we can do to help."

The author beamed in his chair and his head swelled behind the stack of books. He clicked the pen he held several times. My eyes glued to it, remembering why I was putting on the farce. "To get the ball rolling," I said. "Why don't we open up the floor for some questions? Does anyone have anything they'd love to ask Mr. Lee before we give him a chance to talk about his book?"

I felt Archer's satisfied glare at my back and tried to hide the shiver that ran through my body. Any moment now, Joe would ask his question, one that was open ended enough to imply he actually enjoyed any of the preposterous books Archer wrote. We had rehearsed this ad nauseam while setting up, so I knew it was coming. After he was done and Archer was distracted, it was my turn to play. I waited patiently for Joe to clue in it was game time.

"It's crickets in here," Stella mused from behind Archer.

My lips twitched with the need to tell her to shut it, but I kept myself together.

"Hi there," Joe finally said. "Welcome to Orchard Hollow. I wanted to ask you about your exposition of the werewolves in Northern Canada. Were you able to find where the tracks led in the end?"

I did a double-take so fast my neck cracked. Joe Brooks came prepared. I didn't even realize he read Archer's books well enough to ask such a detailed question. Joe was single-handedly saving this entire "event". I whispered a silent thank you to Joe and sat down in one of the chairs closest to the front while Archer Lee went on and on to answer. And on. And on. Honestly, if given the chance, I was certain the man could talk for eternity. Perched behind him, Stella made yawning motions with her hands and I tried not to laugh. Archer spoke for so long, I stopped paying attention, but the gist of it implied he did not in fact find where the tracks Joe asked about went. I had the inkling he didn't find much of anything on his latest hunt for paranormals either. What werewolf would leave tracks so obvious a human could stumble upon them? Not anyone I knew.

"Can you share anything about what drew you to Orchard Hollow? Anything specific?" Cilia asked.

Our eyes met, and I knew instantly what she wanted to know. Why our town and why now? Ray told me they were filming in the hotel, so I assumed it had to do with the supposed hauntings the Rose Hollow boasted online. All the claims were false, of course, but that didn't stop people like Archer Lee from coming. Still, to base an entire tour on one possibly haunted hotel seemed a waste. I feared, as I have since Archer arrived, that he knew more than he was letting on about our town's magic.

"Well, you have quite the views here," Archer said,

grinning. "But other than that, I wish to explore the apparitions mentioned online."

So it was the hotel.

"As for the rest, you'll have to read the book."

The author winked, his hand patting his books. As he sat there, his head tripling in size, I called his bluff. Based on what I'd seen of his books so far, Archer Lee was a phony. Everything he wrote was either untrue or a regurgitation of current online gossip. The Rose Hollow Hotel, while not immensely popular, had grown a bit of a following in the amateur ghost hunting community. It looked that Archer was nothing more than another fanatic chasing a rumor, and without Zeta to do his research for him, I doubted he'd be much of anything else.

I would be lying if I said that his upcoming drop from fame didn't bring me joy. Orchard Hollow didn't need to be in anyone's best-seller, not when there was real magic here. And even if Archer had no idea where to look for it, it didn't mean someone else wouldn't.

The clock on the wall chimed the hour, and I jumped off the petty train and fixed the author with a steely gaze. Time to get down to business. I opened my mouth, ready to ask the questions I'd been rehearsing all morning, when another voice ripped through the shop.

"You never talk about your personal life in interviews; is there anyone special in your life?"

Vivien's voice was much harsher than I remembered it and I had to turn around, making sure it was she who spoke. While I watched Archer's marketing manager, her eyes were glued to the author. I wondered if this was a marketing ploy the two rehearsed to make the less-than-friendly buffoon appear more welcoming. My head spun to Archer, who appeared to be taken aback by the question. He rubbed the ridge of his sharp nose and tapped the end with an index finger. "I have eighteen someone specials," he said, pointing to his books. "These books are my children and unfortunately, they leave very little time for anything else."

Out of the corner of my eye, I saw Vivien's hazel eyes twitch, and she got up, making her way to the drink station. She picked up a latte and downed it in one go. I guessed whatever the two planned, Archer steered off course.

My hand rose, and I settled the shakiness before asking, "How well did you know Tabitha Pogue?"

A commotion ripped through the small crowd and I did my best not to look around. Behind me, I heard Vera and Cilia break out into whispers. I steeled my spine and kept my focus on the author, whose face had sunk deeply. There was a single bead of sweat on his brow and he shifted his weight in his seat repeatedly. Archer white-knuckled his signing pen, answering, "Not well."

*Liar.*

"Wasn't she your financial advisor?" I pressed. "Speaking of, why have an advisor here in our small town and not in the city?" Archer stammered but didn't say a word. "And how do you explain the large sums of money coming in and out of your account when this is the first time you've set foot in Orchard Hollow? I believe you reported Ray for a theft last night, yet the transactions date back to well before your current visit."

I stood, walked over to the register counter, and pulled out the stack of papers I printed off before the event started. My eyes briefly flashed to the window and then to Joe, who held his phone up, letting me know he had the sheriff on the line. With a loud thud, I let the stack drop in front of Archer Lee. The author blinked rapidly and adjusted his glasses as he picked up the first printout. His skin blanched, and he swallowed hard, his Adam's apple bobbing. "What is this?"

"Every single transaction under ten grand leaving your account in the last three years," I answered. "And this page—" I flipped the papers until I reached the one I needed "—is the account the money was deposited into. Oh, and this one. And this one. All in different banks and all in small towns spread around the country."

There was a gasp from someone in the audience, but I ignored it. "Now the oddest thing about all these accounts is the money deposited was in cash and if you look right here," I pointed to another spreadsheet. "When you add up the sums, they are always equal to the amount taken out of your main business account in the King City Bank. And the withdrawals go back for quite some time, long before Ray Langston started working for you."

I crossed my arms. "Care to explain?"

"I-I don't understand," Archer stuttered.

"Cut the pretense. You were smart to keep the amounts small enough they wouldn't get flagged, and you were even smarter to spread them across multiple banks. Ray mentioned you like being prepared, but it was more than that, wasn't it?" I asked, beaming with pride because I knew I had him. "It's almost a quarter of a million dollars. Did you really think no one would find out?"

Archer sniffled and brought the papers close to his nose, reading. "This is.... I don't.... I didn't make these transactions."

As far as confessions go, it wasn't the one I hoped for. I looked at Joe and shrugged, waiting. There was nothing Archer could do now that his crimes were out in the open. We were in a public place with plenty of witnesses and I had the sheriff listening the entire time. If Archer tried to deny what he did, it'd be laughable. I had the proof right there in front of his cocky face.

"You didn't think Tabitha would figure it out, did you? But she did, thanks to your research assistant. Her and Zeta were working together to expose you," I said. "Is that why you killed them? Why you poisoned Zeta's pen and shot Tabitha?"

"That's preposterous!" the author exclaimed. "I didn't do any of this! And I could never hurt someone the way you're implying. What is happening here?"

Stella appeared next to him with narrowed eyes. "I think he's telling the truth."

"Impossible," I said out loud, not caring if people thought I was talking to myself. "Two of the people with access to his banking are dead and one is behind bars, facing charges for murders he didn't commit." I whipped out the USB stick I found in Tabitha's crystal ball and slammed it on top of the paper pile. "You made sure to get rid of anyone who knew the truth, but you didn't count on this. What was the plan? Destroy all the evidence and make out with the cash? Was it really worth it?"

Archer reached for the USB and I snatched it away from him.

"I have no idea what that is," he said, his voice shaking. "Why would I steal from myself? And if what you're implying is true, and I destroyed all the evidence, wouldn't I have to," he winced, "kill everyone who handled the business's banking?"

"You did," I seethed.

The author shook his head, his glasses dipping low on his nose. "Not everyone."

He looked around the shop and I followed his gaze, trying to pinpoint who he was searching for. My attention snapped to the snack table where a lonely cup stood on the table, the latte Vivien held only moments ago. I looked through the audience, checking each face. A movement by the door caught my eye. I was too late to realize my mistake. By the time the bell rang out and the door swung open, the real killer was already making a run for it. Loud shouts of "stop her!" sounded from the chairs, but I couldn't zero in to identify the voices.

My feet swelled inside my boots and I watched in horror as Vivien ran out of the bookshop, the front door slamming closed in her wake.

# CHAPTER 26

My feet pounded the pavement as I gave chase after Vivien. Behind me, Joe yelled for me to stop, but I didn't slow down, nor did I bother turning around. I had to catch up with her.

Passing the hardware store, I jumped out of the way as a woman exited, a large box in her hands. She swung it around and missed my head by a mere inch, giving me a chance to rebound and keep running. Joe wasn't so lucky. I heard a loud thud and some choice words being exchanged as the woman knocked him off course with her package. Their voices faded into the noise of Cliff Row, masked by the sounds of cars zooming by and a child crying in the distance.

My chest heaved and a sharp pain ripped apart my abdomen. I willed myself to keep moving.

I reached the end of the street where Cliff Row branched off into two smaller streets and skidded to a stop. Head swiveling left and right, I tried to gauge which way Vivien might have gone, but I lost sight of her. My eyes peered into the distance and tears burnt my eyes.

A whistle tore through the air to my right.

I spun around, pulse hammering in my ears, and saw Stella standing at a small opening to a random back alley. "This way," she yelled out, pointing into the emptiness.

"Coming!"

I yipped towards her. My legs pumped and the sound of my heart beating thundered in my chest. When I reached her, I spun around quickly, nearly losing balance as I ran into the alley. It was narrow and long, running directly behind a few shops and restaurants. I noticed the back door of the Drunk Elephant and was relieved to find it bolted shut. Other than that door, there were no others visible, so it was a safe bet to assume Vivien was still here somewhere.

Slowing to a jog, I made my way down the alley. The smell of garbage hung low in the air and for a second, I thought to check for Harry Houdini hiding behind one of the dumpsters. I shook my head. Up ahead, the alley came to an abrupt stop and a large brick wall climbed high before me. It cast a dark shadow over the tight space; even the sun was afraid to touch down here. Nearing the wall, I glanced behind me.

If something happened, I was completely alone. No way Joe saw me break off the main part of the street to follow Stella. I looked to my side where my familiar stood with her shoulders pulled back. "I got you," she said.

I didn't want to hurt her feelings, but the woman was as dead as a doorknob. She got nothing.

Though I appreciated the sentiment. "Thanks," I whispered.

There was a flash of movement behind one dumpster and I looked at Stella, pressing my finger to my mouth to motion for her silence. Not that Vivien could see or hear her, so it was mostly for my own sanity. I needed to keep my wits about me if I were to come out of this unharmed. Vivien wasn't all that intimidating but then again, neither was Patty and the antique store owner almost shot me in my face.

My body shuddered.

Tabitha was shot in her backyard. Did they ever find the weapon? I tried to remember what the sheriff said, but I couldn't make anything out. Looking over my shoulder, I prayed for a miracle, wishing to see him and Joe approach.

The alley remained dead silent.

A state I'd be in if I didn't play this right. My gaze rolled down the alley to where I spotted the movement. "Vivien, I know you're here," I said. "Come out, please. I only want to talk."

She didn't move, though I heard more rustling behind the dumpster. With the shadow of the wall, it was impossible to see clearly, and I had to inch closer to get a better look. I immediately felt foolish. Not only was I further away from the only exit and way closer to a murderer than I'd have liked, but I was now also covered in darkness. My eyes blinked to adjust to the low light, and I forced my feet to stop moving. Apparently, they had a mind of their own and really wanted to get me killed today.

"The police are on their way and you're trapped," I said, switching my way of reasoning. "You either come out or they drag you out. At least you know I don't have cuffs on me."

"Don't forget to let her know you don't have a weapon," Stella said, her eyes rolling.

I waved her off with a shaky hand and watched the dumpster. The metal tin groaned, and the wheels squeaked as Vivien made her move. I saw the shadow of her feet under the dumpster, then a flash of dark hair. Where there was once an empty space now stood Vivien. Her sharp nose pointed up and metal gleamed in her right hand. My body jumped to attention. It was the knife I left on the table of the bookshop after cutting the scones. She must have snatched it during her escape.

My voice was hoarse, and I tried not to show my hesitation when I said, "There's no need for that. We're just talking."

"I bet you she was just talking with Zeta and Tabitha, too," Stella remarked.

Crap. She was right. If I was going to avoid getting hurt again, I had better watch what I say. I smiled, a lopsided gesture that made my cheeks hurt, and took a step backward. "Archer was right, wasn't he? It was you who was stealing money from his accounts. It was never Ray."

Vivien sneered.

"Why? You must have known you'd be caught eventually," I continued. "The police here may be on the slower side, but I doubt Ray would sit back and go down for murder."

"I don't care what that idiot goes down for," Vivien shot back.

*Finally, she's talking.* "Then why? What did you need the money for?"

For a second, I thought of the worst. All the

movies I binge watched rushed by me and their plots played out in my head. Someone was blackmailing Vivien, and she needed to pay them off. The mob kidnapped someone she cared for and she didn't have the cash to get them back. Vivien was part of an underground drug trafficking ring and lost a large shipment of cocaine. My stomach twisted with possibilities, none of which were realistic enough to be true. I really needed to stop watching so much television.

"I didn't need the money at all," Vivien said.

Well, that's not any script I recognize. I fidgeted with the zipper on my sweatshirt. "Then why do it at all?"

"Because he has to pay!" she howled. "It should be him in jail right now, not Ray. He should be going down for money laundering, not sitting in your dumb welcoming event and acting like he's a king." Her eyes, wild and dazed, jumped from corner to corner. "Everything was perfect. I planned to expose him at the end of his precious tour. He would be finished. We had it all planned. It wasn't supposed to be this way."

The knife wavered in her hands and she readjusted her grip on it, pointing it toward me. I didn't think she'd use it, not with me a good five feet away from her, but I wasn't willing to take that chance. Then, I realized what she said.

I flicked my gaze away from the weapon and met her eyes. "We?"

"Zeta and I," Vivien said.

My jaw hit the ground so hard I saw stars. "The call Zeta received that night; it was you," I whispered. "But why?"

"Because he deserves to rot in hell for the rest of his miserable life!" The knife was back on me and sweat pooled at the base of my neck. It rolled down my back, chilling me to the bone. "All he does is take and take and take. He doesn't care who he hurts! Once he gets what he wants, he moves along. No worries. No responsibilities. Archer Lee only cares about one thing: his money." She laughed. "We were going to use what he loved most to take him down."

My knees slammed together, and I tightened my hands into fists, my nails leaving crescent-shaped marks in the soft skin. I looked at Vivien, inspecting her face in the low light of the alley. The hazel eyes, the sharp, stoic nose. It all made sense now. My lips fell apart. "You're his daughter."

"I'm no one to him," Vivien bit out. "Archer Lee doesn't know I exist. Same way he forgot my mother existed. They met on one of his pathetic tours and he got her pregnant. The bastard skipped town without so much as a goodbye once his tour was over. When my mom realized she was pregnant with me, she tried to contact him. But guess what? In true Archer Lee style, he left her a fake phone number. I guess he never wanted to see her again after that one night. Mom got the clue pretty fast. She is much too forgiving." Her eyes filled with tears. "Was."

I remembered the conversation I had with Vivien back in the bed-and-breakfast. "You started planning this after your mother died," I said. More of a statement than a question. "How did you get Zeta to help? I thought you two weren't close."

"We weren't," Vivien replied. "It took me some time to convince Archer he needed a social media manager and that I was the right person for the job. When I finally got it, I really thought he would figure out who I was. But nope! Archer Lee is too selfish to notice a thing. Back in those days, Zeta was his right hand and he even treated her like crap. Always ordering her about and making her do all his work for him while he reaped the benefits. I guess she was over Archer's bullshit, too. When she suspected Ray, I knew it would be a matter of time before she figured out it was me. So, I came clean and told her everything. I didn't even have to convince her much. Believe it or not, planning out how we would get Archer arrested for money laundering was the highlight of our relationship. And Zeta was really good at it. She made sure Archer stayed in the dark, she organized the drops. Zeta was a natural. It was going to work too until..."

She didn't have to fill in the blanks for me to know where this was going. "Until she changed her mind and told you she wasn't going through with it."

Vivien nodded, so slow I almost missed it.

Bile rolled into my throat and rolled around in my mouth. I wanted to heave all over the alley's dirty floor. Zeta ditched their plan and Vivien killed her for it. And Tabitha.... I rolled my shoulders back. "How did you find out Tabitha was onto you?"

"She called me after Zeta was—" she paused to rearrange the knife in her hand "—you know. I don't think she knew I was in on it. That it was because of me everything started. She told me she noticed irregularities in Archer's accounts and that she suspected he killed Zeta to cover his tracks."

"So you shot her?"

Vivien's features twisted, a darkness settling over her eyes. Her face growing dimmer before me. "I should have left it alone," she said. "I should have let that woman call the police and sit back and enjoy the outcome."

"But you wanted to be the one to do it," I guessed.

Vivien dipped her chin low. "That and I knew if Tabitha kept digging, she'd find out the withdrawals and deposits were all made by Zeta and I. It was too risky."

"What a piece of work," Stella said next to me. "She's more like her father than she realizes."

I bristled, not showing a reaction to her words, which were very, very on point. An uncomfortable silence rolled through the alley and Vivien and I faced each other, both wondering what to do next. In the distance, loud voices pierced the air, and I cringed, recognizing the sheriff's gruff tone. Vivien must have realized it, too.

Her fingers looped around the knife's handle and she started for me. I didn't know what her plan was— the men were already so close—but I knew she wasn't thinking clearly. The girl killed twice before to get what she wanted and I had no doubt she'd stab me easily if it meant a chance at getting away. I stumbled backward yet remained in her path.

I couldn't let her leave.

Vivien's hair flung from side to side as she picked up her pace to close the distance between us. Next to me, Stella shouted, "Zippity zap!" The urgency in her voice hammered through me. I raised my hands up defensively as Vivien plunged the knife forward, her body toppling onto mine. Blue energy surrounded us and I felt myself fall backward, my head hitting the ground first. Sharp pain exploded behind my eyelids and I pushed my palms outward, feeling them connect with Vivien's chest. The blade of the knife sliced my upper arm, and I winced, pushing Vivien harder. Electricity hummed between us as my magic exploded. Vivien's eyes bulged in surprise, my magic catapulting her through the air. Her back slammed into the brick wall and she dropped to the ground, her legs breaking her fall. Head spinning, I clumsily crawled toward her, keeping my magic at the ready.

I grabbed the knife out of her limp hand and tossed it behind the dumpster.

With two fingers on the inside of her wrist, I whispered, "Please be alive."

A moment later, I felt a pulse.

Garbled voices sounded somewhere near me and I swallowed the nausea coating my tongue.

"Over here!" I shouted, but it came out as "orer hee".

My fingers remained on Vivien's wrist when the alley spun around me and night took me under. Vision flooding with black, I closed my eyes and let my body fall to the floor. My magic vanishing.

# CHAPTER 27

"Clean up in aisle five!" Rory yelled from behind the espresso machine. "It wasn't my fault this time!"

I peered out from behind the book I was reading, not an Archer Lee, and chuckled. The teenager somehow managed to cover every inch of her hole-ridden sweatshirt in matcha powder. Even the apron, which aided little, was stained a new shade of brownish green. *And that's the end of my late lunch,* I thought.

Closing the book and finishing off the last bite of the croissant I desperately needed, I walked over to the counter, ready to clean up. While I wiped away the mess, Rory dolled out the last of the drinks for the few customers waiting. I glanced at the spaceship-shaped clock above the door. Fifteen more minutes and I'm free. It was a long day.

I didn't remember much of what happened after Joe and the sheriff showed up in the alleyway. Apparently, I had a mild concussion and needed to stay in the hospital overnight. It was one of the worst nights of my life. The bed was uncomfortable, my head swelled with pain, and Stella wouldn't shut up about the lack of Feng Shui in the emergency room. By the time the sun came up, I was pretty certain I would have preferred to be back in the alley with Vivien.

My lips turned down at the edges.

"She's not coming back," a familiar voice said, and I followed it to find Joe standing by the front counter.

The vampire made it a point to check in with me every few hours since the alley incident and, while I appreciated the concern, it had been four days of me feeling like I had a babysitter. *Let me live, Joe!* "I know."

Deep down, I knew he was only trying to help. More importantly, he was right, Vivien was never coming back. After she came to and the sheriff drove her to the police station in cuffs, she confessed to everything. It was a sad victory, at best. On the one hand, I was glad Zeta and Tabitha got the justice they deserve. On the other, I felt sorry for Vivien. Her life was turned upside down before she was even born, and a part of me could see why she spiraled out of control. This part, though, I kept to myself. I didn't want anyone to know I sympathized with a killer.

Some good did come out of the entire situation. After Vivien was arrested and Archer Lee found out the truth, he stuck by her. He paid for her lawyer and even had her transferred to a prison in the city so he could visit regularly. In the end, Archer Lee turned out to be a decent person.

Who could have guessed it?

I hoped that he and Vivien could find some peace in the midst of all the ugliness. Again, I kept my lips shut about those hopes. Between my constant involvement in police matters, the uncanny way in which bodies piled up around me, and possibly having Devil magic—I didn't need to draw more attention to myself.

"You there?"

I slapped my cheek to snap out of my daze. "Processing it all, I guess," I mumbled. "Want a drink to carry around?"

"I'm good," Joe answered, gesturing to the green stain on his white sweater.

*Ugh, she got to him too.*

I looked at Rory, who was busy putting on her jacket at the door. Beside her, waiting to drive her home, stood Cilia. The witch caught my eye and yelled out, "You and me, Addison! Friday at nine. Don't be late!"

I nodded in agreement. More than anything, I wanted a night off to myself to watch bad movies and fall asleep on the couch, but there was no arguing with Cilia Craven. She begged me to go out for drinks for days until I finally caved and now that I did, I was somewhat excited for it. To have another witch to talk to was going to be a nice change of scenery. It helped that Cilia was a real live person and didn't disappear on me every time she didn't feel like speaking, unlike someone else I knew.

"What's on Friday?" Joe asked.

I shrugged, finishing cleaning off the counter and waving goodbye to Rory and Cilia at the same time. "Drinks at the Drunk Elephant. I'd ask you to join, but Cilia would probably kill me."

"No worries. I was hoping we could go out for drinks too," Joe suggested. Then adding, "Just the two of us."

My heart pitter-pattered and I dropped the dirty rag on top of my brand new boots. A gross, sloshing sound rose up from my shoes and I refused to look down, knowing they were covered in matcha sauce. *Ew. Ew. Ew!* I scowled. "That sounds great," I said. "It's a—"

Throat suddenly parched, I stopped talking.

"A date, Piper," Joe said. "You can say it."

Reaching to pick up the rag, I tossed it on the counter and took off my apron. My grin froze in place and I tried to appear as relaxed as possible, even though my body was possibly going into shock. "A date then," I said. *Ugh! Why are you so breathy right now?* I leaned on the counter, my hand missing it by barely an inch. Arm pummeling air, my body twisted sideways, and I was free-falling face first into the counter's marble edge before I knew it. Strong hands gripped my waist and yanked me up moments prior to impact.

My head spun as Joe leveled me back on the ground, his hands staying on my waist. His face was so close to mine, I could smell his breath. Which meant he could likely smell mine. I wished I didn't douse that croissant in tuna salad at lunch. Joe leaned in. I stayed glued in place.

*Holy extra large latte! This is happening!*

"Whoops!" a loud, high-pitched voice rang in my ear.

I gasped, Stella's uninvited appearance startling me. Instantly, Joe pulled away. "Hi, Stella," he said. I tried to find the frustration in his voice, but there was none. "I'll call you later, but keep Saturday open for me."

"Oh, she'll open—"

I shoved my fist through Stella's corporeal mouth.

The door opened as Joe walked out and a cold breeze spun around me. Creases formed at the corners of my eyes and I twisted to face Stella, grinding my teeth into pulp. "You have some timing."

The ghost hiked her hands up. "Sorry! How was I supposed to know you'd be all over the blood sucker? Since when do you have guts?"

"Since I almost died," I said. "Twice. Anyway, what did you want?"

Stella winked, pointing to the clock. "You're off shift," she noted and grinned widely. "Meet me at the spear."

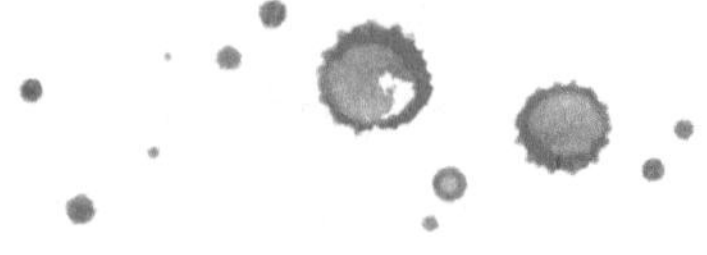

A short drive later and I was standing next to Stella in the cupola of the old lighthouse. The two of us came here every night since I left the hospital. Some nights we talked until I was too tired to stand, others we stood in silence and watched the sea below. But on all those nights, I was grateful to have Stella Rutherford nearby.

It was no different today.

Elbows on the railing, I pressed my nose to the window's glass and listened to the crashing waves. The town looked so different from up here. I didn't notice it the first two times I visited, but it was almost magical. My finger aimlessly traced the carving of the bident on the wall, as it always did when we came here. My mind raced.

"A million for your thoughts," Stella said.

I choked down a laugh. "That's not the saying. A penny. It's a penny for a thought."

"Huh. Well, it should be. What does anyone want with a sad little penny?"

"I'm thinking about mom," I answered, not entertaining her strangeness any further.

My familiar traced my movements, zeroing in on the bident. Her gray body shimmered, less solid today than it was yesterday. Worry was eating away at Stella and I wished I could ask her about it. Except there was no prying when it came to the ghost. She made it quite clear time and time again: if Stella had something she wanted me to know, she would tell me.

Face unreadable, she turned away from me to look at the water. "I think you should call her."

"Mom?" I asked, baffled. "No way. Even if I wanted to, which I don't, I have no way of reaching her. I need to figure it out on my own. Maybe if I can find out who my father is, I can track him down and then.... I don't know what then. But I need to know more about my magic. Especially if it's what you say it is."

"The power of Hades?" Stella asked. Her arms shot up in the air and she shook them twice for emphasis, her voice lowering several octaves. "I grant you the power of the underworld!"

I smacked the air near her. "You're ridiculous."

"And I'm right," she chimed. "You know it."

A rogue smile crept to my lips and while I didn't look at Stella, careful not to give her any satisfaction, pride swelled in my chest. Stella Rutherford was quite clever and though I'd never admit it to her, she was the best familiar a witch could ask for.

We stood that way for a while; staring blankly at the dark sea spreading beneath us. The sun ducked below the horizon and I closed my eyes, imagining what this place looked like when it wasn't a condemned tower of doom. It must have been absolutely stunning up here at night.

"I'm ready to find out."

Stella's voice was so low, I barely heard her. I snapped my eyes open, turning to face her. "What was that?"

"Are you really going to make me beg, Piper? It's uncouth." She crossed her arms and blew out a sharp breath. I had no idea what she was talking about since I didn't properly hear her in the first place. "Fine," Stella sniped. "If you want me to spell it out for you.

I'm ready to figure out what happened to me, and I want you to help."

If I wasn't sure it would make the entire lighthouse fall down, I'd have slapped the wall. Instead, I gripped the wooden railing with all my might and struggled not to pass out. Stella needed my help. Stella Rutherford was letting me into her life. This was a moment to celebrate. I knew we couldn't actually celebrate since we were talking about her death and such, but kick me to next Tuesday, this was momentous. Palms slick with sweat, I let go of the railing and fixed my crooked face. "We'll start tomorrow."

"Can you keep it in your pants, please?" Stella said. "You're much too excited about my death."

"Not your death, obviously. I'm glad you're ready to take the next step."

Stella's features softened and her sheer body took on a little more form. I could barely see through her anymore. "Me too. It's time." She side-glanced my way. "It's also time to discuss the beast you're housing rent free."

"Oh, don't call yourself a beast!"

The ghost pretended to pinch me and pouted her fake lips until they took on the shape of two balloons. "You know who I'm talking about."

"I know, I know," I admitted. "Harry isn't staying with us forever. It's only until I can figure out how to get him somewhere safe. Honestly, this is better than him being at the cafe. At least I don't have to restock the baked goods several times a day now."

"Yes, but I have to restock my sanity. Get him out, please. Before the end of my afterlife, preferably."

Nodding my agreement, I shimmied myself closer to her, and we both turned back to the windows. The sky darkened drastically and there were a million stars covering us in a blanket of twinkle lights. I glanced at my hands and the magic hiding inside them, inside of me. There was much to do. Move Harry Houdini out, find out what happened to Stella, find my father. It was a short list that somehow felt never-ending. Ripping my attention away from my hands, I looked at Stella beside me, her face serene and not a worry line on her. I breathed in her confidence, eating it up until I was no longer afraid.

Whatever came next, I was ready.

# OAT MATCHA LATTE

### *Ingredients:*

Matcha powder

Oat milk

Maple syrup or vanilla extract

Hot water

Milk frother

### *Instructions:*

1. Pour 1 teaspoon matcha powder into a bowl.

2. Add 1/3 cup of hot water and froth until smooth.

3. Add Maple syrup (or vanilla extract) to taste. Stir until it dissolves.

4. Warm oat milk on a stove top or using an espresso machine steamer. Pour into a cup.

5. Add matcha mixture over top and froth until
smooth and frothy.
6. Enjoy!

facebook.com/groups/945090619339423/

**Instagram:**

instagram.com/a.n.sage/

**TikTok:**

tiktok.com/@ansagewrites

**YouTube:**

youtube.com/c/ANSageWrites

9 781989 868317